ALPHA'S PRIDE

IRRESISTIBLE OMEGAS BOOK FOUR

NORA PHOENIX

.

Alpha's Pride (Irresistible Omegas Book Four) by Nora Phoenix

www.noraphoenix.com

THE MEN OF THE PTP RANCH

The Pack Alpha and his men
Lidon Hayes (alpha), pack alpha
Palani Hightower (beta), second-in-command
Enar Magnusson (beta)
Vieno Hayes-Kessler (omega)
Hakon Hayes (alpha-heir, newborn)

Grayson and his boys
Grayson Whitefield (alpha)
Lars Magnusson (beta, Enar's younger brother)
Sven Whitefield-Magnusson (omega, adopted younger brother of Enar and Lars)

Bray and his men
Bray Whitefield (alpha, Grayson's oldest son)
Kean Hightower (beta, Palani's older brother)
Ruari (omega)
Jax (alpha, Ruari's newborn son)

Bray's men (the ones who are named):

Adar (alpha)

Isam (alpha)

Workers:

Ori (alpha, Lidon's cousin)

Jawon (beta, Lidon's cousin)

Servas (omega, Lidon's cousin)

Urien (beta, Lidon's cousin)

Clinic:

Maz (alpha, OB/GYN resident, coworker of Enar's)

Lucan Whitefield (beta, Grayson's middle son, Bray's younger brother)

Sando Melloni (omega, Prof. Melloni's son)

Not on the ranch:

Rhene Hightower (alpha, Palani's youngest brother)

Professor Ricardo Melloni (beta, Sando's father, discovered the Melloni gene)

Dane Whitefield (beta, Grayson's youngest son, brother to Bray and Lucan, physically and mentally disabled)

PROLOGUE

S*even months earlier*

THE CLUB THUMPED and vibrated with the low bass of the music, and Bray sighed with contentment. He'd worked his ass off the last few weeks, trying to impress a rather demanding employer, and he needed this break. A night of fucking was exactly what he craved after spending long days on the job.

It wasn't easy, running your own security company when you were this young. Despite him being an alpha and rather big, people tended to not take him seriously. He hated it, this patronizing look in the eyes of older alphas when they looked down on him, choosing to employ a more established firm even when it charged them double. Their loss, Bray kept telling himself, but it stung.

All he wanted was a shot so he could prove himself. His father had sacrificed a lot to raise Bray and his brothers, and he wanted to make him proud. And since his brother Lucan was a beta and his youngest brother Dane—also a beta— had physical and mental disabilities due an oxygen shortage at birth, he felt it was his job to prove to his father his sacrifices had been worth it.

"What's your plan for tonight?" his friend Jesse asked, leaning back in the black, soft seats of the club's lounge where they were relaxing.

"Fucking," Bray said, his mouth breaking open in a smile. "Lots and lots of fucking."

"You got anyone lined up?" Jesse asked.

Bray shook his head. "No, but I registered a few days ago when I knew I'd be able to make it, so I'm hoping someone has requested me. If not, I'll scout the back rooms to see if anyone wants to play."

The lounge of the club was meant for socializing and dancing, though plenty of couples got their kink on here already. You were supposed to head to the back rooms for the more intimate follow-up, a route Bray knew well. Oh, he'd had a few greedy little omegas on their knees under the table, sucking him off, but he respected the club's rules enough to take them to the back if he wanted more.

Jesse nodded. "Same here. There's bound to be a horny little omega who needs an alpha, right?"

Jesse knocked back his beer and Bray kept himself from frowning. He never drank when playing, and even though Jesse wasn't a serious player by any standard, it still wasn't smart to drink if he wanted to engage later on. Maybe he'd better keep an eye on his friend to make sure he didn't overdo it on the alcohol, or he'd have to report him to the club. That would suck, but Bray took safety seriously, especially in sex and scenes.

Jesse had always been more of a drinker than Bray, who

liked a beer but rarely drank more than that, even back in high school where he and Jesse had become friends. They'd stayed in touch ever since, though they'd had little chance to hang out lately. Bray worked fourteen-hour days and Jesse was trying to work his way up in his father's investment consultancy.

If you saw Jesse now in his brown leather pants with his bare chest, you would never believe he rarely wore anything other than a suit during the day. The same could be said for Bray, whose standard attire was also a lot more conservative than the tight leather pants he was sporting, which made his cock look even bigger and his bare upper body stand out like a freaking wall, as one omega had described it. Hopefully, his pants would do their job again tonight and attract a horny little omega, as Jesse had put it.

Bray emptied his Coke and as he put it down, his phone buzzed with a message. His heart sped up as he read it. The club had matched him with an omega who had requested an alpha to help him through his heat. A slow grin spread across his face as the implications of that request sank in. That meant a solid fuck-fest for at least twenty-four hours, probably longer. Exactly what he craved.

He quickly typed his reply and rose. "I've been matched. Have fun, man. See you next time."

Jesse quirked an eyebrow. "Next time? You won't be back later?"

Bray couldn't help but smile all over again. "My match is an omega in heat. I'll be lucky to come up for air a day from now."

"Damn, lucky bastard," Jesse muttered. "You always get the good ones."

Bray shrugged. "My rep has preceded me, what can I say?"

His cock already grew hard as he walked through the lounge to the back room they'd assigned him, and it wasn't because of the various couples and groups around him who were engaging in all kinds of sexual activities. It had been him and his right hand for far too long, and he couldn't wait to sink himself into a tight, hot ass. Damn, he needed the release.

He loved these kinds of encounters. No need for small talk or awkward conversation or even negotiation. Both parties knew exactly what they signed up for. Hell, he didn't even introduce himself half the time, since it wasn't a date. It was an itch to scratch, a hole that needed filling, simple as that. And it worked well for both alphas and omegas, since the club did thorough vetting on all its members and assured omegas they'd be matched with an alpha who would respect their limits.

Someday, he'd find himself a sweet little omega who'd bear him an alpha son, but for now, he was happy to keep things casual. Extremely casual. Sure, he wanted a family at some point, but not right now. He had time to get serious later on, not when he still had so much he wanted to enjoy first. Like everything the club had to offer.

He opened the door to his assigned room with his club key card and let himself in, his eyes immediately catching sight of the omega waiting for him, stretched out on the bed on his back, already naked, his hard cock making a wet spot on his stomach. Bray's breath caught in his lungs, and he swallowed as his cock grew even harder.

He looked young, so young. Younger than Bray had expected, but he had to be twenty-one, or the club wouldn't have admitted him. His body was slender and tight, but well defined, his abs on perfect display in the pose he'd struck with his hands behind his back. Just then, he shifted on the bed, his hips restlessly moving, even as his eyes sought Bray's.

Bray inhaled deeply, the intoxicating smell of the omega invading his system. It was rich, heavy, pure sex, and it went straight to his cock. God, the guy smelled good. Bray had never smelled anything like him, so hypnotizing.

"What's your name?" he asked, forcing himself to go through the motions and not jump on him instantly.

"Check the sheet," the omega said, his voice thick with want and his body shaking.

Bray nodded, understanding that talking was becoming hard for the omega, about to be overwhelmed by his heat. He rushed over to the dresser where, as usual, a piece of paper was ready for his signature. Omegas prepared this beforehand and alphas had to read it and sign it before doing anything else, then slide it under the door for the club's attendants to find it. It was a safeguard for everyone, so limits and expectations were well-communicated when both parties could still give full consent.

He read through it quickly, in a hurry to get things going. That smell was making his cock leak in his pants, for fuck's sake. Maybe he'd been more desperate for a fuck than he'd realized if this omega had such a strong effect on him.

The omega wanted to stay anonymous, he saw. Not unusual in cases like this, but more than fine with him. At least the guy wouldn't expect roses and Valentine's Day dinners after. Plus, it was a safeguard in case of a pregnancy, so omegas couldn't demand custody payments and alphas couldn't claim parental rights.

The omega had also requested plain vanilla sex, which made sense if he was in heat. Many omegas weren't clear-headed enough to use their safe words if they needed to, so the club didn't allow heavy scenes during a heat. This omega had asked for no scene at all, just oral and penetrative sex. Bray's smile widened. His night just kept getting better.

He signed the paper and hurried over to the door to slide it back to the club's attendants, who would put it on file. Out of habit, he checked to see if the camera was on. It was an unmonitored feed that would never see the light of day unless one of the parties claimed something happened. The club kept it stored for ninety days and after that, it would be destroyed. It was another safeguard for all parties involved that Bray appreciated.

Behind him on the bed, the omega moaned. "Alpha..."

Bray peeled himself out of his leather pants, wishing he'd worn something he could take off faster. Finally, he was free and he dropped his pants on a chair in the corner. God, the boy was beautiful, he thought as he made his way to the bed. Wavy brown hair, stunning blue eyes, and a body that begged to be worshipped. But more than anything, his smell got to Bray, invading his every cell. He wanted to own him, bury himself inside him and not let go.

In wordless invitation that showed his growing desperation, the omega stretched out his arms to Bray. "Please, alpha, please. I need your cock."

Bray smiled at him. He would do perfectly. "I've got you," he said.

He rolled on a condom and lowered himself on the bed, not wasting any time with niceties, but positioning himself right on top of the gorgeous boy. His cheeks were flushed with heat and his eyes glazed over as he pulled up his legs and canted his ass, inviting Bray in. He found his entrance, dripping with slick heat, and eased in. It sucked him right in, this perfect, greedy ass, and Bray didn't linger. Within seconds, he was in balls deep, and he threw his head back and let out a deep alpha-roar.

When he stumbled out two days later, he could barely walk from exhaustion and his cock smarted, but he was happy as a clam. That kid had been the single best fuck of his life—an insatiable, horny, greedy piece of ass who'd even tried to boss Bray around when Bray got too slow for his wanton little hole. It was adorable, though Bray would never tolerate that in a mate. But who needed a mate when you could find a perfect lay like this at the club?

Romance was overrated.

1

A strange vibration hung in the air. Bray felt it in his chest, in his heartbeat, a low buzzing in his blood as it ran through his veins. It rushed through him like adrenaline, the excitement of something amazing that was about to happen. And as he looked around at the other men gathered in the kitchen of the main house, he could see he wasn't the only one affected.

They all sat there, awaiting news about the baby. Bray's father was there—with his two boys, of course. Bray's younger brother Lucan sat quietly at the table, sipping a steaming mug of coffee, with Sando right next to him, looking like his mind was elsewhere, as usual. The omega's brain was always occupied and rarely with something right in front of him. Both of Palani's brothers were present as well, Kean and Rhene. The latter had arrived only minutes ago after Kean had called to tell him he was about to become an uncle.

An hour ago, Palani had come flying out of the alpha's bedroom, calling out for Lucan and Maz. Sven had grabbed a checklist from the refrigerator and had started boiling water and gathering supplies, which had been carried in as soon as he was done. Lucan had been assigned a task as well and went running to grab medical bags and rush them to the bedroom. After that, all they could do was wait.

Sounds drifted in from the bedroom, which wasn't that far from the kitchen. Vieno was in pain, crying out. Bray winced a little, not entirely comfortable with listening in on something so private.

"It's not supposed to go that fast, is it?" Lucan asked.

His question wasn't aimed at anyone in particular, but Bray wasn't surprised when his father answered. "It happens sometimes, especially with male omegas. It's called precipitous labor, and Enar and Maz must've seen this plenty of times. They'll know what to do."

It was a stark reminder that out of everyone in the house, his father was the only one who had experience with this. Three times, actually, though the last time it hadn't ended well. Bray's daddy had died giving birth to his brother Dane, who had ended up with severe disabilities due to the complications of the delivery. Bray couldn't remember his daddy clearly, but he remembered sitting on his lap as he held him and Lucan. It was a vague memory, but one that brought love to Bray's heart. Of course, his father had completely forgotten about his first husband.

Bray stole a glance at him, noticing the way he sat with Sven on his left and Lars right next to him. Those three were always touching each other. Bray couldn't understand why no one else objected to that sickening level of PDA.

When his dad had started seeing those two boys, Bray had been appalled. They were younger than him, for fuck's sake, younger than Lucan, even. What the hell was his dad thinking? At first, he'd figured things would come to an end all by themselves. After all, how could an old guy like his dad keep up with two men, one of whom was a super horny omega, affected by the Melloni gene?

That had been a miscalculation on his part, he admitted. Not only had his dad kept up, he'd done a terrific job, according to the rumors flying around the ranch. Talk about TMI, ugh. Bray shuddered at the various comments he'd had to endure about his own father's sexual prowess.

What was even more worrisome, was that their fling had turned into something far more, something much deeper, and Bray no longer held the hope they'd break up any time soon. Hell, his dad had even managed to make Lars behave, and no one, including Bray, had thought that possible.

Granted, the pack alpha and his mates weren't much better when it came to public sex. They were worse, actually, as Bray had caught them in compromising positions multiple times, and he wasn't the only one. It was a running joke among his men, the number of days they managed to not catch the alpha's mates in a sexual situation. So far, their record had been four days. Maybe that would change after the baby had arrived.

Still, it was different when it was the alpha and his men. Bray had no desire to see his father and his two boys get it on, though he had to admit his men didn't object so much. That morning, one of his guys had caught a rather arousing view of Lars getting a spanking and had joked with the others he wouldn't mind being on the receiving end of one as well.

"You're staring." A soft voice startled him in his thoughts.

He averted his eyes and focused on the guy who said it. Kean, who else? Just as observant as his brother and equally stubborn, Bray had discovered the last few months. For a beta, he was damn opinionated, another trait that ran in the family, though Bray couldn't deny Palani was doing a phenomenal job as second-in-command of the pack. As much as he hated to admit it, he couldn't think of a single alpha on the ranch that would've done better than him at bringing the pack together and expanding their operations, all while researching and blogging about current affairs.

"Just staring into space," Bray said, annoyed Kean had caught him.

Kean rolled his eyes. "Sure."

Bray wondered why he always reacted so strongly to whatever Kean did or said. He usually didn't have that much of a trigger temper, but with Kean, it was different. The beta managed to easily see through his mask, get through his defenses, and Bray didn't like it one bit. One of these days, he was gonna put him in his place. Maybe they should battle it out sometime, he thought. Just to see who was boss, which would be Bray, obviously. He would never let a beta best him.

It wasn't the first time he'd considered it, hooking up with Kean. They were both single and neither of them was looking for anything serious. Bray sure wasn't, still content with his monthly trips to the club. To his disappointment, he'd never run into that omega again he'd fucked through his heat over six months ago. That still stood in his memory as the single best fuck of his life, but who knew, maybe he and Kean could make those sparks between them work in the sack.

It was funny, because the beta wasn't even his type. Bray preferred omegas, their slender, boyish bodies. He loved the contrast between their build and his, especially when fucking. It was such an arousing sight to see them take his cock, to watch them surrender to his dominance. Then again, he couldn't deny the idea of conquering Kean appealed to him on a deep, primal level as well. The beta was anything but slender, but what would it feel like to make a body like his submit and take his dick? Hmm, definitely something worth considering.

Bray wanted to react to Kean's little taunt when the energy in the room shifted, and he went weak and dizzy in an instant. He couldn't explain it, but it felt like all the power was sucked right out of him, leaving him trembling and boneless in his chair.

Bray's hand shot out at the table for support, but before he had a hold, Kean grabbed his arm and steadied him. "You okay?" the beta asked.

"Daddy?" Lars called out, his voice filled with concern. Any other day, Bray would've been annoyed by that term for his father, but not this time.

Bray blinked, his head light and dizzy. "Is he okay?" he asked Kean. "My dad, is he all right?"

Before Kean could answer, another wave of power hit Bray, but this time it was the opposite. Energy slammed into him so hard it took his breath away, making his body jerk in shock as if he'd been electrocuted. His muscles contracted painfully before releasing with a force that made him feel like he could fly.

And then he knew. Even before they heard the sounds from the bedroom, he knew. He couldn't explain how, except that his alpha recognized his leader.

When the howl drifted in from the bedroom, Bray sank to his knees on the floor, his body shaking. Around him, the others were doing the same, forced to their knees by a power they couldn't see, only feel.

Tears started running down his face even as his mouth split wide in the biggest grin he'd ever felt. His body was pumped with adrenaline, his cock rock hard, his whole being emitting energy and joy. He'd never felt this alive, this in harmony with his alpha, who roared with power inside of him.

And when a large, gray wolf slowly stepped into the kitchen a little later, Bray did the same as everyone else. He fell flat on his belly, bowing down to the magnificent creature in front of him. He had no doubt, no qualms, no reservations whatsoever. This was Lidon, their pack alpha, and they owed him their allegiance.

The wolf—Lidon—let out a satisfactory howl, then trotted over to Bray's father, who lay prostrated on the floor like everyone else. Bray turned his head so he could see what happened. His father lifted his head when the wolf approached, and it recognized him with a big lick over his face. The joy on his dad's face had to mirror his, Bray thought, still unable to stop smiling.

He'd never seen an animal so magnificent, so majestic and powerful. And to know it was one of their own, their pack alpha...it was hard to believe, except he felt it to be true in the very core of his soul. His breath caught as Lidon made his way over to him. He bowed his head in recognition of Lidon's power, and then he, too, felt the wolf's tongue on his face.

It was powerful, that touch, like Lidon claimed him somehow. He was almost ashamed to admit it felt sexual too, his cock growing even harder in his pants. He had to resist the urge to seek friction against the floor, the sexual energy in his body almost too much to take.

Lidon licked them all, one by one, going by rank from alpha to beta to omega, from old to young. It was dead quiet in the kitchen, though a gasp of awe broke the silence every now and then as everyone stared in amazement at what transpired. Bray couldn't even find the words to describe it himself, and he saw his sense of wonder reflected in the others.

It lasted a few minutes, and then the wolf left them to trot back to the bedroom, where sounds of a crying baby were making Bray's heart sing. The baby had been born then, and by the sounds of it, it was healthy. Thank god for that.

He wondered if Vieno had been right about it being an alpha son, an alpha heir to Lidon. Then he caught himself. Could he doubt that, after everything that had happened? After what he had witnessed? It had to be true. Everything had turned out to be true. Lidon was the true alpha and the wolf shifters had returned.

Bray threw his head back and let out deafening alpha roar that mingled with one of his father's, and seconds later, Rhene joined in as well. The wolf shifters had returned.

2

Kean was a little freaked out by what happened. When that massive wolf had trotted into the kitchen, his heart had stopped. Rationally, he'd known it had to be Lidon, but he'd still been scared. No, he corrected himself; it hadn't been his brain that had recognized the wolf. It had been his beta, his soul. Just like everyone else, Kean had dropped to his knees and then flat on the floor, compelled by a deep desire to honor his pack alpha.

His ears still rang with the deafening roar of the three alphas in the kitchen, and Kean felt its power roll through him. Once Lidon had left, they had all scrambled to their feet, somewhat dazed. The blast of energy that had brought them all to their knees still hummed in Kean's veins. He was restless, on edge, and undeniably aroused. Man, his cock was throbbing in his pants, and he had to restrain himself to keep his hands off. A quick glance at Bray, who stood right next to him, confirmed he wasn't the only one.

Hell, Grayson's two boys were already plastered against him, with Sven shamelessly rutting against his alpha.

Grayson's hand found Lars's neck as Kean watched, dragging him close for a deep kiss that left little to the imagination of what they were about to do. He wasn't surprised when seconds later, Grayson and his boys headed to their bedroom, dropping clothes in the hallway. Kean caught a glimpse of Grayson's bare ass before he entered their room and suppressed a sigh of admiration. The man was built, there was no denying that. And his two boys weren't a hardship to look at either.

Their departure left Kean, his brother Rhene who looked hyper as fuck, Bray, Lucan, and a dazed and flushed Sando. Kean liked the shy, smart omega and had even hoped for more of a connection, but there was nothing more than friendship between the two of them. It was for the better, as he was a bit stubborn and strong for the soft-spoken omega.

Bray, however, was a different story. As much as his lazy arrogance infuriated Kean, he couldn't deny his attraction to the alpha. Hell, he'd been fighting it since they'd met, when he and Rhene had visited Palani for the first time. When Kean's eyes had caught sight of Bray, something had sparked, something he hadn't been able to let go of since. Not even the discovery that Bray could be a massive ass had taken it away, sadly.

Bray noticed him too, he was sure of it. There had been lingering gazes, some definite checking out of his ass, which admittedly was one of his best features. That, and his cuddliness. For a beta, he was on the big side, his body toned and muscled from working outside without having the perfectly sculpted pecs or the drool-worthy six-pack Bray had. A friend he'd hooked up with multiple times had called Kean "a cuddly bear but without all the fuzz."

Apparently, that did not appeal enough to Bray to make

a move. That was a damn shame, because he still harbored hope that if they hooked up once, Bray would realize their attraction as well and would want more. Kean had even thought they might be... No, he had to forget about that. If that were the case, Bray would've felt it as well, right?

He adjusted himself, resigned to the fact he'd have to make do with his right hand. "I'll catch you guys later," he said, hoping he'd come off casual.

He hoped Bray would come after him, but when he didn't, Kean retreated to his room where he jacked himself off until his cock stopped throbbing so damn much and the muscles in his hand were screaming with fatigue. It worked, but it was a damn downgrade from what being taken by Bray would have been like, he guessed. A guy his size had to pack a big tool, and that would've been so much better.

No one got much work done that day, he noted, as they all walked around half dazed and still aroused. What the fuck had happened there to cause that massive blast of power?

The next day, Palani called a pack meeting in the new barn they had built. The living room had become too small considering the pack size, so Jawon and his men had built a large barn and painted it red. It could serve as a meeting room, party barn, and whatever else they needed it for. It was still sparsely decorated, but Palani had ordered a bunch of wooden picnic tables so they had a place to sit and eat if they wanted.

Kean made sure to be there early, wanting to have prime access. He slid his frame into the table at the front, turning his body half around so he could watch the others come in. Everyone was expected to show up, Palani had stressed in his announcement. Kean hadn't spoken to his brother since the day before, when Lidon had shown up as a wolf, so he had no idea what this was about. They certainly had something to talk about after what had happened. Even Rhene had hung around an extra day, too curious to go back to the city just yet.

Kean studied Bray as he walked into the barn, dressed in his usual tight black shirt and cargo shorts. The man had calves that were as big as Kean's thighs. He sighed inwardly. Hot damn, he was one sexy motherfucker. What would it be like to be the recipient of that strength? The man would undoubtedly fuck like an animal, and damn if that didn't appeal to Kean.

Much to his surprise, Bray dropped on the bench next to him. "Hi," the alpha said after a short hesitation.

Kean suppressed a smile. He didn't leave Bray as unaffected as the alpha would like to pretend, now did he? Did that mean he was finally getting through to him? Or maybe —he barely dared to hope—the alpha had sensed their bond as well?

"Hi," he replied, then decided to poke the bear a little, if only because Bray was so fun to tease. Besides, he had nothing to lose. "How's your right hand doing? Or did you find a willing omega to oblige you?"

Bray's head shot to the side and his eyes widened. Kean grinned. "You didn't think you were the only one to walk out of there with a dick hard enough to pound nails, did you?" Bray's mouth opened, then closed again, and Kean's grin broadened. "Sorry, little too direct for you?"

"I'm not used to discussing my sex life with others," Bray said.

"Huh, interesting."

"What's that supposed to mean, 'interesting'?" Bray's tone was sharp.

Kean shrugged. "Just a little surprised. Wasn't expecting you to be a prude."

Bray's eyes narrowed, but before he could respond, Palani took his position and spoke. "Hey guys, thanks for joining us tonight for a pack meeting. It was an eventful day yesterday, I think it's safe to say…"

Snickers and laughs rolled through the pack, and Palani grinned. "Eventful covers it nicely, I thought," he joked, then turned more serious. "I'm sure you all have questions, as do we ourselves, so we'll try to explain as much as we can and allow you to ask anything. But before we do that, we have something special to show you, or rather, someone special."

The back door opened and Enar wheeled Vieno in, sitting in a wheelchair, holding his son. Kean's "Aw…" joined a chorus of similar reactions from the others in the barn. Vieno beamed as he held his son close, who was swaddled in a light blue blanket, only his red little face peeping out.

Lidon stepped forward, bending to kiss Vieno, then gently took the baby from him, holding him with his face turned toward the pack. "Meet our son and alpha heir, Hakon Hayes."

Kean loved how Lidon said "our," even though everyone knew damn well it was his biological son and not Palani's or Enar's. But these four were a united front as they stood there, beaming with pride.

Then Grayson's voice rang out. "In the days of old, the pack alpha's heir was honored by the pack swearing allegiance to protect him. Please join me in renewing this tradition."

Kean couldn't get off the bench fast enough, and it was the same for everyone else. Once they stood, Grayson said, "Kneel for your alpha's heir," and as one man, they sank down to one knee.

"Hakon Hayes, as our alpha's son, we swear allegiance to you. We swear to protect you at all costs, and we would lay down our lives to keep you safe. We bless you with a full moon, a loyal pack, and a long life. To Hakon!" Grayson shouted.

Kean's mouth opened without him realizing, and he joined the rest of the pack as they raised their voices in unison. "Hakon!"

When he rose again, he found his eyes tearing up, and he wiped them, a tad embarrassed until he saw others do the same. He couldn't explain it, but it was like his soul recognized these traditions, like it knew what to do even though he'd never done this before. And what was even more amazing, was that he had meant every word of the vow that Grayson had spoken. He was willing to lay down his life for Hakon, and wasn't that the strangest feeling ever? Sure, that tiny little baby was his nephew, but still. He'd never felt this deeply about anything in his life, and it would scare the hell out of him if it didn't feel so right.

BRAY'S HEAD seemed to spin. Or maybe it was his heart, his soul. What the hell had happened? He'd always prided himself on being a rational person, but that moment had been fully emotional. He hadn't even thought about it, had sunk to his knee and made that pledge without a second's hesitation. What had motivated him to do that? He had no idea, but he stood by it.

He took his seat again, noticing that Kean seemed just as thrown off-kilter as he was. A quick look around confirmed that everyone looked a bit out of it. This whole pack business was some seriously weird shit at times.

"Wow," Palani said. "That was a moment so special I can't even put it into words."

"If you're speechless, that's saying a lot," Kean called out, and a relieved laughter rolled through the room, breaking the tension.

Palani gave him the finger, which caused more laughter. "You'd better be careful with that with a little one around," Grayson warned him. "Before you know it, your son will copy that gesture...at one of his dads."

Palani looked a little embarrassed as he laughed. Enar tapped his shoulder, and at that signal, Palani leaned in to kiss Vieno, who was holding Hakon again. Lidon did the same, and then Enar disappeared, taking Vieno with him. No wonder, the omega probably needed lots of rest the day after giving birth.

Once they had left, Palani turned to face the pack again. "Okay, let's talk about the shifting, because you all must be curious and have questions. Alpha, your turn."

As always, Bray felt compelled by Lidon's quiet power. It hung in the air, even now, when he hadn't said a word. Over the next few minutes, Lidon explained how he'd felt changes in his body the last weeks of Vieno's pregnancy, a premonition of the impending shift. This wasn't news to Bray, as Palani had kept him apprised for obvious security reasons.

Then he talked about the birth of Hakon, discussing how the four of them had shared a power that had given Vieno the strength to get through the dangerous delivery. Bray hadn't realized how close a call it had been, but Lidon's quiet words brought that point home with a sobering shock.

"I can't explain how I shifted," Lidon said. "I just did. I realize that must sound unsatisfactory to you all, but one second I was a man, and the next I was shifting. It was like my body knew how, or my soul, I don't know. But it was the baby who brought forth the shift. As soon as I held Hakon, I felt it, that he and I were connected and that we shared power somehow. It was like he transferred power to me and then took it back, or the other way around. I'm not even sure what happened."

"You also took power from us alphas, alpha," Grayson said.

Lidon's eyebrows rose. "I did?"

"Yes. I was in the kitchen with the others, waiting for news, and there was a moment when my alpha powers were sucked right out of me. I almost fainted. You felt that too, right, Bray?"

Bray saw no reason to deny it now that his father had admitted to it. "Yeah, I did. I felt like Jell-O."

"Huh," Lidon said. "I didn't realize that, I'm sorry."

Bray debated if he should mention the release of power. Maybe that was something better mentioned in private, as it could lead to embarrassing discussions about sex. But once again, his father had no such qualms.

"Once you shifted, alpha, there was a release of energy," he said, his voice more matter-of-fact than Bray could have ever pulled off. "And it had quite the impact on everyone, not only alphas."

Lidon pulled up one eyebrow. "Impact how?"

Bray's stomach twisted at the fat grin on his father's face, like a cat who'd cornered a mouse and was about to eat it. "Let's just say everyone's libido got a massive boost."

Lidon seemed to be embarrassed while Palani held his hand in front of his mouth, doing his best to not laugh at Lidon, but seconds later, he lost that fight and snickered. Even a slightly peeved side-eye from the pack alpha didn't bring down his mirth, and there were quite a few who laughed along with him.

"Oh my god, imagine that every time you shift, you make them horny as fuck," Palani said to Lidon, wiping tears of laughter out of his eyes.

"Imagine that," Lidon responded dryly, but the corners of his mouth twitched enough that Bray knew the man wasn't upset.

"Well, truth be told, you were horny as fuck as well afterward," Palani then said, and Bray almost choked on his breath.

Lidon's hand shot out and grabbed Palani's wrist, pulling him first toward him, then on his knees. The beta went willingly, Bray saw, his eyes still dancing with laughter.

"Do I need to put your mouth to use to get you to shut up?" Lidon asked, and everyone laughed when Palani shrugged with a smile. The alpha bent toward his mate and kissed him in front of everyone, and not a subtle peck on the lips either.

Bray snuck his hand under the table to adjust himself and promptly bumped into Kean, who was doing the same thing. Kean's mouth split open in a grin that made him the spitting image of his brother, and suddenly Bray had no trouble imagining how and why the pack alpha wanted to put that mouth to use. Judging by Kean's wink, the beta knew where Bray's thoughts had gone.

"Okay," Palani said when Lidon let him go. "I think you've made your point, alpha." More laughter ensued.

"Now, let's get more serious," Lidon said as Palani got back to his feet, then took position next to his alpha. "Grayson, is this a known effect of shifting? Do we know if this has been reported before?"

"Not this specifically," his father answered. "But many of

the legends and stories of old are from times when shifting was normal and when they didn't discuss sex openly, at least not in stories. After this happened yesterday, I did a little digging..." Someone snickered. "Yes, that kind of digging as well, as both my boys were more than accommodating," he continued, and Bray's mouth pulled tight. Why did his dad always have to rub his relationship in everyone's face? Why couldn't he keep shit private?

"I tried to find any similar tales. I didn't find this specific thing, but I did come across several mentions of new pack recruits experiencing an increased sex drive the first months after joining. They worded it differently, but the picture that emerged was clear. I thought this might be because they weren't yet used to the pack's energy or the pack alpha's energy, so kind of what happened yesterday, alpha."

"You're saying this may occur more often in the beginning until we're all more used to it," Palani said.

"That's my assumption based on what I've read, but it's not conclusive."

"Thanks, Grayson," Lidon said. "That's good to know. Apparently, I have to apologize in advance for boosting all of your sex drives. Or not, depending on how much of a success yesterday was for all of you."

Bray mentally cursed. If this happened more often, he'd need to find a better outlet. He'd jerked off till his dick had become too sensitive to touch—and he'd still been hard. And it wasn't like he could head out to the club that easily, not with how far the ranch was from the city. Now, he'd have to find someone on the ranch, someone like...

He stole a careful glance to his side. Maybe he *should* act on the chemistry he and Kean had, because there was no denying they sparked. Surely the beta would be up for a little casual fun between the sheets, especially if he shared this problem, right? All they'd do was work off a little steam, get rid of that pent-up sexual energy. They'd both benefit from that, since it wasn't easy to find another partner.

Bray's options were limited, since he didn't want to ask Palani for permission to approach an omega—plus, with omegas there was always the risk of unwanted entanglements caused by pregnancy—and the number of betas was limited.

No, Kean would do. Now all Bray had to do was convince him to bend over for him, but that shouldn't be too much of a problem, right?

3

Kean let out a happy sigh as he walked into the house, reveling in the way the air-conditioning breathed cold air over his hot body. It was hot as hell outside, and catching an ornery goat that had escaped from his pen—again—hadn't exactly helped him cool down. By the time he'd finally caught the little shit, he'd been about ready to offer him as a sacrifice to the weather gods in exchange for a good thunderstorm.

Why the hell had he ever proposed they get goats? What the fuck had he been thinking? Sure, they kept the grass nice and short, and with the removable pens they were easy to move across the ranch, but that one little fucker kept escaping.

Truth be told, he did like them. Not that Houdini-wannabe, but the goats in general. He liked their milk, and if he had a little more time, he'd love to experiment with making goat cheese. He'd never expected to be as busy as he was, but at some point, he'd have to ask his brother to get an assistant for him, especially since he'd been looking into going back to school and getting his degree to become a full-fledged veterinarian.

Right now, he wanted nothing more than to jump into the pool to cool off, but sadly, duty called. In this case, duty was his brother, who had requested him to stop by at his earliest convenience. Nothing urgent, Palani had assured him, just something he needed to discuss. And even though Kean was the oldest, older than Palani by a year, this was not a request he would ignore. He respected his brother's position as second-in-command of the pack too much.

It made him wonder what was going on. The pack meeting a few days earlier had run long, with Lidon and Palani answering all questions as best they could. The bottom line was that everyone had been wondering the same thing: would they be able to shift as well at some point? No one knew, but they'd sure had fun speculating.

As he rounded the corner to enter the hallway to the kitchen, he narrowly avoided bumping into Bray. The alpha's face resembled a thunderstorm, and Kean suppressed the urge to roll his eyes. For someone who was supposed to be as cool as a cucumber considering his job, the man was a bit of a drama queen at times.

"Don't go into the kitchen, unless you want a live porn show," Bray said, the disdain in his voice communicating loud and clear who was getting their dirty on. If it had been the pack alpha's men, Bray wouldn't have had such an issue with it.

"I take it your dad is having a little fun with his boys?" Kean said, unable to resist the challenge to poke Bray a little.

Bray's mouth tightened even further. "I wouldn't call it fun, but yes."

Kean's eyes lit up. "Oh, awesome. I'm going to have a look."

"You're gonna have a... Are you crazy? Why would you want to see that?"

"Because it's hot as fuck? Dude, your dad is sexy as hell and observing him with those two is the best live porn ever."

Bray shivered. "That statement is so disturbing, I don't even know where to start. How are you okay with seeing that? Don't you think it's an invasion of their privacy?"

Kean huffed. "If they wanted privacy, they would've done it in their own room. I'm sure you've realized by now Sven has a little exhibitionist streak and a weakness for humiliation play, Lars doesn't give a crap who's watching, and Grayson loves pushing the boundaries of his boys. Trust me, they want others to see this."

Bray's eyes widened and his head reeled back as if he'd been slapped. Kean frowned. This couldn't be news to Bray, could it? He'd performed a little digging after overhearing a remark from Grayson and discovered Bray had experience as a Dom in a club Kean had visited a few times to discover if it was his scene. Spoiler: it wasn't. The various kinks he'd engaged in had done little for him. Well, he'd liked some of them, but not enough to make going to the club a regular occurrence. But Bray was a member, so the alpha had to be familiar with humiliation play and exhibitionism.

"That's my father you're talking about. I have zero desire to see him naked. I'm not a perv like..."

He stopped talking, but Kean had no trouble finishing that sentence. It was crystal clear Bray still hadn't gotten over his objections to Lars and Sven, which was ridiculous, because anyone could see how well they fit together with Grayson. If ever there was a match made in heaven, it was the three of them.

The only objection Kean had was that it raised the bar for the kind of relationship he now aspired to. After seeing how happy his brother was with his three men and how sweet Grayson and his boys were, Kean was determined to not settle for anything less than that. He wanted someone who looked at him the same way Grayson looked at Lars and Sven. He wanted a mate who was as in tune with him as the pack alpha and his men were with each other. There were times when Kean had to look away instead of observing them, because their closeness made his insides squeeze painfully in a reminder of what he didn't yet have.

He'd hoped to find that with Bray, after he'd experienced that attraction the first time, but when even weeks, months later, Bray hadn't acted on it, he'd concluded it was hopeless. Maybe he'd been wrong, or it worked differently than he had imagined. Hell, even after that massive power boost that had all of them hard, Bray hadn't approached Kean—and he'd been all but ready to bend over.

"For someone who's active in that lifestyle, you're pretty narrow-minded at times," Kean said. "I can understand you don't want to watch your dad, but—"

"I'm not narrow-minded."

Kean lifted an eyebrow, meeting Bray's eyes dead on. "I wasn't done talking."

"I just wanted to stress I'm not narrow-minded."

Kean was pretty even-tempered, but frustration bubbled up inside him at Bray's careless arrogance. "You could've done that without interrupting me, by waiting until I was finished speaking," he said, his tone sharpening.

Bray looked startled, frowning. "You don't have to make such a big deal out of it."

"I wouldn't if I had even the slightest impression you regretted it, but I don't. You seem to think it's normal behavior to be interrupting other people. Would you do that to your dad?"

Bray's frown deepened. "Of course not. He wouldn't let me, and besides, he's my father."

The unspoken assumption was crystal clear to Kean. "So it's not okay to interrupt your father, because he outranks you, but it's okay to do it to me because I'm a beta?"

"No, that's not what I meant. It's..." He stopped talking and Kean saw the moment he realized he'd been painted into a corner. His shoulders dropped, and with a sheepish look on his face, he said, "It's never okay to interrupt someone."

Kean nodded, satisfied with that conclusion. "On that we agree, so do me a favor and let me finish my sentences. It *is* a big deal, and if you keep doing it, I'll make an even bigger deal out of it. Now, if you'll excuse me, there's a live porn show I need to watch."

He'd already turned around and taken a few steps toward the kitchen when Bray's voice rang out. "What did you want to say? When I interrupted you, I mean. You were saying something about my dad and those two. What was it?"

Kean slowly pirouetted. "Those two? You can't even bring yourself to say their names, can you?"

"They're younger than me, than my brothers. How could I be okay with that?"

For the first time, Kean sensed the underlying hurt in Bray's anger. "I can understand that will take getting used to, but try to see how happy your dad is. Watch him with Lars and Sven. Just watch the three of them interact, and you'll see how good they are for him. He loves them, and they love him. Are you begrudging them that? Besides, they didn't choose this. They're fated mates."

"Fated mates," Bray harrumphed. "I don't believe in that."

Kean couldn't help himself from reacting with a little shock. "You don't believe in fated mates? How can you not after watching the pack alpha and his men?"

Bray shrugged. "It's obvious that they're in love with each other, so I'm not refuting that. I just don't think it was a fated thing, just four men who fell in love with each other. It seems to me fated mates is a rather dangerous, manipulative strategy to tie someone to you, rather than letting them decide to stay all on their own. If someone believes they're mated to you by fate, how much does their declaration of love even mean? How could you ever trust it to be real, rather than someone feeling pressured to say it, or even feel it?"

Whoa, dark much? Kean didn't say it, but that was a bleak view the alpha was expressing on something Kean experienced as magical and beautiful. He was entitled to his own opinion, obviously, but Kean couldn't help but feel a little sorry for him. He sounded so negative and jaded and even a little sad.

"Well, I do believe in fated mates, and I hope that some-day, you get to experience it yourself when you meet your intended mate," he said.

Bray shook his head. "Not gonna happen," he said with conviction. "And I pity the guy trying to convince me he's my mate. Dude, I'm not even interested in a relationship in the first place, but if I were, it would not be with an omega trying to convince me he's my fated mate. Someday, I'll settle down with a sweet, pliant omega who loves me and not someone who tries to trick me into a relationship."

Something sharp stung in Kean's heart, but he pushed it down. This was not the moment to let his thoughts linger again on his weird attraction to this man he wasn't even sure he liked. That first time they had met, he'd felt like he'd known Bray, somehow. He hadn't, but his beta had stirred, insisting on a sense of recognition where there was none.

Ever since, he'd wondered why he was attracted to Bray, when the alpha was arrogant and prickly and not even his type. The idea of being fated mates had crossed Kean's mind more than once, but he'd reasoned that if that were the case, Bray would have felt it as well and would have approached him. Since that never happened, he'd concluded that he must be mistaken. Bray's little confession about not believing in fated mates invalidated that whole theory, but Kean didn't want to spend any time on the implications right now.

"No matter if you believe in fated mates or not, it's hard to deny the obvious love between your dad and his two boys. And I have a hard time understanding how someone with experience in the scene could have a problem with any kink at all, let alone the mild daddy kink they're obviously enjoying," he brought the discussion back to their original topic, not willing to let it go just yet.

Bray was a man who wasn't used to being challenged in his viewpoint, Kean had come to see over the last few months. He was super bossy and dominant, causing many around him to be hesitant in expressing conflicting opinions. Kean, of course, had no issue with that. Neither did Palani, much to Kean's enjoyment.

Their mother had often joked that the two of them should have been twins, they were so much alike, both in appearance and in character. They shared the same analytical mind, as well as stubbornness and refusal to back down, even when challenged by authority. Kean loved seeing how his brother was growing in his role as second-in-command,

and he agreed that Lidon couldn't have picked a better man for that position.

"How do you know about my involvement in the scene anyway?" Bray asked him. "You referred to it twice now, so I'm curious how you even know about it."

There was a sharpness in his question, the hint of an accusation, and Kean had no issue following Bray's line of thought. "Palani didn't tell me anything, in case that's what you're wondering. I overheard your dad mention something to you about a club, and I got curious. I did a little researching, and it turns out you belong to the same club I visited a few times. Apparently, we managed to not run into each other there back then, or we did and neither of us remembers."

Bray's eyebrows shot up in surprise. "You belong to the club? How...?"

"Nah, I never became a member. You know they let you visit a few times to try it out. I did, but it wasn't my thing."

A smile ghosted Bray's lips. "I can see why you'd have trouble submitting."

Kean shrugged, not in the least embarrassed. "Yeah, that didn't do it for me. Tried some stuff with a friend of mine who's a Dom, but it never went beyond okay for me, so I decided vanilla plus, as I call it, is fine with me. I'm fine with experimenting a little, but I don't want to go to a club or push my limits. Do you still go?" he asked.

Bray's Adam's apple bobbed as he swallowed, and Kean was strangely satisfied by making the alpha uncomfortable, if even for a bit. "When I can get away," he said evasively. "Which is not easy, as I'm sure you know."

Kean did understand that part, how hard it was to get away from the ranch. It was difficult to explain, the pull the ranch had on him. Or maybe it was the land or the pack,

Kean wasn't sure. Whatever it was, it made it hard to leave for an extended period of time, even so much as a night. He felt uneasy whenever he wasn't there, missing the men, the silence of the ranch, the animals, everything.

The silence hung heavy between them with Bray studying Kean, who stood patiently as the alpha seemed to make up his mind about something. Finally, the alpha jammed his hands into his pockets. "We could play sometime," he said, his voice gruff.

It was the least sophisticated proposal Kean had ever had, but he couldn't say no, not when it was what he'd wanted for so long. It was pathetic that even this small crumb Bray threw him was enough to make his heart skip a few beats.

"Sure," he said, keeping his voice level, determined not to show his hand. "That'd be cool."

4

———

Palani had warned the pack they wanted to do experiments that night with Lidon trying to shift. He'd joked that they'd better find privacy in case the effects were the same as last time. Kean had made a mental note to do that, not wanting to find himself in a similar predicament as two weeks ago when Lidon shifted for the first time, but he'd had a complication with a baby goat who refused to be born and as a result, he was running late.

Plus, he'd hoped Bray would contact him during the day to make good on his vague promise to play sometime, whatever the hell that meant. Hell, that was ten days ago and the alpha still hadn't made a move. What was he waiting for, a handwritten invitation?

He was still dropping off that day's fresh eggs in the kitchen when the wave hit him, raising goosebumps all over his skin, as well as one excited cock. Dammit, he hadn't even had dinner yet, and he was fucking starving.

He tried to ignore it for the first minute as he put the eggs in the fridge, but his cock signaled it wasn't planning on backing down anytime soon. But it wasn't just that; the whole energy in his body was impossible to ignore. He felt like he'd done drugs, too high to sit still, too wired and wound up to even try. With a frustrated sigh, he decided to head back to his bunkhouse to get some exercise in for his right hand.

He'd barely made it into the hallway when he heard footsteps behind him. Before he could turn around, a big hand grabbed his shoulder and spun him. Bray stood in front of him, his eyes blazing with the same sexual heat Kean felt thundering through his own veins.

"You want this?" the alpha growled, his voice reaching deep inside Kean.

He didn't even think. Fucking finally. "Hell yes."

Bray grabbed his wrist, pulled him into the first bedroom they could find, then locked the door behind them. For a few seconds, they stared at each other, a wordless battle. Then Kean stepped in and offered his mouth to Bray, content to let the alpha dominate him. For now.

There was nothing sweet or hesitant about Bray's kiss. He took Kean's mouth with a confidence that bordered on aggression, and Kean was fine with it. He opened up, let Bray in, then kissed him back for all he was worth, their tongues dueling even as their bodies found each other. Bray pushed him against the wall, his hard-on connecting with Kean's, who pushed right back. God, yes, this was exactly what he needed right now to get rid of that crazy energy in his body.

Bray didn't even have an inch on him, which put their heads at the same height as they kissed furiously. Bray's hands were flat against the wall behind Kean, boxing him in, and for some reason that made Kean's stomach go weak.

Those biceps right next to his face were massive and so fucking masculine.

The alpha gyrated his hips, grinding into Kean with slow but coordinated moves. If he kept that up, they wouldn't get far. He wriggled his hands between them and went for Bray's belt. He had it unbuckled in a second, then dragged the man's pants and underwear down to his thighs, where Bray took care of the rest and pulled them all the way down and kicked them off. They let go of each other for a few seconds to take their shirts off, and Kean figured he might as well get rid of his pants.

There was no doubt anymore where this was going, so no need to be delicate. They both knew what they wanted, and Kean saw no reason to deny himself. He'd waited long enough for Bray to get a clue.

Bray plastered himself against Kean again, and the connection of their naked bodies against each other sent a shock wave through him. It had been a while since an alpha had fucked him, and it was what he needed right now. Bray was hot as fuck, and his body was absolutely fucking perfect. That included his cock, which now rutted against Kean's, both slick already.

Kean dragged his mouth away. "Lube. We need lube."

Bray looked at him as if he were speaking a foreign language, then understanding dawned in his eyes. "You're not an omega," he said, and that struck Kean as funny. Apparently, their sexual chemistry didn't leave Bray unaffected either if he was so into it he'd forgotten Kean was a beta, not an omega whose hole would get slick all by itself.

"Last time I checked, no," Kean said.

His eyes lit up when he saw a bottle of lube on the bedside table. This was Lars's old room, so the beta must've left it behind when he moved into Grayson's room. Or those three had stashed bottles everywhere, which wouldn't surprise Kean either, what with their sexual appetite. On that thought, it could have been one of the pack alpha's men as well. Not that he was going there, because that would mean his brother and he was so not thinking of his brother when he was about to have sex with a hot alpha.

He pointed toward the bottle. "There you go."

For a second, Bray hesitated, as if he wasn't sure he should be the one getting it. Kean waited. If the alpha wanted to fuck him, he could damn well make the effort of getting the lube. That was his job as a top, right?

Bray let go of him and walked over to get the bottle. Kean wiped off his mouth, his lips throbbing with the aftermath of their frantic kissing, and took the opportunity to admire the guy's body. Damn, there was not an imperfect spot on Bray. It was a little disheartening, really, that one man could be so perfect. Good thing he was a bit of an ass, otherwise it would be too much in one person.

When Bray turned around, Kean had his first opportunity to study his front in a little more detail. Yup, not a damn thing out of place, including a large, thick, perfectly curved dick. He would feel that tomorrow, he was sure, but damn, it would be worth it.

"That's one hell of a cock you got there," he said, not seeing any reason he shouldn't be honest.

Bray looked a little startled. "Thank you," he said, then seemed to catch himself at the somewhat stupid reaction. It looked like he'd wanted to say something more, but he didn't, and Kean suppressed a laugh. He liked unbalancing him, making him question himself. It was fun, even in a situation like this.

"You want to head to the bed?" he asked Bray. "As much as I appreciate a good wall fuck, it might be easier to start in bed. I'm gonna need some prepping time considering your size."

Bray's eyes darkened. "You've done this before, right?"

Kean grinned. "I'm not some delicate virgin flower."

"That's not what I meant. I meant, you've done it with an alpha before?"

"Have you ever done it with a beta before?" Kean shot back. "If we're comparing sexual history."

The muscle beneath Bray's right eye twitched. "I'm not sure what that has to do with anything."

Kean's eyes grew big. "Oh my god, you haven't, have you? Dude, I'll be taking your beta virginity, how cool is that?"

"You're being absurd," Bray said, but Kean noticed he wasn't denying it, merely deflecting.

Oh, this was gold. Pure, precious gold. "You do realize we're not the same as omegas, right? That's we need a little more TLC beforehand?"

"Of course," Bray said stiffly.

Kean took pity on him. "Bray, it's okay if you've never done this before. There's no reason to hide it or be ashamed of it."

Bray's eyes flashed with annoyance as they met Kean's. "I don't like to be in a position where I'm the weaker one."

"Admitting you don't know something doesn't make you weaker," Kean said, his tone mellowing. "It makes you smart, because you're being honest and clear. It's no biggie, you know?"

Then, to lighten the mood, he let his eyes drop to Bray's cock. "Well, maybe in this case it is."

He was happy to see Bray's lips curve upward in a smile. "You like my dick?" the alpha asked, and beneath the arrogance Kean tasted something else, a hint of insecurity.

Maybe even perfect Bray wasn't always as self-assured as he appeared.

Kean sent back a broad smile. "I really do. Do you think we can make this work anytime soon?"

In response, Bray grabbed his wrist and pulled him toward the bed, letting the two of them tumble on the mattress on top of each other. Of course, the big guy rolled right on top of Kean, but when he fused their mouths together again, Kean reasoned that it wasn't the worst thing in the world to let Bray win every now and then.

BRAY CURSED KEAN'S PERCEPTIVENESS, even as he kissed him till they both ran out of breath. It wasn't elegant, their mouths fusing, but damn, it had him hard. He'd been hard ever since that wave rolled through him, but kissing Kean had made it almost painful. But how the hell had the beta figured out Bray was a little out of his depth here? He'd never fucked a beta before, and truth be told, he was unsure of the logistics involved.

Not that he would ever admit that to Kean. It was bad enough the guy had sniffed out the truth. It was easy for him, a beta, to state that admitting you didn't know something made you smart, but it was different for an alpha. Alphas couldn't show weakness, not ever.

Kean moved beneath him, spreading his legs wide, and Bray gasped into the beta's mouth as their groins connected even more intimately. He couldn't wait to get inside him, that sexual frenzy still buzzing inside him.

"We good?" he asked, dragging his mouth away. Kean was gorgeous, all flushed and with swollen lips, that sturdy body of his trembling.

"I'm perfect," Kean grinned. "Put some lube on your fingers and stretch me, and we're good to go."

Okay, he could do that. He leaned over to grab the lube he'd deposited on the floor next to the bed, then squirted some out. It made him realize that he'd never done this. He'd never put his fingers inside another man. With omegas, you didn't need to. If you went a little slow and careful in the beginning, they were fine, since their holes slicked up by themselves. And he'd never touched himself there, obviously. He was an alpha, and his body wasn't made to be penetrated.

He rolled off Kean and kneeled between his legs. What if he did something wrong? Something that made it clear he didn't have a clue about this part? Kean would laugh him out of the room. Dammit, he should've never done this, not with a beta, and not with Kean. He was not only sharp as a tack, but Palani's brother, so this could go wrong on so many levels.

Then Kean's strong hand circled around his wrist and brought it close to his ass. "Push in slowly with one finger," the beta said softly.

"I know how to do this."

"Shut up, Bray," Kean told him mildly. "We don't need to talk this to death but don't fucking lie to me."

Bray clenched his teeth as humiliation flashed through him, but when Kean didn't say anything else and let go of Bray's wrist, he focused on the pink hole in front of him. It was pretty, he had to admit, surrounded by a pair of pale, luscious globes. His skin was super smooth there, unlike his hands, which showed he was a working man. Bray didn't mind so much, he discovered. He loved the forceful way Kean grabbed ahold of him.

He painted a slick trail with his lubed-up right index

finger, starting at the top of Kean's crack and descending until he'd reached that little pucker. It was stiff at first, unyielding, until he circled around a bit, massaging and pushing. It softened then, and he pushed the tip of his finger in. Kean let out a breathy sigh, which Bray thought was a good sign, so he slid his finger in and out.

Damn, he was tight, even around his finger. Was that normal for betas? How did getting fucked not hurt? Maybe they were wired differently and enjoyed that. He wouldn't, he was sure.

After a bit, Kean's hole relaxed around him, giving way. Hmm, would it be enough? Kean had said stretching, though, so he should try adding another finger first. His cock was much thicker than that, so he'd better make sure he wasn't hurting him.

"Add another one," Kean told him.

"Hold your horses," Bray snapped, pissed the beta had spoken before he could've done it himself. Now it looked like he needed instructions, dammit.

He slid two fingers back in with a bit more force than he'd intended to, feeling guilty until Kean moaned and pushed his ass back at Bray. "God, yes, like that."

Huh. Apparently, a little force was a good thing. Who the fuck knew? He pumped his fingers in and out, Kean loosening up around him.

"Fuck, that feels good."

Bray watched his fingers disappear into Kean up to his knuckles and decided he liked this. It felt a little weird at first, but seeing how much Kean enjoyed it spurred him on. The beta kept making little grunts of pleasure, sounds that Bray found wonderfully erotic. Then he realized that two fingers were still a lot less than his dick, and he added a third.

"Oh, damn," Kean sighed. "Oh, fuck."

Bray kept watching him as he closed his eyes, biting his lips as his hole stretched around Bray's fingers. There was something powerful about this, something magical to see his body respond to Bray's touch.

He changed his fingers' position, curling them, and Kean catapulted off the bed. "Okay, that's it. I'm ready," the beta declared, and Bray pulled out. As much as he enjoyed fingering him, his cock was leaking and dying to get inside that tight hole.

He rolled a condom on within seconds, then applied extra lube, figuring it couldn't hurt to be on the safe side, and was back in position, Kean watching him with hungry eyes. Just as he wanted to slide in, the beta said, "Bray, one more thing. In case you forgot: no knotting. That's a little more than I'm willing to do for a first time."

Bray's brain registered the "first time" part first, already reveling in the fact that Kean wasn't excluding a follow-up, but then the previous part sank in. No knotting. He hadn't even thought of that, that betas might not like that part. Or maybe it hurt too much? That made sense, since they weren't as flexible on the inside as omegas, who were built to bear children. As much as he hated to admit it, it was good Kean had warned him. Shit, he could've fucked that up.

He wanted to wave him off, but instead opted for a little more honesty here, since Kean deserved that much. "Okay. Tell me if I'm hurting you, okay?"

Kean's blue eyes sparkled as they met Bray's. "What if I want it to hurt a little?"

Bray's mouth dropped open and stayed that way for a few seconds, before he caught himself. He swallowed thickly, looking down on Kean as he rested himself on his arms. "You like it rough?" he checked to make sure he understood.

"Yeah. I'm not some fragile omega, Bray. I won't break. I may bruise a little, but given the right circumstances, I may not mind so much."

Bray swallowed again. "That's a lot of trust you have in me."

Kean's grin softened. "I know you'll respect my limits."

"Always," Bray swore.

"I know. Do your worst, alpha. Have at it."

Call him weird, but hearing Kean call him "alpha" did something to Bray. He said it so rarely, and to hear him say it now, in that low, growly voice, when Bray was about to take him...man, he wanted to do things to him. Dirty things. Hot things. All-night-long-and-then-again things.

The buzz in his veins that had simmered down increased to a roar. His cock found Kean's slick hole, and he pushed in, less worried now about hurting him. It was an unfamiliar feeling, to not have to be careful. Even in the club, with subs, he was still always aware omegas were fragile compared to him. Delicate was a better word, and that sure as fuck did not apply to Kean Hightower.

He plunged in, delighted when Kean let out a low moan of pleasure, opening wide for Bray's onslaught. He pinned Kean's arms down—loving the way their bodies fit together with him on top—then planted his knees for a better angle and went to town. It was rough, deep, deliciously slick and so fucking tight.

Kean's tan body moved with his, his hips snapping up to eagerly meet his thrusts, the two of them finding a rhythm as old as time. "Damn, Kean," he grunted, sweat pearling on his body.

"Alpha," Kean moaned, jamming his ass down, allowing Bray to sink his cock in even deeper.

Bray lowered himself on top of Kean, blanketing him, trapping the beta's cock between them. He held on to Kean's wrists, still pinning them against the mattress, though he wasn't even protesting it. He'd never felt a body like this underneath him. Not this strong, this smooth, this soft and tough at the same time. His skin was like velvet, glowing and slick, setting Bray on fire everywhere their bodies touched. He'd always thought Kean gorgeous, but right now, the beta took his breath away.

He lowered his mouth, hovered until Kean's eyes found his, then closed the distance. His teeth found his bottom lip, that stubborn lip that could smirk like no one else. He nipped, delighted when Kean let out a little growl, then bit again before soothing the sore spot with his tongue. Kean let him, surrendering fully, welcoming Bray's invasion in his mouth and his body. It was magical, Bray thought, then his mind shut down to everything else but the urge to claim Kean.

They were in sync, their bodies moving in a flawless harmony, Kean's choppy breaths mingling with Bray's. His balls churned, communicating their desire to unload, and he sped up. Kean met his pace, a string of moans falling from his lips now, each one spurring Bray on even further. He pressed down his stomach, increasing the friction on Kean's cock, which was leaking like crazy.

"Bray..." the beta grunted, then louder, "Bray!"

Bray's eyes screwed shut as he bent over deeper, every part of his body touching and claiming Kean's. He started shaking, the tingle that inched down his spine settling in his balls, his cock, until the pressure was unbearable. He held on as long as he could by sheer will, not wanting this pleasure ride to end. Then he couldn't take it anymore, the pleasure blazing through him unstoppable. He allowed it to overtake him, and then he soared, flew. He vaguely registered Kean letting out a choked cry, but Bray was lost to his orgasm. Stars. He saw actual fucking stars explode right before his eyes as he emptied his balls and filled up the condom.

He barely had the strength to pull out after, holding the condom, then tying it off and dropping it on the floor for now. His body was still shaking as he gathered a trembling Kean close and claimed his mouth again, greedily swallowing the beta's gasps as he rode out the last waves of his orgasm.

Kean's arms found his biceps, then pushed off and rolled both of them over, with Bray on the bottom on his back, Kean splayed out on top of him, his hungry kiss signaling they weren't done yet.

"That was an excellent first round," Kean whispered a little while later, and Bray smiled.

Kean put his head on Bray's shoulder, and Bray's hands explored his back, smoothing down the planes of his shoulder blades, his spine, his lower back, and then those perfect globes. Kean had a clear tan line from working without a shirt outside, his pale ass in sharp contrast with that tan skin everywhere else. It was endearing, and Bray found himself wanting to explore that ass in more detail. Much more detail.

His fingers trailed lower, dipping down Kean's crack. That was the downside of wearing a condom, he thought. One day, he'd love to see his cum drip down a man's ass. How gorgeous would that look on Kean, those luscious cheeks all pale and white and then cum seeping out? He could picture it and was hard thinking about it. Then again, his erection had never gone down even after coming, the boost from Lidon's shift still humming through him.

Bray smiled when Kean spread his legs wider, allowing him more access. The beta was clearly on board for more. He dragged his head up for another searing kiss.

"Let's see if we can make round two even better."

5

Ruari woke up from a slumber when his ten-week-old son started crying.

"What's wrong, Jax?" he whispered, dragging himself out of bed to pick his son out of the crib. "Are you hungry?"

He checked the clock. Two hours since his last feeding. He shouldn't be hungry, then, since he'd finished the whole bottle. He cradled him against his shoulder and slowly walked around the room, making swinging motions with his upper body. Hopefully, Jax would fall asleep again without needing the baby carrier, 'cause once he was in there, Ruari couldn't get him out without waking him up again, which meant he'd be stuck for hours.

Jax's cries decreased in intensity, and Ruari hummed a song. His son seemed to love that, but whether it was because of the sound or because of the vibrations in Ruari's chest he found soothing, Ruari wasn't sure. Jax had just closed his eyes again, letting out a last feeble whimper, when Ruari swayed, a dizziness enveloping him. He had to

lean with a hand against the wall for support to keep from
stumbling, his heart racing as he waited for the dizzy spell
to pass.

This was, what, the fourth time this week? He let out a
shaky sigh as he felt his body return to normal. This
couldn't go on. One of these days, he would fall down the
stairs with Jax, or stumble and fall on top of him. He needed
to have his blood work checked, but how?

He once again cursed his body as he'd done so many
times before. Even as a teen, something had been off with
him in comparison with other omegas. His heat had been
late, for instance, really late. Plus, he'd been so tired and
slow, fighting some days to get out of bed. Depressed, too,
but that could have been because of his parents. Well, his
father.

His mother had taken him to the doctor plenty of times,
but the man had never found anything abnormal. Of course,
that was before he'd become a prisoner in his own home,
before his father had decided he needed to be locked in his
room. Ruari had never gotten an explanation, had never
understood why, what he'd done wrong. Had his father
discovered how much Ruari knew about his activities? That
he'd overheard more than one conversation he shouldn't
have?

Whatever the reason had been, for the six months
before his first heat had arrived—finally—he'd only left his
room to spend time in the garden every day, 'cause his
mother had insisted he needed sunlight. He'd been ready to
kill himself, and that was not even a joke.

Then his heat had come, that horrible, horrible heat,
and they'd shoved an alpha into the room who'd gone all
but feral on him. Not that he hadn't wanted it at that point—

he'd been clawing the walls for release—but he'd imagined his first heat a little differently. Thank fuck he hadn't been a virgin, 'cause that would have been a fucked-up introduction to sex.

Jax let out a little smacking sound, then fell asleep—thank god—and Ruari lowered himself into the rocking chair, the only decent chair in his tiny one-bedroom apartment. As his son nestled against him in his sleep, Ruari thought about his predicament. Something was wrong with him, something serious enough to make him dizzy all the time, and he needed to get it checked out.

He couldn't go to a regular doctor. His father would keep tabs on doctors and hospitals, somehow, probably through the electronic patient information system most of them used. The man had informants everywhere, including on the police force. Ruari had a fake ID, but it wouldn't stand up to that level of scrutiny.

Even if he could find a doctor, payment was also an issue. He was low on funds, dangerously low, in fact. He had two, three months left at most—if he budgeted carefully—and that was it. That budget left no room for blood tests and a consult that could run up to five hundred dollars without insurance.

No, he needed a free clinic, but those were scarce for omegas. And many of them had long waiting lines outside, which would be impossible with Jax. Hell, he didn't even want to bring a baby into a clinic like that in the first place. Fuck knew what it would expose him to, but what choice did he have?

Maybe he should see if there were other options. He reached out for his phone, one of the few things he'd taken from his parents' home when he'd ran away, though he'd had to switch to a prepaid plan and had to limit his data usage. It took a little while, typing and holding the phone with the same hand, since his other was wrapped around his son, but he managed to start a search for free clinics for omegas.

The first few hits were the ones he already knew about. One was way too close to his father's office, the other in a neighborhood Ruari didn't dare to venture in even during the day. The third one had a good rep, but was notorious for its waiting lines, which could be as long as four hours. Not an option with his dizziness and Jax with him.

Then his eyes fell on a mention of a clinic he'd never heard of before. Hayes Clinic. Huh, that had to be a new one. He clicked on the link, which led him to a basic website. He first checked their location. Damn, they were way out in the boonies. That would be a major hassle with public transportation, since he didn't have a car. Then again, it was also far off the beaten track, so his chances of running into anyone were slim.

He scanned their FAQs, since that usually told him whether they charged for anything and if there were any special requirements he needed to be aware of. It all looked legit, and he got the sense this doctor—Enar Magnusson—cared about his patients. There was something about the tone of the website that was different, something warm and caring. It drew him in, like that clinic was a safe place to be. That made zero sense, and yet Ruari couldn't shake it off.

He glanced through the rest of the questions, stopping when he saw something he didn't quite understand. It said the clinic offered free testing for the Melloni gene. What the hell was that? He clicked on the name, which was a link to a different website, some kind of blog. Palani Hightower. The name sounded familiar, but Ruari couldn't place it.

The blog post was a long one, he saw. Did he need to know all this? Then he saw a bullet list of symptoms and read through them. Delayed heat. Intense heats. Increased fertility. Depression. He almost dropped the phone, his heart racing as he recognized each and every one of them. It was describing him, this list.

He read the rest of the article, his heart speeding up even faster as he tried to take it all in. But when he saw that unsuspecting women had been injected by their OB/GYN with something that had created this genetic mutation, his heart all but stopped, and he got dizzy all over again.

This was it. This was what had happened to him. Oh god, it all made sense now. And his parents knew. That's what had happened the six months before his heat. Those heated fights between his parents about his mother going behind his father's back when she was trying to get pregnant, seeking help from this fertility specialist who'd injected her with that gene. He hadn't been able to make sense of it back then, but now he understood.

That's why they had locked him up, since apparently, his smell was irresistible to alphas. It also explained why that first alpha had gone nuts on him. And it was how Ruari had ended up pregnant, despite using condoms. This explained everything.

He had this gene. There was no other explanation. He had to get to this clinic and get tested. And if he was lucky, they could check up on Jax as well. His mind made up, Ruari started looking for a way to get there.

LIDON WAS balls deep inside Palani for one of those quick fucks they both loved so much, when his phone rang.

Palani's look was almost comical, like he was personally offended that someone had the audacity to call at this time. Then again, Lidon was pretty sure he was sporting an identical expression. Their eyes met, the temptation to let it ring unspoken between them, then Palani shook his head.

"You should get it. You don't get that many calls, so this is probably important."

Lidon pulled out with a frustrated sigh. "We will get back to this after."

Palani grinned. "Is that a threat or a promise?"

Lidon was still smiling as he picked up. It only took seconds for that smile to disappear, and when he hung up, Palani had picked up on the fact that something was going on.

"That was Watkins," Lidon told him.

"The PI? I thought he didn't work for us anymore since he couldn't find anything about Melloni or the fraud case against you?"

"He doesn't, but he wants to meet with us. He says he has new information."

Palani's face showed the same surprise Lidon was feeling. "Now?"

"I told him we'd meet him in the city in an hour," Lidon said. "I've never met him in person, so I don't want him inside the gates."

"Obviously. Let's get dressed."

Minutes later, they were on their way to the city, where Lidon had agreed to meet the PI in a restaurant. When they walked in, the man was already sitting there at the table they had agreed on. He was younger than Lidon had expected, in his early forties, a sturdy alpha with sharp, gray eyes and a face that showed he'd seen his fair share of shit.

"Mr. Hayes," the PI said. "It's a pleasure to meet you in person." His handshake was firm.

"Likewise. This is my mate, Palani. You've spoken before."

"Yes, the reporter. Pleasure to meet you. I admire your investigative journalism," Watkins said. "It's a crying shame they fired you from your job, but I think your reach and influence have grown bigger since."

Lidon wasn't sure if the man did it on purpose, but showing Palani respect was a surefire way to gain Lidon's respect. He appreciated when people could look past labels and admire a man for their character and their talents rather than for their status assigned at birth.

When the server appeared, they all ordered, and as soon as the woman was out of earshot, Watkins leaned forward, lowering his voice. "I know that technically, I am no longer on a retainer, but I happened to come across some information that is of crucial importance to you."

Lidon nodded. "We appreciate it. Please, go ahead."

Watkins looked around, as if he wanted to make sure no one was listening in, then lowered his voice even further. "I have credible information that Professor Melloni is still alive."

Lidon's heart skipped a beat before continuing its usual rhythm. "He's alive?"

"Yes. You have to understand, I'm in a gray area here, as I discovered this information through another client who hired me, a client whose name I cannot reveal."

"We understand. We appreciate you sharing anything with us that you can," Palani said. He of all people would understand confidentiality of sources, Lidon thought.

"This client who has hired me, he has a son who has run

away from home. My job is to find him. I haven't, yet, but in tracking potential leads my employer provided me with, I checked out some properties he owns. He is...not exactly legal in everything that he does, let's put it that way. One of the properties was owned by a dummy corporation. I did a cross check to see what other properties this corporation held and discovered industrial buildings in another city. Even though my client hadn't told me to investigate those, I did, wanting to be thorough, and one of those buildings turned out to be some kind of lab, which struck me as unusual. I didn't manage to get inside, but I did talk to one of the guards there. The fact that it even had guards alerted me something was going on, as this was a rather rundown neighborhood that didn't look like it needed private security from one of the most expensive firms in the country. To make a long story short, the young guard and I connected well..."

It didn't take Lidon but a second to get the meaning of that statement, and he couldn't suppress a smile. "Please, continue," he said.

"Let's say in our case pillow talk was a little less sexy and romantic and a whole lot more about him trying to brag about guarding some top scientist. I'm almost sure he was talking about Melloni."

Next to him, Palani let out a soft gasp. "He's alive, then."

Watkins nodded. "I think so, yes."

The server returned with their food, and they were silent as she handed them their plates and refilled their drinks. When she was gone again, Watkins spoke up.

"Here's my problem. I know you hired me months ago to track down Melloni, and I wasn't successful. The problem is that I'm now on someone else's payroll, and his interests are in a direct conflict with yours. If I had known that when I started working for him, I wouldn't have accepted the job, but I didn't. It sounded like a simple case of a missing person, quick money, since he pays me well. But it turns out he's got a lot of shady dealings that I'm finding out while investigating his son's disappearance, and some of those dealings are a direct threat to you."

Lidon's adrenaline spiked. "Threat?" he repeated, keeping his voice soft.

"Yes, but that's all I can say."

Lidon studied the man in front of him. He didn't appear to be the type that was intimidated easily, but his eyes sure held fear now. "Your client, he's not someone you want to get on your bad side," Lidon concluded.

"Very much so, Mr. Hayes. Trust me, if I'd known who he was, I would've never taken the job."

"If we act on the information you've given us, we might put you in jeopardy," Palani said, showing he had reached the same conclusion Lidon had.

"That's my gut feeling right now. My client is suspicious of everyone around him, trusts no one. My guess is that if the information about Melloni leaks, he'll know it was me, and I don't think that would end well for me."

"Is he being treated well, as far as you know? Or are they torturing him?" Palani asked.

Watkins did a quick shake of his head. "I have to go on what the guard told me, but it sounded as if they're treating him relatively well. They're forcing him to work on something, but the guard had no idea what. But he confirmed it's a lab, and that this scientist has access to laboratory equipment, as he called it."

"Are they holding him there? Is that where he lives?" Palani asked.

"Yes. They built a bedroom for him in the back of the building."

"You want us to sit on this information and not act on it," Lidon clarified.

Watkins shot him an apologetic look. "I know that's a lot to ask, since his son must be desperate to hear something about his father. And it's hard for me to ask you to value my safety over that of Professor Melloni."

"But you came to us with this information," Palani said. "So my guess is you have a plan, or at least a specific request to us, right?"

The corners of the PI's mouth pulled up in a smile. "I see your reputation is well deserved. Yes, I do have a plan. Or at least, something resembling a plan. This client is dangerous. Deadly dangerous."

"What do you propose?" Lidon asked.

"I am asking you to trust me. I need to find my client's son first, so I can end my contract with him. Meanwhile, I will continue to find out what I can about Melloni. If I suspect at any point he's in real danger, I will act, I promise. I need a little more time to figure out what's going on."

Lidon and Palani shared a look. It shouldn't surprise Lidon anymore, that they could communicate without words, and yet as he locked eyes with his mate, his right hand, it amazed him all over again how in tune they were.

"We can live with those terms," Palani said, and how Lidon loved that he was confident enough to communicate the decision to Watkins without deferring to Lidon. "But we would appreciate if you could tell us a little more about what threat your client poses to us. We don't need names, because we understand the difficult position you're in, but can you give us anything more so we can prepare?"

Watkins studied them for a long time, his face tight.

Lidon could all but see him going over every option in his mind.

"My client was behind the attack on your ranch," he said finally. Palani's hand shot out to grab Lidon's arm in an iron grip. "That should tell you enough about what kind of threat he poses to you. He's not done with you by far."

6

Even though he'd done it dozens of time by now, Ruari still triple-checked to make sure the baby sling was fastened securely before he let his son's weight settle. Jax had been fussy all morning, so hopefully being nestled against Ruari's chest would make him fall asleep.

Maybe he was teething, Ruari thought as Jax let out another cry of protest. He caressed his son's baby fuzz. Or was that too early? Babies could get upset from something as small as some air in their stomach or intestines, he remembered from the baby book he'd read. If the sling didn't work, he could try belly rubs or trying to make him burp. Well, after he came back from the clinic.

He slung the backpack with all Jax's stuff over his shoulder. He'd never known how much a tiny little infant could need in a few hours' time, but every time he took him outside, it was like a small move. By now, he had a standard backpack to go out, one that he refilled as soon as he came home. After running out of diapers once when he'd forgotten to restock it, that would never happen to him again.

Ruari could only hope the wait in the clinic wouldn't be too long. He'd wanted to leave earlier, but everything always took more time with a baby, even something as simple as taking a shower. He couldn't remember the last time he'd spent more than three minutes in the shower and a bubble bath had become a thing of the distant past. When Jax slept, Ruari slept, and when he was awake, Ruari was busy with him.

Going on a trip like this, where he'd be gone a few hours, that was something he rarely did. It sucked up too much of his already precariously low energy. Plus, he was too scared to run into someone he knew, someone who could rat him out to his father. But knowing he had that gene was all the motivation he needed to make this trip. He was almost sure he had it, but he needed to get tested. Plus, they could check him out and find a cause for those dizzy spells. Still, it had taken him a week to gather all his courage and head out to the clinic.

The trip was long and cumbersome, switching buses three times, and by the time he was nearing the clinic, he was exhausted. The last bus hadn't gone farther than the crossing of the road that led to the clinic, and it had been at least a two-mile walk from there. Jax had slept for a bit, but was starting to get fussy again. "Hang on just a little longer, baby. Daddy will get you out in a few minutes, okay?"

A sign indicated the clinic's entrance was just a little farther on the right. He hoped it really was, because his body was telling him it was reaching the end of his energy reserves. He needed to sit for a bit and maybe eat something, because he was getting light-headed again.

He tripped and stumbled, instinctively cradling Jax, but

a strong arm gripped his elbow and held him up. "Whoa, careful there," a concerned voice spoke.

When he looked up to see who had saved him from falling, the blood withdrew from his head, and he felt himself go weak as jelly. He let out a cry of anguish as he sagged, but even as his vision went black, hands held him and he collapsed against a body strong enough to hold him.

Ruari came to in an air-conditioned room, blinking to clear the fog from his mind, still dizzy and weak. He panicked when the baby sling was missing from his chest. "Jax," he cried out. "Where's my baby?"

"He's right here, and he's fine," a soothing male voice said. "I'm taking good care of him."

Ruari turned his head. A rather sturdy beta was tenderly cradling Jax as if he did it every day, while his blue eyes were fixed on Ruari. It made for quite the picture and Ruari's heart eased a little.

"Who are you?" Ruari asked. The guy was dressed in cargo shorts and a T-shirt, not the kind of uniform he'd expect from medical personnel.

"I'm Kean Hightower. I'm the one who found you outside when you were feeling unwell, so I carried you inside. Enar is with another patient, but he'll be with you shortly. I promised him I'd stay with you."

"Enar?" Ruari asked, confused. The name sounded familiar, but his head was still too foggy to remember.

"Sorry, Dr. Magnusson. He's my brother-in-law, so he's Enar to me."

"Ah, okay," Ruari said, his head clearing a little. He studied the man who was holding his son so gently. Jax was awake, making the soft smacking noises that always made Ruari tear up with tenderness. "He's hungry," he said.

"Okay, do you want me to bring him to you and give you

some privacy so you can feed him?" Kean said, as if it was the most normal topic of conversation between two people who had just met.

Ruari felt a blush creep up his cheeks. "I eh... He's bottle-fed."

Kean nodded. "Okay. I assume you have everything in your backpack? I can make a bottle for him if you want?"

Ruari's blush deepened. "I can do it myself, but thank you."

"My instructions were to make sure you stayed in a reclining position—quoting my brother-in-law here—until he's had a chance to examine you, so that option won't fly."

Kean's voice was kind and friendly, but Ruari had no trouble detecting the steel spine inside. And while he usually didn't back down from a fight, he was just too tired right now.

"Okay," he capitulated. "You do it then."

Kean handed him back his son, and he cradled his soft body while he told the beta how much water to add to the powder already in the bottle, and how to shake it. To his surprise, Kean washed his hands first in the basin in the exam room, then rubbed hand sanitizer on them before he even touched the bottle. Someone had been trained well, Ruari thought.

Kean seemed to have no trouble with the instructions Ruari gave him, and Jax's bottle was ready in no time. Just when Kean handed it to him, the door opened and an alpha dressed in scrubs came in.

"Ah," he said. "I see you're awake. I'm sorry for the delay, but we had an emergency delivery happening right when Kean brought you in. We're not equipped for emergencies, so sorry you had to wait for a bit."

"No problem," Ruari said. Once upon a time he would

have seen a private doctor without waiting at all, but all that had changed with Jax. Now, he was grateful to even be seen at all.

"So, I'm Dr. Magnusson, but please, call me Enar."

Ruari could barely hide his surprise at that un-alpha-like breach of protocol. "Ruari," he said, using his new chosen name and omitting his last name. He wasn't revealing that, knowing the uproar it might cause. His father was too well-known.

"Let's talk about what brought you in here today."

"I need to feed my son," Ruari said. "He's already hungry so he won't stay quiet much longer."

"Oh, okay," Enar said. "How about you do that and I'll pop back in as soon as my schedule opens again? It might be a little while though, if that's okay with you."

Ruari was stuck. What did he do now? He didn't want to lose his chance of being checked out, but he had to catch the last bus back or he'd miss his connection and end up stranded at the bus terminal. But if he didn't feed Jax now, he'd have a fit, and he'd be off his schedule.

"I don't mean to interrupt," Kean said, startling Ruari who had forgotten the beta was still there. "But if it's okay with you, I can feed the baby while you talk to Enar. I'll bring him back as soon as he's done."

"No!" Jax started crying at Ruari's sharp voice, and he hushed him, rocking him and kissing his head until he calmed down. "I need to be in the same room as him."

Enar and Kean shared a look he couldn't decipher, but this was not something he would budge on. Losing Jax was his biggest fear, and he didn't know this man, no matter how kind and dependable he looked. His father had men everywhere and if they took Jax from him, they could make him do anything.

"I can sit here and feed him," Kean said hesitantly. "But I'd overhear your conversation with Enar, so you'd have no privacy."

A memory flashed through Ruari's mind of giving birth with only strangers around him. He'd lost any sense of privacy a long time ago. He would do anything to keep Jax safe, even if that meant bearing all in front of strangers. "That's fine," he said. "I just want to be able to be near him."

"Okay," Kean said. "That okay with you, Doc?"

Enar smiled. "Absolutely. Thanks, Kean. Go sit in that chair, I'll hand you the baby. Does that work for you, Ruari?"

Ruari nodded and watched as Enar took Jax from him and then handed him to Kean, who settled in a comfy chair, the bottle ready. "You need to hold him..." Ruari started, then stopped as he saw how expertly Kean held both baby and bottle.

"Do you have kids?" he asked.

Kean smiled, looking up from Jax. "Baby goats, lambs, and calves," he said and when Ruari frowned, he added, "I'm a vet tech here at the PTP ranch, and I've bottle-fed more than a few baby animals in my life. Babies are babies, you know?"

He smiled at Ruari, who couldn't help but smile back. The guy's genuine friendliness was contagious.

"Thank you," he said.

"Okay, now that that's settled, let's talk," Enar said.

KEAN LOVED the little sucking sounds the baby made as he fed him his bottle. He was drinking greedily, and Kean had to tilt the bottle back every now and then to make sure he wasn't drinking too fast. Kean thought babies were cute in general, but this one was exceptionally gorgeous with round, pink cheeks, a little button nose, and a pair of dark blue eyes that looked like they would turn brown.

It was no wonder the kid was beautiful, considering his daddy, though his eyes had to come from his alpha-father, since Ruari's were a deep shade of blue, Kean had noticed. Enar had pulled a privacy curtain around them so Kean couldn't see them anymore—not that he would have looked anyway—but he had no trouble picturing Ruari. The omega was gorgeous, though Kean had also spotted the dark circles under his eyes that spoke of exhaustion and a too thin frame that betrayed he wasn't eating enough.

"What brings you in today?" Enar asked.

"I read about the Melloni gene and that you offered free testing," Ruari said, and Kean's insides clenched painfully. Every time he heard stories of omegas with the gene, it broke his heart all over again. Palani had shared only a little of what Vieno had been through, but it had been enough to ensure Kean understood how awful that gene was for omegas.

"We do," Enar said. "Can you tell me why you think you may have the gene?"

"My first heat was late," Ruari said, his voice detached. "I think my parents knew about the gene, since they locked me up the last months before my heat came. They arranged for a caretaker for me, and when he walked into the room, he went crazy with my smell."

His voice broke a little for the first time, and Kean struggled not to say anything, his whole heart going out to the omega. Instead, he pressed a soft kiss on the baby's head.

"I remember little, but I know he couldn't satisfy me. I needed something more, and he got angry with me when I kept begging him to fulfill me. Even knotting didn't work."

"I assume he was wearing a condom?" Enar asked.

"Yes. I didn't want to get pregnant."

"I'm so sorry to hear this, Ruari. I'll ask you a few more questions before we do the testing, okay? Do you have any siblings?"

"No. And yes, my mother had trouble conceiving and used the services of a fertility specialist, albeit behind my father's back. I heard them fighting about it, but it didn't make sense until I read about the gene. I think my father recognized the symptoms in me, as I did when I read Mr. Hightower's blog posts..." His voice trailed off. "You said your last name was Hightower. Are you...?" he called out to Kean.

Before Kean could answer, Enar spoke up. "Yes, Kean is his brother."

Kean wondered if the omega would make the connection, but he didn't have to wait long to find out. "He said you were his brother-in-law, does that mean you're with his brother?" Ruari asked Enar, the puzzlement in his voice clear.

"Yes, but not just with him. There's four of us."

Kean all but held his breath, wondering how Ruari would react to that news. He knew they were pretty open about it, but not everyone reacted with understanding. "Oh," Ruari said. "That's cool."

Kean could practically hear Enar's sigh of relief. "It is," he said. "We're very happy together, and we're the proud fathers to a baby boy, an alpha heir. His name is Hakon."

You couldn't miss the pride in his voice, and it gave Kean all the feels all over again. It was amazing to see how deeply Enar and Palani loved that baby, even though biologically, it wasn't theirs.

"Congratulations on your alpha heir," Ruari said.

"He's not my heir, Ruari. He's our alpha's son."

Kean could only imagine Ruari's confusion right now. It had taken him a little while to get used to seeing Enar as a beta, but now it was routine. He couldn't blame Ruari for being a little confused, however, and was waiting for him to ask for clarification. Instead, the omega softly said, "He's still your son, then, isn't he?"

"Yes, he is. Very much so," Enar said, gratitude and pride ringing in his voice. "But let's get back to you. Did that first heat result in your pregnancy?"

Ruari let out a deep sigh. "No, that was the second one. My parents kept me under lock and key, but I managed to get away. I found a club that offered secure heat-services, and so I stayed in a hotel right next door for two weeks and then rode it out in the club. I'd taken heat blockers, but I'm not sure they had much effect. I had an alpha helping me, and while it was a little better than the first time, it was still intense. I'm sure he had a great time, but it once again left me unsatisfied and struggling. We used condoms, but I got pregnant anyway."

"I'm sorry for your negative experiences, Ruari. It sounds like you have the symptoms of the gene, but we'll know for sure after we test you. It'll take two weeks for the results to come in," Enar said. "Have you had a heat since you gave birth?"

"No. But I'm not breastfeeding, so it shouldn't take long, right?"

"No. On average, your first heat will be about three to six months after giving birth if you don't breastfeed. How old is your baby?"

"Almost ten weeks. What do I do if my heat comes? Is there a medicine I can take to make it less intense? I can't leave Jax to fend for himself for two days."

Ruari sounded close to panic, and Kean couldn't blame him. It was a horrible position to be in as a single daddy. His hands itched to offer help, but that was ridiculous, of course.

"We're experimenting with various meds to see what works. There's still a lot we don't know about how this gene works. What we do know is that you need alpha sperm, so you'll need to find an alpha you can trust and go without condoms. The proteins in the sperm help quench that desperate need you have during your heat, no matter if they enter you orally, anally, or even on your skin."

Kean's cheeks flushed, and he could only imagine how mortified Ruari had to be knowing that someone else was listening in on this private conversation. To distract himself, he focused on the baby, Jax. The name fit him somehow, this tiny little human. He was done drinking and Kean put the bottle aside, then put Jax against his shoulder and patted his back.

"Okay, that's good to know," Ruari said, much calmer than Kean had expected him to be. "But how will I prevent another pregnancy?"

"I can prescribe meds, but know that these are not one hundred percent effective. There's still a risk of getting pregnant, which is why I recommend asking an alpha you trust to avoid nasty legal situations."

Ruari was quiet for a long time. "I'm... I'll have to think about this. I lost my support network when I got pregnant, so I don't have a lot of options right now. I'd also need to find care for Jax, and that's not easy either."

"I understand. Let's do the testing first and wait for the results. That will take two weeks. We can talk about all this once we know for certain, okay? That way, you'll also have more time to consider your options."

Jax let out a burp, and Kean chuckled, joined in by the

other two men. "There ya go," Kean whispered to the baby. "That was a good burp, my man."

"Did you have a checkup since you gave birth?" Enar asked Ruari.

"No, and that was another reason I wanted to come in. I've been having dizzy spells, like what just happened outside. I don't want to fall and accidentally hurt Jax."

"Okay, let's have a look at what's going on, then. You can get undressed and put on the gown, and I'll be right back. I'll draw some blood from you and check you out, okay?"

"Doc, when you're done with me, could you please check out Jax as well?"

"Ruari, I'm not a pediatrician," Enar said.

"I know, but I have nowhere else to go. I don't have insurance, and I can't go anywhere where they'll register me."

Kean wondered what had Ruari so spooked that he was this careful with his identity. Clearly, something was wrong. Was it the baby's father? It wouldn't be the first time that an alpha demanded custody of a child he'd fathered, especially if the baby was an alpha. The law was still on the alpha's side in cases like this, though Prime Minister York wanted to change it. His Conservative Wolf Party had managed to affect some changes that benefitted omegas, but the opposition against them was growing.

"In that case, I'd be happy to check him out," Enar said, his voice warm and kind.

Kean tuned out what happened behind that curtain, wanting to give Ruari the privacy he should have had. He cradled Jax, rocking him until he fell asleep minutes later against his chest. He had a ton of things to do, but right now, Kean was a happy man, just sitting here, holding that baby.

7

"We need a pediatrician in the clinic," Enar told Palani later that day.

They were sweaty after a round of flip-fuck sex where they'd switched off until they'd both come hard. That would make his hole nice and ready for Lidon to take him later, Enar thought. Vieno wasn't healed enough yet to be sexually active, and though Lidon's libido had receded somewhat as a result, he still came to Palani and Enar more than usual. Not that they minded, hell no, but it helped if they were ready for him.

"Kean told me you had an omega collapsing right outside the clinic today?" Palani said as he gathered Enar close and held him against his chest, an experience that still made Enar's heart sing. How he loved to be held, especially by Palani who could be so tender.

"What else did he tell you?" Enar asked, wondering for a second if Kean had breached patient confidentiality. He wasn't a doctor or a nurse, so technically, you couldn't fault him, but it was something Enar would be bummed about.

"Nothing," Palani assured him. "He said he'd seen an

omega collapse and that he'd brought him into the clinic and had stayed with him for a spell."

"Yeah, we had an emergency come in, a pregnant omega who went into early labor, so Kean stayed with the omega who fainted until I could see him. That's why I said we need a pediatrician. He asked me to check out his baby, and that's the fifth one this week. We need to find a pediatrician so we can offer free checkups for the babies as well."

Palani kissed his head. "Okay, Doc. You know we can expand the clinic if we have to. It's set up for that. Do you know anyone?"

"A few, but Maz may have some ideas."

"Okay, we'll see what we can do."

Enar's thoughts went back to Ruari. He'd been exhausted, and Enar was certain that had caused him to faint. He was waiting for the results of the blood work to come back, but he was sure the omega was anemic and malnourished, his pale skin and protruding bones clear indicators. Ruari had been open about his experiences and his pregnancy, but he'd been tight-lipped about his personal situation. Enar got the sense he was hiding from someone. His baby's father, maybe? Or his parents, since Ruari had mentioned they were not on speaking terms since his pregnancy.

"I may have an omega we need to take in," he said. "I'm pretty sure he has the gene. He doesn't have a support network, and he has a ten-week-old son."

"Hmm," Palani said. "If he has the gene, he'd be best off in a self-contained unit, right?"

"I think so, also because he's super protective of his kid."

He understood that better now, that instinct to protect your child. He'd known it existed on a rational level, but since Hakon's birth, he'd come to a whole new level of understanding. Hakon might not be his biologically, but he was his son nonetheless, all of theirs. Ruari had understood that, even if Enar hadn't told him all the details.

The door to the bedroom opened and Vieno poked his head around the corner. "You guys done?" he asked with a strained smile.

"Hey, baby," Enar said, his heart warming when he saw him. "I haven't seen you all day. You want to come cuddle with us?"

Vieno seemed to hesitate, then closed the door behind him and made his way over.

"Hakon asleep?" Palani asked as Enar moved over to make room for Vieno in the middle.

Vieno kept his tank top and shorts on as he climbed in, Enar registered. It was one of the many small signals he'd picked up lately that something was off with their omega.

"Yes, Sven has the baby monitor," Vieno said. He nestled between them, and they both cuddled with him, Palani from the front and Enar spooning him from the back. "He said I looked like I needed some downtime."

Sven had been wonderful since the baby had been born, always willing to step up and take over for Vieno. And he had a way with babies, as he loved taking care of Hakon. Vieno should use him much more than he did, Enar thought, but for some reason, he was reluctant.

"Lidon is outside making his rounds, so he'll be in shortly as well," Palani said.

Enar couldn't see Vieno's face, but he felt his body tighten in response before he relaxed again. "I don't think I can stay till he's back. I don't want to leave Hakon for too long," he said, and Enar's alarm bells went off. His eyes met Palani's and while the beta didn't react, Enar knew he'd picked up on it.

Palani kissed Vieno's forehead. "I'm gonna take a shower. Why don't you cuddle with Enar for a bit?"

Vieno dutifully turned toward him as Palani got up and headed into the bathroom. There was little of his usual joy in the omega's face. He didn't look exhausted, Enar noted, more lifeless.

"What's wrong, little one?" he asked, his voice soft. "Won't you talk to me?"

Vieno's eyes filled with tears. "I don't know what's wrong," he whispered, his voice thick with emotions. "I'm just...sad."

"Okay," Enar said. "That's okay. Can you tell me what you're sad about?"

Vieno gave a frustrated gesture. "My head is a mess. It's so full of thoughts that I can't think, you know? I know that doesn't even make sense, but I don't know how to explain it."

Enar took his hands and kissed them, then held them against his heart while his mind was busy analyzing what Vieno had said. "Can you share one of those thoughts?"

Vieno's bottom lip quivered and Enar's heart broke a little, seeing him so sad. "I'm scared you'll get upset. Well, not you, but Lidon."

"Honey, you know how much he loves you, how much we all love you. I can't imagine you could ever do anything that would make him or us upset."

A big tear rolled down the omega's cheek and Enar wiped it away. He patiently waited till Vieno was ready.

"I don't feel like me, it's like someone else has taken over my body. I'm fat, my belly is still so flubby, and I'm just so sad all the time..."

"Oh honey," Enar said, gathering him close as Vieno burst into tears. He knew better than to counter anything his mate had just said. "Tell me everything. What else?"

Vieno sobbed against his shoulder, his body shaking with the force of it. "I'm broken. I want to so badly, but I can't. It doesn't feel right. Nothing does."

"What doesn't feel right?" Enar asked, already guessing the answer, but Vieno needed to say it.

"You, me, us. Everything. Like, you're naked and holding me and I'm supposed to want you but I don't. I really don't, and I'm broken. What happened to me? How do I fix this? I don't want you all to start hating me. And Lidon needs me, but I can't. I just can't."

And with that, Enar had his diagnosis, or at least a part of it. But before he could say anything, the door opened and Lidon came in. Vieno reacted to his presence as if he'd been slapped in the face, withdrawing from Enar, pushing him back with both hands. "I have to go," he said.

"What's wrong?" Lidon asked, hurrying over to the bed, picking up on Vieno's distress.

At the same time, Palani walked in from his shower, a towel wrapped around his waist. Vieno looked from Lidon to Palani and then to Enar, his eyes showing an intense despair.

"Sweetheart, talk to me, what's wrong?" Lidon asked again.

"What happened?" Palani asked.

Vieno sank to his knees in the middle of the room, then clamped his hands over his ears and started rocking back and forth, and Enar knew he had to stop this.

"Lidon, back off," he said. "Let me handle this."

Lidon frowned. "I want to—"

"Back off," Enar repeated with more force. "Please, alpha," he added to placate him.

Lidon's eyes blazed with indignation at being overruled,

but with a look at Vieno, he stepped back and allowed Palani to drag him to the side.

Enar focused on Vieno, who still sat rocking himself, his eyes closed. He lowered himself on the floor, not caring he was still naked and still had Palani's cum dripping out of his ass. "You're not broken, honey," he said softly. When Vieno didn't react, he said it again. "You're not broken, I promise."

Finally, Vieno looked up with tear-stricken eyes. "But something is wrong with me."

"I wouldn't call it wrong, but yes, there's something happening in your body and your mind."

"Can you fix it?" Vieno asked and the mix of hope and despair about killed Enar.

"We'll make it better, I promise. The four of us, honey, we've got this."

"W-what is it? What's wrong with me?" Vieno asked, and for the first time, Enar saw a spark of something in his eyes.

"You had one hell of a delivery, and it's going to take a while for your body to return to normal. So all those things that are feeling off, they're a sign you're not healed yet. Your body went through hell to deliver Hakon in such a short time, so it'll take longer for you to recover compared to others who had normal deliveries. It's not even been six weeks since you gave birth."

"Is that why my body feels so different?" Vieno asked, and Enar had no trouble picking up the veiled reference.

"Baby, if you don't feel ready yet for any sexual activities, that is okay. None of us expected you to jump back into that within weeks after your delivery. Your body went through a lot, and you need time to heal, both physically and mentally."

"But I looked it up, and it said most omegas are sexually active within four weeks of delivery. I'm so scared," Vieno said. "I've never felt this way, to look at one of you and not feel the attraction."

Enar wanted to hold him so badly, but he knew he would have to wait until Vieno indicated he was ready for that. But it broke his heart to see the omega so dejected and sad. "I know, baby. I can't even imagine how confusing that must feel for you, but you need to know none of us blame you for this. You take as long as you need to heal, and we'll be here. And those are just averages, and they're not based on precipitous labor."

Vieno's eyes were full of tears once again as he lifted his head to face Enar. "What if it never comes back? What if I am broken forever?"

"You won't be, baby, I promise. But even if that were the case, we would still love you. We don't love you for your body, as amazing as it is, or for the sex, as much as we enjoy that. We love you for who you are. I won't deny that it would be hard for all of us to adjust if that were the new reality, but we would find a way."

Vieno shook his head. "I hear you say the words, but somehow, I find it hard to believe. It's not just my body that's struggling. There's more, right? I'm thinking my depression has returned?"

Enar hesitated. He wasn't sure how much to tell Vieno. The omega had every right to know, but there was a balance to be struck between comforting him and scaring him. Then he saw Vieno's face, looking up at him with a mix of hope and horror, and Enar knew he had to tell him.

Before he could say anything, Vieno spoke up again. "I'm so scared it will come back. You don't know how much I struggled before we met you. Those dark days, when I would wake up, not sure if I would have the strength to make it to the end of the day. That black darkness that sucks all your energy and joy, I don't know if I can face that again."

"I know, baby. That must've been hell for you and for Palani, having to watch you struggle. But you're much stronger now, and you have all three of us. You have a big support system here, all these people wanting to help you every way they can. Plus, you have Hakon."

Vieno's shoulders dropped. "It's back then, my depression?"

Enar had to be honest. "In a way. It's not the same, but I think you have the symptoms of a postpartum depression. It's not uncommon after precipitous labor, but I am so sorry you have to go through this. But we are here for you, baby, you know that."

Even as he spoke, Enar heard a double gasp coming from the two men behind him. Lidon and Palani had not seen this coming, that much was obvious. He hated to spring it on them this way, but he had no choice. He owed Vieno the truth. Plus, they were in this together. This was not a battle Vieno would have to face alone.

"Is that why everything feels like a struggle?" Vieno asked.

Enar nodded. "Your body isn't fully healed, that's a fact. But your depression complicates things, because it makes it hard for you to distinguish between what's physical and real and what your mind is telling you. Your judgment is clouded, so to speak. Like, I told you we would love you no matter what, and you found that hard to believe. That's your depression talking, because a few months ago, you wouldn't have doubted that truth. But it's okay, baby. We understand, and we will help you through this."

Enar saw emotions flash over Vieno's face. It was a lot for the omega to take in. But at least they were talking about it now, and it was out in the open. That was an important first step, and the next would be to get Vieno to accept help. He had been struggling on his own, not sharing this with them, and that was unacceptable. The only way they would get through this was together. That thought triggered something in him, and he cocked his head.

"This is in no way an accusation and please don't take it that way, but am I right that you've been avoiding us? I've barely seen you the last two weeks, and I know that every time the three of us were intimate in some way, you weren't there. Is it too hard for you to watch?"

Vieno's eyes dropped to the floor, and it took a long time for him to answer. "It hurts to see you and not be a part of it. But at the same time, I don't want to be a part of it, and I'm scared that if I join, you guys will expect me to. I didn't want to have to say no, but I didn't want to be a cock tease either, I guess."

"Oh baby," Enar said. "You can always say no to us. We would never be upset with you for that. And you know we would never put pressure on you to do anything you don't want."

Vieno's eyes rose from the floor to look at Enar, and there was something in his look at that Enar didn't like at all. "Do I? Have you ever tried saying no to the pack alpha? You know what he can do, how strong his powers are. He could make me do anything he wanted, and we all know it."

LIDON HAD GOTTEN hurt in the line of duty multiple times, including a few injuries that had been rather painful. But the pain he felt in that moment as Vieno's words registered with him was so intense that it took his breath away. His heart felt like it was being stabbed with shards of glass. Cold, sharp glass that hurt deeper than he had ever thought possible.

Palani reached out to him, but Lidon stepped away, unsure if he could trust himself right now. He felt like his world had just fallen apart. How was it possible that after everything they had shared, Vieno would feel this way about him? When had the omega he loved so much that he would die for him become afraid of him? And not just intimidated, but scared to the point where he feared Lidon not only could force him to do anything, but that he would?

"I need to go," he managed, surprised that he could even still talk.

"Lidon, don't. It's his depression and anxiety talking. He doesn't mean it," Enar said, his voice pleading and emotional.

Lidon refused to look at him, too afraid he would have to face Vieno and that the fear and rejection on the omega's face would literally bring him to his knees. Without another word, he left the room, breaking into a run once he was in the hallway. He needed to go, outside, somewhere where he was alone and that no one could watch him fall to pieces.

He had just stumbled through the back door when his body started tingling, and he recognized the feeling. God, yes. He embraced it, the drive of his alpha to take over, surrendered to it fully while whipping off his shirt and kicking off his shoes. He was still wearing his underwear and shorts when he shifted, ripping them to shreds.

Darkness was falling outside, but he didn't care. It was perfect, because no one would be able to see him. All he wanted to do was run as far away as possible from everyone.

He heard someone call his name, but he ignored it. The first time he'd shifted, he'd been surprised that even in wolf form he could still understand language. Somehow, he had expected to lose that, to become fully animalistic. But apparently, that wasn't how it worked. Even as a wolf, his human side was still there.

And so he ran, cutting across the pack land in no time at all. He hesitated when he came to the border. Wolves weren't common in this area, so if he went outside of pack land, he better make sure no one saw him. He didn't want to end up getting shot by a hunter looking for a deer or something. Still, he had to run, had to get this deep emotion out of his system.

He left the pack land behind him, choosing to head to the mountains that were still in the distance. They were in a designated wilderness area, all but desolate and devoid of any human interaction. People were allowed, but few ventured out that way because there was nothing there. If you wanted to hike there, you had to bring everything, as even water was hard to find. It suited him well, and as he stretched his legs and broke out in a wild run, he marveled at his own speed.

It was such freedom, being in this form, uninhibited by a human body with all its limitations. He could see much better, his eyes having no trouble in the dark, even with only a pale moon guiding him. His hearing was stronger too, and his sense of smell was even better. A few miles in, he smelled wildlife before he ever saw the deer, and he smiled mentally. That would make hunting so much easier. But he didn't want to hunt now, he wasn't hungry for food. He kept running until he had reached the foot of the mountains, and it wasn't till then that he slowed down.

He found a spot to lie down and rest, amazed that his brain worked the same in this shape, even if his body and senses were different. His alpha still functioned as well, and he could sense Vieno's distress, even at this distance. That was interesting, he noted, that distance didn't make a difference in how he was connected to his omega.

Had he hoped differently when he ran this far? Had he hoped to disconnect from Vieno for a while, to escape the stress and anguish he knew his sudden departure would bring to his mate? He wasn't sure, but maybe he shouldn't ask himself that since he wasn't convinced he wanted to know the answer.

As his breathing slowed down, so did the frantic barrage of thoughts in his head. He wasn't prone to anxiety, like Enar was at times, and Vieno even more. In that sense, he and Palani were more alike, systematic and rational in their thinking. But that didn't mean he was without feelings, that his emotions couldn't get the better of him now and then. They had now, and as he felt himself settle down, he realized how deeply Vieno had cut him, probably without intending to.

No, not probably. Certainly. There was no way his mate, his wonderful, sweet Vieno, had hurt him on purpose. Even if he had lashed out in his current state of mind, it had to be because of what he was going through, as Enar had pointed out. Lidon hadn't been able to process that at the time, but now he realized that Enar had been right. It hadn't been Vieno talking, it had been his depression and anxiety.

And if Lidon was honest, his anger and hurt hadn't been aimed at just Vieno either. Yes, his omega's expression of distrust and fear had cut deep, but Lidon's anger encompassed more than that. There was a good portion of him upset with the others for missing all the symptoms Vieno must've had indicating he wasn't doing well. And the biggest part was rage with himself for missing them.

He and Vieno were connected on such a deep level, so

how could he have missed this? He'd kept his distance from him, not wanting to pressure him into something he wasn't ready for. And he missed him, god, he had missed him. Not just physically, though he couldn't deny that was the case. But he missed their emotional connection even more, the merging of their souls.

The first week after Hakon had been born, Lidon had still sought his company, had cuddled with him while holding their son together. But after a week, he noticed his own body reacting to Vieno's, and he had withdrawn, not wanting to appear like he was only after sex. Sure, he noticed Vieno had looked confused at times, but he figured it was better to keep a little distance from him. How wrong he had been. And how unbelievably fucking stupid.

He tried to recall what he knew about postpartum depression, but it wasn't much. The word depression indicated enough, he figured, which meant it wasn't something that could be healed overnight. Then again, Vieno's earlier symptoms that had been a result of the gene had all but disappeared after he connected with Lidon, hadn't they? Lidon and Palani had even discussed this, how stunned they had been to see not just Vieno's physical symptoms disappear but his mental symptoms as well. Could that be the case again?

Lidon mentally frowned. What if the solution to Vieno's current physical and mental struggles was the same as it had been before? He thought back to the delivery, and how sharing the power in that room between the four of them had proven to be what Vieno needed to survive the delivery. Lidon had asked Enar a few days after if Vieno would've made it without that, and Enar had shaken his head after a short hesitation. "Precipitous labor for omegas is extremely dangerous," he said. "Their bodies need the time to adjust before the baby is born, so the mortality rate for cases like this is high, about seventy percent. I've never seen an omega come through it as unharmed as he has, so yes, I credit your alpha powers," Enar had said.

"Our powers," Lidon had corrected him. "You know damn well it wasn't just me. It wasn't till we were connected with the four of us that he felt it work."

That exchange made Lidon wonder if that was what they needed to do again, somehow create that same connection. It was worth a try, right?

But first, he had some things to make right with his omega, his mate. It was a sobering thought that a few weeks into the whole fatherhood thing, he had already fucked up big time. As he rose from his spot under a tree where he'd been resting, Lidon vowed to do better.

He started the run back at a much lower speed than before, his body tired from the miles he'd already put in. It was interesting, though, that he'd managed to shift so easily. The previous time, when they'd announced to the pack they were experimenting, it had taken him two hours until he'd managed. This time, it had been a matter of seconds, of instinct, not a conscious and deliberate attempt. What had made it work? He kept pondering this as he made his way home, but couldn't come up with a satisfactory explanation.

He shifted back near the back door, not even sure how he pulled that off either. One second he had been a wolf, and the next he realized he couldn't open the door in wolf form, and he had shifted back to being a man. Hmm, he needed to figure out why it was so easy now when it had been so hard when he'd tried before.

He should have known Palani would be the one waiting for him, sitting in the kitchen with a large cup of coffee. Palani looked up from a book as Lidon entered the kitchen, naked, shivering, and dirty. He slowly rose from his spot at the table, putting his coffee mug down. Lidon tried to read him, to get a sense of what his mate was feeling, but for the first time ever, he couldn't.

Palani walked over to him, his face still unreadable. "Don't you ever, *ever* run away from us like that again," Palani said, and now the beta allowed his emotions to show. His eyes spewed fire, his face pulled tight. "Do you know what time it is? Do you realize how long you've been gone? I was worried sick you'd either gotten shot by some overzealous hunter or that you'd shifted back and were lying in a ditch somewhere, and we would have no idea where and how to find you. You can't do this, Lidon, you can't take off like that."

Palani's eyes welled up, and hell if that didn't make Lidon feel like the biggest asshole ever. His eyes stole a glance at the clock, and dammit, it was five in the morning. He'd been gone the whole night, and all that time, Palani had waited for him. If there was a bigger sign of how much the beta loved him, Lidon didn't know.

He reached for him, but Palani stepped back, and Lidon's heart clenched in his chest. Palani had never done that before, had never avoided his touch. Had he fucked it all up, the most important thing in his life?

"I'm sorry," he said. "I'm so sorry. I didn't realize. I wasn't thinking, I swear."

Palani studied him for what felt like a minute, then slowly nodded. "I believe you, but I'm beyond angry, Lidon, so it'll take me a while to cool off. I'm going to bed now that I know you're safe. We'll talk tomorrow."

The cold, hard lump in his heart grew bigger. "I'll do whatever it takes to make this right," Lidon swore.

"Right now, you can sleep in the guest room so you don't disturb Vieno and Enar," Palani said, and walked out.

Lidon sat for a long time before he finally made his way to the bedroom, where he lay awake even longer, hoping and praying his mates would forgive him.

8

Bray lounged on his bed, watching some TV while forcing himself to eat a microwave meal. He'd worked out earlier, and after taking a shower, he was just too tired to cook. That happened too often, he admitted to himself. He worked long days and at the end of the day, he was often too tired to bother with a decent meal.

It was stupid, because ever since the bunkhouse he was staying in had been finished—and Bray didn't know why they called them bunkhouses, when there were no bunk beds—he had a full kitchen at his disposal. And it was stocked, too, the grocery ordering system Palani's brother Rhene had developed assuring everything was restocked on time.

They'd named the buildings that were ready. Omega One was the omega building that was finished, and it was the home of Sando, who seemed to be settling in well. Bray admired Enar's vision of opening a safe place for omegas, especially those with the gene, but he'd be lying if he said it didn't scare him a little as well. His encounter with Sven was still burned onto his mind, one of his biggest moments of shame ever. He could only hope that keeping the omegas separate would prove to be enough.

The building he was staying in with Adar, Isam, and Maz—when the latter was staying on the ranch—had been dubbed the Alpha House for obvious reasons. Jawon, Servas, and Ori stayed in another one, which they called the Workers' House. As an omega, Servas could've stayed in Omega One, but since they were family, he'd opted to share housing with his brother and cousin. Kean shared housing with Lucan, who, like Bray, had left the main house when their dad had started seeing Lars and Sven. Their house was dubbed the Beta House, which wasn't gonna win prizes for originality, but was aptly named.

Bray liked staying in the bunkhouse. It beat the hell out of the main house where he risked coming across his dad with one of his boys on his knees servicing him, as he'd been unintentionally subjected to once. The only downside was that it made seeing Kean difficult, at least without everyone else finding out. They'd met a few times now to hook up. He suspected others knew but were too polite to say anything about it. That worked for him. He didn't care if people knew, as long as they kept their mouths shut.

He'd just shoveled the last few bites into his mouth and put the plastic tray on the floor when a wave rolled over him, sucking his strength out in a second. Bray lay down on his bed, gasping with the force of it. Lidon was shifting, he thought, but why? Palani hadn't announced anything, so it was a spontaneous thing. Was something wrong? Or was it someone else?

He braced himself for what he knew would follow, and seconds later it came, this surge of power that made him jerk, his muscles contracting all at once. Damn, that shifting-shit was powerful. Lidon really needed to learn how to control that. His heart raced and of course, his cock was hard in an instant. Hmm, maybe the latter wasn't so bad? He wouldn't mind rubbing one out, though he remembered from last time, that hadn't done much good.

Now he really wished he lived in the same bunkhouse as Kean. He could find him, though. The beta had to be affected as well, right? They could help each other out. Before that thought had fully formed, he stood next to his bed. He found his shoes, didn't even bother to tie them. In the hallway, he stopped when he heard unmistakable noises coming from one of the other rooms. Maz's room. It sounded like the alpha was having one hell of a good time. Who did he have in there? Bray wasn't about to wait and find out. Not now. Not when his cock was leaking at the thought of being inside Kean again.

He met him halfway between their houses, Kean apparently having the same thought. Bray grinned, then jerked his head toward Kean's house. "Your place," he said. "Maz has someone in his room."

They spent precious little time talking, both stripping naked as soon as Kean had closed the door behind them. Bray had him flat against the wall a second later. God, he loved the strength in Kean's body as he pinned him with his own. He relished that he got to be more aggressive with him, that Kean could not only take it, but welcomed it.

Their mouths met, hot and wet, fueled by the same restless energy. Bray gently bit his lower lip, and Kean moaned. "God, I love it when you do that," the beta said.

"I love the sounds you make when I do that," Bray said with a grin.

His right hand snuck in between their bodies, finding Kean as hard and leaking as he was.

"I need to feel you," Kean groaned into his mouth. "Hurry the fuck up, please."

"Lube?" Bray asked.

"On the bed."

"On the bed?" Bray said, smiling. "Were you expecting company?"

"I was literally fucking myself with a dildo when that surge hit. I came on impact," Kean said, and Bray almost choked on his breath at the visual those words gave him.

"That means you're..."

"Yes. No prep needed," Kean confirmed. "So hurry the fuck up."

The bossy beta was a far cry from the more timid omegas Bray preferred, but he'd be lying if he said Kean's verbal matches didn't amuse him. And turn him on, because that impatience was intoxicating.

"Bend over, hands flat against the wall," he told him.

The wicked grin Kean shot him as he obeyed made his cock even harder. He grabbed the lube, found a condom on the nightstand, and rolled it on with impatient fingers. When he turned around, Kean stood ready for him, a bronze display of smooth lines and curves, that pale ass sticking out, demanding to be seen.

"You really need to sunbathe naked some time. Your pale ass could use some sunlight," Bray said as he walked over and slapped said ass, resulting in a satisfying jiggle. Oh, there was a sight. He did it again on the other side, his hand-print leaving a mark. "Though I have to admit, that's a damn fine ass you have. I think it would look even better after a solid spanking," he decided.

Kean rolled his eyes at him even as he moved his ass backward against Bray's hand, which was kneading it none too gently. "You're such a romantic. What's next, Shakespeare? You're gonna compare my ass to a summer's day?"

Bray shoved his head down to make him bend over deeper and lined up behind him. "There's nothing summery about your ass."

Whatever Kean wanted to say turned into a long grunt as Bray pushed in with one deep surge, not stopping until he was buried deep and his balls slapped against Kean's cheeks. Kean pressed his face against his arms, pushing back, and how Bray loved to see him like this, so greedy for more. He slammed in hard, the choked gasp from Kean music to his ears.

Bray found himself wanting to hurt Kean just a little more because of the glorious sounds the beta made. He might not be a sub, but he endured Bray's rough treatment so beautifully, his strong body taking what Bray dished out. He wanted to explore that more, to see what other intoxicating sounds he could elicit from him.

His orgasm snuck up on him, slamming into him before he realized it, making him pant with the force as he pumped the condom full.

"Bray..." Kean said, coming close to whining.

He pulled out and got rid of the condom. "You're even prettier when you're desperate."

That got Kean to look over his shoulder. "You think I'm pretty?"

Was that a weird term to use for a beta, Bray wondered? Maybe he should've used handsome or gorgeous. "You are when you're in a little pain," he said, his voice hoarse. "Those sounds you make are addictive as hell."

Kean's eyes widened before a blush crept up his neck. "I've been tested recently," he said after a beat.

Bray raised an eyebrow. They all were, courtesy of a

requirement for monthly testing from Enar. What did...? Oh. He considered it, then decided he'd love to see his fantasy of his cum dripping out of that bouncy ass come true.

"You sure?"

Kean nodded, a slow smile spreading over his face. Bray's heart skipped a beat. He grabbed his cock with his right hand, Kean's throat with his left, and held him tight as he pushed in.

"Dammit, Kean, I wanna keep doing this until we're both too exhausted to come," he grunted as he rammed right back in again. "Can you take this? Can you take me?"

Kean's breath came out a half-sob. "Anything," he promised. "Anything you dish out."

His fingers dug into Kean's hips as he fucked him relentlessly, his cock throbbing deep inside him, unencumbered by even the thinnest barrier between them. Kean's arms buckled from their hold on the wall and Bray reached under his arm and held him up with his left arm, continuing his assault on his hole with long, deep strokes. Both their breaths came out harsh now, shallow puffs increasing in frequency.

Bray found Kean's neck with his mouth, sucked hard, then bit down. Kean was now making sounds Bray had never heard before, almost animalistic. The beta's body trembled against his, and Bray held on tight in case his legs gave out. He sneaked around with his right hand, gripping Kean's cock with a tight fist. He swiped his thumb over the slit, catching his precum, then stroked him firmly.

It only took four, maybe five strokes before Kean exploded against the wall, shooting rope after rope, tremors wrecking his body. Instinctively, his ass clenched, and that was enough for Bray to release. He fucked Kean brutally through his orgasm, not stopping until he'd deposited every last drop of cum inside him, both of them shaking with the effort.

He let go of Kean's dick and rested his head against the beta's sweaty back. "That was..."

"I need to lie down. My legs are shaking."

Bray pulled out, and they stumbled to the bed, crashing on it together. A relaxed smile curved Kean's mouth as he nestled against Bray's shoulder. He looked blissed out, Bray thought, then realized he probably sported an identical look.

"That was perfect," the beta sighed. "Man, I love your cock."

Bray decided Shakespearean poetry was overrated.

FOR THE FIRST time since his men had moved in with him, Lidon woke up not only alone, but feeling lonely. He let out a deep sigh as he pushed himself out of bed. A faint headache brewed behind his eyes. No wonder after the all-nighter he'd pulled, and the day ahead.

He wasn't sure what today would bring, but groveling would be involved and lots of it. God, he'd fucked up. He had no idea how to make things right with his mates. It wasn't just Vieno, he'd realized last night. Palani had been beyond angry as well. The man had stepped away from his touch. That said enough, didn't it? And he had deserved it. Hell, Palani hadn't even given him half of what he deserved. He'd been selfish, too caught up in his own pain to realize what he was putting his mates through. Lidon couldn't believe he had been that stupid.

He debated taking a shower, then decided he wasn't that

much of a coward. He had to face the music. Wasn't it strange how he had no problem facing a drug gang, but now shook in his metaphorical boots at facing his mates? He wasn't used to failing on this level.

Maybe it was good that he was taken down a peg. That was something Palani would say, and Lidon smiled. The beta was never one to mince his words. How angry and hurt he had been. Vieno had lashed out because of what he was going through, Lidon realized that. But Palani, that had been different. That had been fueled by the beta's love for him, by him being worried sick something had happened to Lidon, and that was not so easy to dismiss.

He got dressed before he could talk himself out of it, then made his way to the kitchen, where much to his surprise, his three mates were sitting at the table having a late lunch. They all looked up as he walked in, and the tension hung thick.

"I'll make you something to eat," Vieno said, not even bothering to greet him.

Lidon's heart squeezed painfully. "Guys," he said, his voice pleading. "I fucked up, big time, and I am so, so sorry."

Vieno spun around and looked at him with eyes blazing. "Yes, you did. I hurt you with my words, and for that, I'm sorry. I didn't mean it, you have to know that."

"I do," Lidon assured him.

"But if every time we hit a snag or do something you don't like, you turn into a wolf and take off on us, this is not gonna work. You can't run, Lidon, not when we can't follow you. We were worried sick about you."

How humbling it was to be chewed out by his omega. It was effective though, more than when Enar or Palani had spoken up.

Lidon swallowed back the bile that rose in his throat.

"I'm sorry. I wasn't thinking. I was hurt and ran, and I swear I didn't realize how long I was gone."

Vieno studied him, both hands on his hips, and Lidon was so worried his mates wouldn't forgive him that he went to his knees. He was not too proud to beg if that was what it took. "Please, baby, please. I never meant to make you worry." He looked to the others, noticing the shock on Enar's face and a look of approval on Palani's. "That goes for all of you. I was so in the wrong, and I'm sorry."

Vieno's eyes filled with tears and that stabbed Lidon in his heart even more.

"You were running from me," Vieno whispered. "I thought you regretted marrying me, claiming me."

"Never," Lidon swore, still on his knees. He yearned to close the distance between them, to gather his sweet omega in his arms, but he didn't dare cross that line, unsure if his affections were welcome.

"What if I can't have sex with you for a long time?" Vieno asked, his voice barely above a whisper.

"Then I will still love you, baby. Nothing will ever change the way I feel about you. But please, baby, don't hide it from me, from us. Let us help you carry this burden."

He spotted the doubt still lingering in his mate's eyes, and it killed him. He hated that the old insecurities that had plagued him before were back.

"Do you promise?" Vieno asked.

"I promise. And baby, none of us will ever put pressure on you to do something you don't want to. We want you to be with us, but if seeing us being intimate makes you feel uncomfortable, we understand. Talk to us, that's all we're asking."

Vieno slowly nodded. "It's the talking part that's so hard," he admitted. "My head is a mess, and there are so many thoughts in there, it's hard to figure out which are truths and which are lies."

Lidon had no idea how to respond, but Enar came to his rescue. "How about we promise we won't get angry with you if you voice your thoughts or ask us to help you figure them out, no matter if they're hurtful to us or not?"

And with blinding clarity, Lidon understood how deeply he had failed Vieno the day before. It wasn't just that he had run and made them all worry about him. But he had run after Vieno had voiced a thought that felt true to him. Lidon had taken it personally, hadn't given him the opportunity to explain or ask for verification.

He shook his head at his own stupidity. "I am sorry that when you told me something you experienced as real, I didn't take the time to tell you it was a lie. This is all on me, baby, not on you. You have nothing to apologize for. God, I am so sorry."

It was as if Vieno had waited for him to grasp that deeper level, and when he did, he closed the distance between them, almost knocking Lidon on his back with his hug. He sat down on the floor, pulled Vieno on his lap and held on for a long time.

"I am so sorry you're going through this," he whispered in his ear. "I promise I will do my best to be there for you. This is not something I'm good at, the talking stuff and the emotional support, but I'm willing to learn if you have a little patience with me."

Vieno snuggled close to him, and Lidon realized again how much he had missed him. Not just the sex, though he had to admit he missed that, but the intimacy, the deep sense of calm and peace his alpha had when he held him.

"I always feel a little better when you hold me," Vieno said softly.

Lidon thought of his realization earlier. Should he bring it up? They had just promised each other to be honest, hadn't they? To communicate?

"Remember what worked before, when you weren't feeling well?" he asked, keeping it vague so the omega would hopefully draw his own conclusions.

Vieno looked at him for a few beats before his eyes lit up. "Connecting with you," he said.

"I don't mean a sexual connection," Lidon said quickly, before his words could be misinterpreted. "But you might benefit from being close to me, like during the pregnancy and the delivery. Maybe you can find a way to draw on my power, so it can help you. It was a thought I had when I was running. Fleeing," he corrected himself wryly.

"I think that's worth a try," Enar said. "It worked before."

Lidon waited for Vieno's reaction, still a little scared the omega's trust had been broken too much for this. But Vieno nodded in agreement. "You realize that means I'll be pretty much glued to your side, right?" he asked and Lidon had no trouble spotting the insecurity even in that statement.

As if he would ever object to having his mate by his side. He looked him deep in the eyes as he answered. "Baby, it would be my pleasure. I will do whatever you need me to do. And if I do something that makes you feel uncomfortable, you tell me, okay?"

With Vieno now plastered against him, Lidon looked up at Enar and Palani. "Please, will you forgive me as well? I'll do whatever you need me to to make it right."

It was a little easier now that he knew he'd at least patched things up with Vieno, but he needed their forgiveness as well. This weight on his heart wouldn't let up, not until he knew he hadn't lost them.

Enar came first, rising from the table and sitting down

on the floor right next to Lidon and Palani. He put his head on Lidon's shoulder. "I was worried sick," he said softly.

"I'll never run from you guys again, I promise," Lidon said, his heart lifting a little when Enar offered his mouth for a kiss.

He kissed him softly, almost reverently. When Enar snuggled close, Lidon raised his head to meet Palani's eyes. His proud and strong beta, never scared to tell him the truth. He'd wounded him so deeply, and he worried his apology wasn't good enough. God, how he wished he was better at words, better at saying what mattered so much.

Finally, Palani got up as well and kneeled on the floor in front of him, then leaned in for a kiss. It was hard at first, as if the beta was still angry, but then it softened as Lidon allowed him to set the pace for the first time. It was a deep kiss, a long one, but Lidon surrendered, his heart finally released from its heavy burden.

When he pulled back, Palani wiped the moisture off Lidon's lips with his thumb. "Don't do it again," he said, his voice thick.

Lidon let his forehead rest against Palani's. "You have my word."

9

Fiery hot water cascaded down on Kean's back, pummeling his upper body and making the cramped muscles in his shoulders and back weep with relief. His whole body hurt, courtesy of the stubborn calf that refused to be born without him pulling the damn baby cow all the way through the birth canal. He had managed, and both calf and mom had survived, but his body had suffered. Bless the person who had insisted on installing high quality showers in the bunkhouses. Probably his brother, he thought, knowing Palani and he shared an affinity for long, hot showers.

He took his time cleaning himself, though not so much because he worried about actual dirt as because he was too tired and aching to move. Even the thought of having to towel himself off made him want to curl up into a ball on the bathroom floor on that fluffy, soft bath rug.

He was still in the shower, fighting the urge to stay there, when he heard someone enter his room. Shit, he forgot. That had to be Bray. They had texted earlier that day to meet. That was before the little calf had turned out to be such a problem child.

"I'm in the shower," he called out, then realized the stupidity of that statement, as Bray could hear the water run.

He wondered if the alpha would walk in. Showering together, now there was an appealing a visual. God, he loved that man's body. Kean was decent-sized for a beta, but Bray dwarfed him. Every time he looked at the man's arms and chest, he went a little weak in the knees.

"I'll wait here," Bray called out.

No need to stay in the shower any longer then, Kean thought, a little disappointed. He groaned as he dried himself off, every move sending painful stabs through his abused muscles. He slung the towel around his waist, unsure if Bray would appreciate him walking in naked. It was ridiculous considering why the alpha was there in the first place, but somehow, Kean knew the man had lines that shouldn't be crossed. He had made it clear this was about sex, so Kean better not venture into relationship territory.

Bray's eyes did light up when he spotted Kean, then narrowed into slits as he caught his cautious moves.

"What happened to you?"

Kean groaned as he put his boxers on with slow, careful moves. Damn, bending over was hell. He better be careful not to make it worse, or he wouldn't even be able to go to work tomorrow.

"I had a stubborn calf that needed to be born," he said between clenched teeth as he managed to pull his underwear up.

Bray whistled between his teeth. "Looks like you pulled a few muscles."

Kean had never realized how many muscles he used

putting on a shirt, but he was discovering now. Holy hell, this was far beyond painful.

"More than a few," he said, trying to make light of it. "If there is a muscle in my shoulders and back that doesn't hurt, I haven't found it yet."

Bray had found a spot in a reading chair, and Kean lowered himself on his bed. "But enough about me. How was your day, honey?"

It took a few seconds before Bray realized it was a joke, Kean saw. Did he really think...? He mentally shook his head. He had to remember that Bray was a literal guy. It wasn't that he didn't have a sense of humor, but he tended to take things literally at first.

Bray shrugged. "Nothing special."

His eyes told a different story. There was a wariness there that was new. "I assume that's code for something happened but you can't tell me about it?" Kean said lightly.

One corner of Bray's mouth tipped into a hint of a smile. "Close enough," he said. "There have been some developments that have me worried," he added, and it surprised Kean he even shared that much.

"It's a big responsibility you have here."

"It is, and I won't deny it weighs heavily on me."

He was answering Kean's questions, sharing more than Kean had counted on, and yet he couldn't shake the impression that Bray wanted to end this line of conversation. Or was Kean misinterpreting his signals?

Then it hit him. Bray sucked at making small talk. Maybe he didn't have much experience or maybe it was just not a natural skill, but the alpha struggled with making simple conversation. Was it weird that he found that endearing? Probably. Not that he cared.

"I already told Palani I need an assistant at some point," he said. "Today was really a two-person job."

Bray cocked his head as he studied him. "Aren't you technically the assistant yourself?"

He was right, Kean reminded himself. No need to get all upset about something that was factually correct.

"You're right, but I'm the only one here who can even do this kind of work right now. I'm hoping to go back to school and become a full-fledged veterinarian."

Bray raised an eyebrow. "That's gonna be a challenge, the combination of school and working here, especially considering how far away you are from the university."

"I know, and I haven't quite figured out how I will do it, but it's definitely something I want."

"Veterinarian, that's pretty much alpha territory, right?" Bray asked.

"It is," Kean confirmed. "Most veterinarians are alphas, but that doesn't mean a beta can't do the job, you know that. My experience here will definitely help me as I'm doing a lot of work most vet techs can't even dream of. I'm sure that will come in handy for my degree."

"You and your brother, you guys really don't like to make it easy for yourself, do you?"

Kean decided he would take that as a compliment. "Nope, we don't. Nothing wrong with setting a challenge for yourself, right?"

Bray kept looking at him, then said, "I don't want you to get in over your head."

He was concerned for him, Kean told himself. He ignored the voice in his head that said it could also be interpreted as if Bray didn't have much faith in him, or even in betas in general. Surely the alpha hadn't meant that, right?

"Not to be rude, but you don't look like you're in the

mood to hook up," Bray said, his voice as emotional as if he was discussing the weather.

Kean's fleeting fantasies of Bray massaging his neck and shoulders vaporized. "I guess I'm not," he said.

"No worries, I understand. Make sure you take painkillers and get a good night's sleep," Bray said. "Text me when you're recovered."

Before Kean realized it, the alpha walked out, leaving him bewildered. What the hell had just happened?

He didn't sleep well despite taking the painkillers, and when he woke up, the strange evening was still on his mind. He popped two more ibuprofen after breakfast, then set out to work, his mind still on Bray. It didn't hit him till the end of that day, a day where he'd subconsciously been expecting a text from Bray, asking him how his back was doing. It never came, and when they ran into each other during lunch, the alpha barely spared him a glance. Not that that was unusual, as he rarely did in front of others, which Kean thought was because he didn't want others to know they were together.

It wasn't till he was in the shower that night, a feeble attempt to get his cramping muscles to relax, that he realized where he'd been wrong. They weren't *together*. Not in Bray's mind.

Kean couldn't believe he'd missed it the night before, but he blamed it on how exhausted he'd been. They didn't have a relationship, no matter how much Kean wanted it. And they never would have. Bray didn't even consider him relationship material. All he would ever be was a good fuck.

And as the warm water eased his muscles, Kean took a long, hard look at himself and wondered if he wasn't worth more.

SVEN'S BODY had felt off ever since his last heat, but he'd blamed it on the weird energy bursts Lidon's shifting kept causing. It affected all of them, and he'd figured maybe that was why he'd been feeling weird, tired and not himself.

But now, seven weeks after his heat, he couldn't deny the obvious truth anymore. He sighed as he examined himself in the mirror. Was it his imagination or was his stomach a little more rounded than it had been before? A pregnancy lasted six months, and it had been seven weeks since his heat, which meant it would be detectable by now. Yeah, it would be, as he remembered from Vieno's pregnancy. He sighed as he let his fingers trail his stomach. What the hell would he do now?

Even though he'd witnessed Vieno's pregnancy from the sidelines, he still knew little about the whole process. Getting pregnant hadn't been on his radar at all. At first, his biggest goal had been to get out of his father's house with Lars and find their own place to live. Then when they'd moved into the ranch, it had been to get through his heat. Then they'd met Grayson and well, life had been good. They were happy, the three of them. Happier than Sven had ever thought possible.

Yes, he loved taking care of little Hakon, and he had thought about a baby of his own lately. But Grayson was a dad already, with grown children. They had never talked about kids, and with a sickening feeling to his stomach, Sven considered that the man might not want more children. Then what would he do?

He needed to be sure first, though he had little doubt. The changes were too obvious to be denied. He wasn't throwing up, like Vieno, but his stomach was a little woozy in the mornings. He'd come to hate the smell of coffee, though he'd always loved it. And his whole body felt different.

So, he needed to get tested, which was easier said than done. It wasn't like he could go to the city on his own and buy a pregnancy test. Sure, he could tell Lars, but he wasn't sure he wanted to do that yet. They'd been making decisions together for a long time, but this was different. Lars would have strong opinions, as he usually did, and Sven needed more time to figure things out. Plus, he might want to tell Grayson, and Sven wasn't ready for that yet.

No, there was only one solution right now. He timed it so he ran into Enar when he was done in the clinic, where the man was always the last one to leave. Well, Sando was still in his room in the back, working on whatever all those formulas were about, but he wouldn't pay attention. Sven had discovered that the omega wouldn't hear a bomb go off when he was concentrating on his work.

"Hey, Sven," Enar greeted him when he spotted Sven walking in.

"Can I talk to you?" Sven wanted to get right to the point, before someone could interrupt them.

Enar's eyes tightened in worry. "Sure. What's up? Are you okay?"

They'd made small steps in the last months to get to know each other better, and while they weren't close by any standard, Enar was unfailingly kind toward him and even Lars.

Sven took a deep breath. "I think I'm pregnant."

Enar's eyes widened. "You think the birth control didn't work?"

"Yeah. I feel different. Slightly nauseous. Tired. And just off."

"Okay. There could be several reasons for that, but pregnancy could be one of them. The meds I have you on are ninety-five percent effective, but there's no data yet on using them with omegas who have the Melloni gene. It could very well be they don't work—though I've used them on Vieno twice before he got pregnant. Would you like to do a pregnancy test first, so we know for sure?"

Sven was ever so grateful Enar went into doctor-mode, sensing Sven didn't need reassurance or comfort, but facts.

"Yes, please," Sven whispered.

"Sure. Go into the first exam room while I grab supplies, okay? I'll be right back."

Enar was only gone for a few minutes, and Sven tried to keep himself calm. His mind wanted to panic over even the possibility of a pregnancy, but he refused to entertain it. One step at a time.

When Enar came back, he explained how the test worked and Sven went into the adjoining bathroom. He dutifully peed on the stick, stuck it back into the holder-thingy, washed his hands, and walked back out with trembling hands, holding the stick. He handed it to Enar.

"It's positive," he said, his voice barely audible. He cleared his throat. "It's a double line. I'm pregnant."

Enar studied the stick, then put it down on the desk. "It looks like you are. I'll draw some blood to double-check, but how are you feeling about this, Sven? Talk to me."

Sven sat down on the chair next to the desk, his insides strangely calm. "I don't know. Shocked, I guess. Do...do I have to tell Grayson?"

Enar shook his head. "You don't have to tell him anything. This is your body, Sven, and it's your decision. If you want to keep it, alone, with Lars, or in whatever way, we'll support you in that. If you decide to give it up for adoption, there's a great adoption agency that would be happy to find a good home for your baby."

"And if I wanted to...terminate the pregnancy?"

"Then that's your choice and we'll respect it."

"Grayson could forbid me," Sven said. "As the alpha-father, he could—"

"He wouldn't," Enar said. "And even if he did, I wouldn't honor his decision. It's your call, Sven, and no one else's. You can talk to as many people as you want or to none at all, and I will do whatever you decide."

Sven sat on the bed, his arms wrapped around himself, and tried to imagine himself with a baby. It was surprisingly easy but maybe that was because of the hormones? He loved holding Hakon, and Vieno had said more than once Sven had a good instinct with him, but was that enough? Watching Hakon for a few hours wasn't the same as having a kid of your own.

"What do you think I should do?" he asked Enar. "I'm so young to have a kid, and Lars too, and I don't know how Grayson would feel about this. He already has kids, so I'm sure he wouldn't want to start all over again."

Enar smiled at him. "I can't make the decision for you, but I can offer you a few things to keep in mind. Medically, having an abortion has risks, and it has a higher risk of complications with future pregnancies. That's something to keep in mind. If that's the way you want to go, the earlier you let me do it, the less those risks will be, so you're a little pressed for time."

Sven's head shot up. "You would do it?" he asked, surprised. "I thought they were illegal under these circumstances."

"They are, but I do them anyway. I hope I can trust you with this information."

Sven nodded quickly. "Yes, yes, absolutely. I was surprised. I didn't know."

"Now you do," Enar said. "And I trust you'll keep this to yourself. As for Lars and Grayson, you can't decide for them how they would feel. You don't have to consult them as it's your decision, but don't make the mistake of assigning them reactions and emotions in your head without testing those. Grayson may surprise you. He loves you and Lars so much. There's nothing that man wouldn't do for you."

He was right. Sven wasn't sure of many things in his life, but Grayson loved him, and Lars too. That was a fact. The three of them were like a puzzle that fit perfectly, even though they were oddly shaped pieces. But what if he added a baby to that mix? What would that do to their relationship, to their dynamic? Lars still needed Grayson in a big way, and the daddy-care Grayson offered meant so much to him. Would that have to stop?

God, his head hurt already. And Enar was right, Sven couldn't know for sure how they would react until he told them. But did he want to? They could influence his decision, make him do something he didn't want.

"Take at least a day to think it over. Whatever you decide will be okay, Sven. Come find me when you're ready to talk, okay? This is your call."

10

R uari received a call two weeks later that his test results had come in, and that Dr. Magnusson asked him to stop by the clinic at his earliest convenience. It was a hassle, making that whole trip again, but he didn't hesitate, not after the doctor had confirmed it sounded like he had the symptoms of the gene. He needed to know for sure, and if he indeed did have the gene, he needed advice and as much of it as he could get.

So Ruari made the long and complicated trip to the clinic again, happy that Jax was a lot less fussy than last time. When he walked to the clinic's entrance, he caught himself looking around to see if he spotted Kean. The beta had been such a big help, and he had been so nice about it too. Ruari had been forced to accept a lot of help over the last few months, but sometimes, people made it feel like they were doing you a favor, rubbing it in. Kean hadn't been like that at all, and Ruari's heart had melted at the tender way the man had held his son.

But he knew he shouldn't be on the lookout for Kean.

Even if they had shared a connection, and Ruari was willing to admit that they had, he wasn't in a good place for a relationship right now. Plus, he wasn't even sure if Kean was single, and if he was, what man would want an omega who already had a child? And not just that, but a child from an alpha whose name he didn't even know. That was what he kept telling himself as he forced Kean out of his mind.

He didn't have to wait long for the doctor to see him, and Enar got right to the point. "I'm sorry to inform you that you do have the gene, Ruari," he said. "I'm sure you must have a lot of questions, and we are here to help you in any way we can."

Ruari wasn't as shocked as he had expected himself to be, maybe because over the last few days, he had already come to accept this diagnosis. That didn't mean he didn't have questions, however. "Is it hereditary?" he asked. "Or can only omegas get it?"

"We don't know yet," Enar answered. "So far, we have tested a few dozen kids of gene carriers, and none of them have tested positive, but there were few omegas among these babies. In fact, we suspect that gene carriers are far more likely to have alpha sons, as the rate of alphas among those babies was statistically significantly higher than among the general population."

Ruari let out a sigh of relief. At least his baby would be okay. "But you'll still test him, right?"

Enar nodded. "Absolutely. In fact, we would like your permission to enroll him in a series of tests. Both of you. I have an associate who is doing research into the gene and who could always use more participants."

"What is the goal of that research, finding a cure?" Ruari asked.

"Ultimately, yes. In the short term, we would be happy to learn more about how the gene works, how it affects the body, and how we can ameliorate its effects. The strong heats are not only a nuisance, as you know better than I do, but have led to dangerous situations and sadly, many cases of sexual assault and rape."

Ruari swallowed. Even though his first heat hadn't been a good experience, and his second had not been as satisfactory as he had hoped, at least he hadn't gone through the horrors Enar was hinting at. Even in his situation, that was something Ruari was grateful for. No matter how much he struggled, things could be a lot worse.

"I would love to participate in the research, but if it means coming to the clinic on a regular basis, that might be a problem. I don't have a car and the public transport here is not a walk in the park, especially with a baby. And I expect it only to become more of a hassle the older Jax gets."

"I understand, and before we get into that, we have more test results to discuss."

"The dizziness," Ruari said.

"Yes. You're anemic, probably still from giving birth. I can prescribe iron supplements for that. But you're also malnourished, Ruari. You're not giving your body the nutrition it needs. Vitamin supplements can help, but I would like to look at your eating habits to combat this in the long term. You need more vitamins, more calcium, and more proteins."

Ruari shrunk in his seat. How the hell would he be able to afford it? He barely had money left as it was, and he had to prioritize Jax's formula and diapers. "Healthy food is so much more expensive," he whispered.

Enar's expression showed nothing but understanding.

"Bad luck Jax wouldn't take to breastfeeding, huh? Formula costs an arm and a leg." He leaned forward, his eyes kind. "You don't need to tell me anything you don't want to share, but are you in a position right now where you can take good care of yourself? Because having this gene alone has a lot of implications for the future, especially around your heat, and you're not in a good physical condition to begin with."

Ruari leaned back in his chair, rocking Jax, who had fallen asleep against his chest. He had taken him out of the sling as soon as they had arrived, because he'd read that it wasn't healthy for their bones to be carried in a sling for too long.

How much would he tell the doctor? How much could he tell him? The man had patient confidentiality, but this was a private clinic on private property, and Ruari knew damn well different rules applied here. And if his father ever found out, Ruari had to wonder if the good doctor would be strong enough to resist the pressure his father would put on him to disclose Ruari's records. And then he would be up shit creek without a paddle.

But what was the alternative? He left home with enough financial reserves to last for a little while, but the bottom of those reserves was in sight. He'd need to start looking for a job soon, which presented so many complications he didn't even know where to start. Moving to another city was still his best option, one where his father had less of a reach and network, but how would he manage that without a car? And without money, because the little he had left was not enough to finance a move.

Even with the changes in the law the government had made, the system was still stacked against omegas like him. He didn't have any work experience, and he wasn't suitable for many jobs because of his status as an omega. Many employers were still hesitant to hire omegas, and there was now the added complication of him having these intense heats, where he apparently attracted every alpha in a five-mile radius. How the hell would he be able to hold a job under those circumstances? And that didn't even include finding a babysitter for Jax he could trust.

All that time, Enar had patiently waited for Ruari to answer, and he was grateful for that moment to gather his thoughts. He shook his head. "Honestly, I feel like I'm drowning right now. I'm running low on money, and I don't know what to do. I doubt it will be safe for me to have a job where I'm around people, especially alphas, so I'm lost on how to make this work."

KEAN HAD BEEN FEEDING the chickens when his phone had buzzed, and to his surprise, it had been Enar. He wasn't sure why, but his first thought had been that the call was about Ruari. He hadn't been able to put the omega out of his mind ever since he met him, thoughts of his sharp blue eyes, and his tight body, and that sweet baby popping up in his head all the time. It was a strange combination, these thoughts, the first two making him rather horny whereas the latter made him dream about being a dad—in itself a new experience.

It had confused him, this strange attraction to someone he'd just met, especially since he was still with Bray. Sort of. They hadn't spoken since their talk three days before, Kean's back still painful enough he didn't want to even consider having sex. Was his attraction to Ruari proof he should forget about Bray, that he'd been wrong about their connection?

Within seconds of taking the call, he was surprised to discover his instincts had been right. Enar was calling him about Ruari, asking Kean to give him a tour of the ranch and explain how they operated.

"He needs a safe place to stay," Enar explained. "I talked to him about staying here at the ranch, at least until he's figured some things out. He seemed very interested, but before he can make a final decision, I'd like for him to have a tour and know more about the way we operate. By the time you're done, it will probably be too late for him to head back using public transport, so can you either give him a ride back to the city or offer that he can spend the night? You may want to put him up with Sando. I think knowing there's another omega staying here will help Ruari feel safe."

"You want me to tell him about the pack?" Kean asked, just to be sure how much he was authorized to reveal.

"Yes. We've discussed it, the four of us, and we want everyone who considers living on the ranch to be fully informed. There's a legal aspect, to be sure, but to us it's more about their well-being. If we advocate the importance of making informed decisions, for instance for omegas when it concerns their bodies, we need to set the right example."

Kean couldn't deny that made total sense, even if being so open about the pack scared him a little. He'd learned about the attack on the ranch months ago, and even though they had received no threats since, it was still a concern. Especially now that the rise of the Conservative Wolf Party had agitated the Anti-Wolf Coalition and all its rather short-tempered members, the news of the Hayes pack's existence falling into the wrong hands could lead to violence. Still, he would follow Enar's instructions.

"Sure, no problem. Give me a few minutes to finish what

I was doing and get cleaned up. I've been working all morning, so I'm pretty sure I stink."

There was no way he was showing Ruari around looking and smelling like this. Granted, it wasn't as bad as it was on certain days, since he hadn't done any deliveries or procedures on animals today, but he still was sweaty, looked like he hadn't showered in a week, and smelled like a farm. Or, a farm animal, more precisely.

Enar chuckled. "Are you sure that's the only reason you want to get changed?"

Even though Enar couldn't see him, Kean blushed. Was he that transparent? "Why did you ask me to give him the tour?" he asked instead.

Enar's voice was soft and kind as he answered. "I thought you two had a connection, and it seems to me Ruari could use a friend."

He didn't elaborate, but they both knew how much Kean had overheard while Enar was examining Ruari. Enough to realize Enar was right and that the omega had been through a lot.

"I'll be there as soon as I can," Kean promised.

He didn't care what Enar would say or think, but Kean did take a shower before he headed to the clinic. It was a speed-shower of the two-minute variety, but it was enough to at least smell a little better and not have his hair look like he'd put his fingers in a socket. He threw on a clean pair of shorts and a fresh shirt and rushed over to the clinic, where he found Ruari in the waiting room, Jax strapped to his chest in a sling.

Kean shoved his hands into his pockets, suddenly more self-conscious than he'd been in a long time. "Hi."

Was it his imagination, or did Ruari look a little flustered as well?

"Hi," the omega said back.

"Enar said you wanted a tour of the ranch?"

"He suggested you could do it. I hope that's not too much of an inconvenience for you?" Ruari said.

Kean thought of the long list of tasks on his to-do list and shook his head. "No, not at all."

They walked outside, where Kean matched his pace to Ruari's much shorter legs. He showed him the fields first, as they were closest, then led him toward the area where the animals were.

"This is mainly where I work all day," he said. "We have a chicken coop that provides us with fresh eggs daily, we have cows for milk and to slaughter for meat—though we outsource that as I don't slaughter—we have pigs and goats, basically every animal you would expect at a working farm. And we're looking into buying horses, as well as some tom cats and a few guard dogs. And maybe some other animals, I don't know yet. The goal is to make the ranch as self-sufficient as possible, especially in terms of food."

Ruari looked around with more than just a polite expression. "You do all of this by yourself?"

Kean nodded. "For now, yes. But I need to talk to my brother about finding me an assistant. It's getting a bit much for me to run by myself."

He couldn't interpret Ruari's expression, but it looked a lot like he was impressed. They walked closer to the main house, and Kean pointed out all the buildings they had built. "That's Omega Two, one of our omega buildings. It's not finished yet, but it should be in a week or two. We have another one that is finished and suitable for omegas to live in, called Omega One. There's one omega living there right now named Sando."

"Why are these buildings separated from the main house?" Ruari asked.

Kean shot him a careful look, I'm sure of how much detail he should provide. "For safety reasons," he said. "Since Enar and Palani are both so closely involved in the research into the gene, they're expecting gene carriers to live here. That means they would need to stay away from any alphas during their heat, which is why they built these houses so they're disconnected from the main house. First, the wanted to connect them but later, they decided not to, also because of the prefab construction they used which made that idea hard to realize on short notice. Not that all the alphas are in the main house. There are many people living here on pack land, and most of the single men live in dormitory style cottages with four people, spread out all over the pack land. We call them bunkhouses."

Ruari studied him out of the corner of his eye for a second or two. "Is that where you live?" he asked, and Kean wondered if it was an indirect way of inquiring whether he was single. Or was he overthinking things and attaching meaning to an innocent question?

"Yeah, I share a bunkhouse with another beta, with room for two more. I could've moved into the main house since my brother is there, but..." He stopped talking, unsure if this was a topic he should bring up with Ruari. He wasn't sure if his negative experiences in the past with alphas had traumatized him in any way, and Kean didn't want to stir up any bad memories or make him feel uncomfortable.

"But what?" Ruari asked.

Well, he would find out at some point if he moved in, Kean reasoned. It wasn't like it was a secret, and the men talked about it amongst themselves all the time. "There are two groups of mates living in the main house, first of all the pack alpha and his three mates, one of whom is my brother. Then there's Grayson, an alpha who lives there with his two mates, Lars and Sven."

Ruari looked at him quizzically. "Yeah, so?"

Kean wasn't shy about sex, but this was a rather awkward situation with a man he had just met, in a context where sex was not an expected topic of conversation, and with someone he liked. Was he about to ruin his chances of anything more with Ruari? He would have to risk it, because lying was not an option since Ruari would find out the truth himself soon enough. It was a rare day when you didn't spot someone getting it on.

"Let's just say they all have a voracious sexual appetite," he worded it carefully. When Ruari still looked confused, he added, "And they don't always bother to retreat into the bedroom before they engage in said activities."

Ruari's eyes widened, and then he smiled. "Oh, that has got to be awkward when it's your brother."

Kean grinned, relieved that Ruari had taken it well. "You have no idea. Bray, our head of security, and Lucan, who I share housing with, are in the same position, as Grayson is his father. And to make it even worse, Grayson's two mates are Enar's brothers. It's all super complicated, these relationships and family lines," he said when Ruari frowned. "But they all love each other very much, so we try not to make a big deal out of it, but it made me decide to not live in the main house. There are only so many times you can see your brother sexually active before it becomes too much."

"Live porn shows in the main house, noted," Ruari said, and Kean couldn't believe he used the exact same expression he himself had used to describe it to Bray. "But I have another question. You've used the term pack a few times now. Does that refer to what I think it does? Are you guys living in an old-fashioned pack?"

"Yes. We have a pack alpha, which is Lidon, and a second-in-command, which is my brother Palani. We follow the old pack traditions as much as we can, and that means that on a day-to-day basis, we follow the commands of our alpha and his second-in-command. Pack law supersedes any other law or family bonds."

Ruari was quiet for a bit, and Kean allowed him the time to let this unusual news sink in. "You guys must have been happy with the election results, then," he finally said, and Kean was surprised that was the first thing he would think of. There was an edge to Ruari's voice he couldn't place, like he was saying more than Kean picked up on in that statement.

The answer to Ruari's question about the election, of course, wasn't as simple considering what they knew about the election fraud, so Kean decided to let that go. Instead, he figured it was time to share the biggest and most shocking revelation.

"There's more," he said, then tried to explain Lidon's shifting powers as best as he could.

"He can shift?" Ruari asked, shock painted all over his face. "Like, shift into a wolf?"

"Yes. So far, he's the only one of us who can, and he doesn't even know exactly how he does it. But I've seen him as a wolf, and it is the most amazing, magical experience you will ever have."

Ruari put a hand on Kean's lower arm and made him stop. "You're serious? He can shift and you've seen it?"

Kean nodded, not surprised in the least at Ruari's reaction. It was hard to believe when you hadn't been a part of this pack for the last month and hadn't experienced it yourself. "Yes. I haven't seen him shift, not the actual process, I mean. But I have seen him in wolf form, and I've experienced the effects of a shift. It's quite powerful."

"What kind of effects? How can his shifting affect you?"

Dammit, he boxed himself into a corner again. "It's erm... It affects all of us, our libidos?"

Ruari stared at him for a few seconds, then slowly shook his head. "What is this, a pack or some kind of sex club?"

11

Grayson sat on the couch in the living room, reading a book. Lars was working out in the gym, but Sven—who usually accompanied him for that—had said he was tired and wanted to stay with Grayson. So he'd found a spot at Grayson's feet, content to lean against his legs and rest while Grayson scratched his neck and stroked his hair.

Usually, this was a time of intense relaxation for Sven where he'd drop into subspace or something close to it, but tonight, he was restless. He'd been off the last few days, in fact. Something was wrong with Sven, something Grayson couldn't put his finger on, and he was worried.

The kid was distracted, for starters. Where his sweet eyes were usually focused on Grayson—a habit the alpha loved—Sven was now all over the place with his attention. Grayson had found him staring into the distance the last couple days, biting his lips or playing with his hands. He'd done his job, had done everything Grayson had asked of him, and he'd provided all the right answers and reactions, but his mind had been elsewhere.

But it was more. He wasn't just distracted; he was also... different. Grayson studied the omega at his feet, trying to pinpoint what it was. What was different about him? It was subtle, but it almost seemed like he... Grayson's heart skipped a beat.

Like he *glowed*.

Sven's skin was subtly glowing, radiant.

He was pregnant.

Just then, the omega looked up and Grayson wasn't fast enough to change the expression on his face. Sven froze.

"I didn't mean to..." he said, his whole body rigid with shock and fear. "I wasn't ready to tell yet."

Grayson did what his instinct told him to. He bent over and picked him up, cuddling him on his lap. His boy needed him right now, needed to be assured that whatever it was, it would be okay. "Shush, honey. No need to explain or apologize."

Sven put his head against Grayson's shoulder in sweet surrender. "I'm scared," he whispered. "I don't know what to do."

Grayson held him tight, a storm of emotions whirling through his head. "I'm here for whatever you need, honey. You're not alone."

Sven sat quiet on his lap for a long time, his body relaxed and his breathing even. "I tested positive," he finally spoke.

Grayson fought hard to stay calm when the omega confirmed his suspicions. His boy was pregnant. There were a million things going through his mind, but they'd have to wait. Sven needed him. "Are you okay with this news?"

"Are you? I figured you'd freak out, since you already have three kids."

He'd been worried about Grayson? God, the kid was

such a sweetheart. "This isn't about me, honey. What I think or feel doesn't matter. How do you feel? Did you tell Lars?"

"But...but you're the father. That gives you a say, every say, according to the law."

Grayson kissed his head. "This is a pack, honey. Pack law comes first, and Lidon has made it clear omegas have equal say. But aside from that, I would never overrule you, and you know that, deep down. You get to make all the decisions here."

"Oh." The word was loaded with meaning. "I'm scared to tell Lars," Sven whispered.

"Why? Do you think he'd be upset?" Grayson knew the answer as soon as he'd asked the question. It wasn't about Lars being upset. The beta would be reminded all over again of what he couldn't give Sven. It wasn't as much of a pain-point for Lars as it once had been, but there were still times when he struggled with what Sven could get from Grayson but not from him.

"I hate hurting him," Sven said.

"It's not your fault, honey. Don't take this on yourself. You can't help this."

"You're not mad at me?"

The question broke Grayson's heart just a little, and his arms tightened around the omega. "Of course not. How could I be angry with you for something you didn't do? The birth control didn't work. It happens."

"Do you want me to get an abortion?"

Grayson should've known this question would come up, what with Enar being Sven's brother. It was clear he could and would deliver anything Sven needed. On one hand, it would solve the unexpected problem of an inconvenient pregnancy, and yet... The image of Sven, swollen with child, popped into Grayson's head. Then another picture of Sven, cradling a newborn baby, so easy to picture since Grayson had seen him snugging with Hakon. Grayson's alpha stirred, wanted.

"No, I don't. I'd love for you to keep the baby, but I will support you no matter what you decide. If you decide to keep it, I'll be here for you with whatever you need. And if you're not ready yet, I'll accept that, too. It's your call, but Sven, I'd really advise you to talk to Lars. You can't keep him out of this. He'd be so hurt if he found out that we didn't tell him."

"You want to keep the baby?"

"Did you think I wouldn't want it?"

When Sven didn't answer, Grayson pushed back his head so he could look at him.

"I figured you'd be done with kids, since you already have three."

Grayson smiled. "If you'd asked me beforehand, I probably would have hesitated. But now the idea of you having my baby is..." He stopped himself. "I don't want to influence your decision, and I could do that if I go on. You'd feel obliged to me, and that's not my intention."

Sven shook his head. "No, Gray, I needed to hear you say this. I thought you wouldn't want it, and that was a big reason for me to consider an abortion."

Grayson's heart stumbled at Sven's abbreviation of his name. He'd never used it before and how cute was that? But even more important was what Sven was communicating. "You want this baby?"

"I do," Sven said, his voice barely audible. "I wouldn't have planned it like this, but I've always dreamed of having kids, even though that wouldn't be possible with Lars."

A little shard stabbed in Grayson's heart. They'd grown so close over the last few months, the three of them, but sometimes, innocent remarks like this made him feel like an outsider again. There was no mention of him in there, no reference to Sven being happy it was Grayson's baby. It made him feel like a sperm donor, and he didn't like it one bit.

"This feels like a gift, like a once in a lifetime chance that I shouldn't let go," Sven continued.

Grayson pushed his pain down. This wasn't about him, and once the emotion had settled, he'd know Sven hadn't meant it as a dig at him. The boy was high on hormones, still confused and scared. He needed Grayson to be there for him.

"Honey, I would love to for you to keep the baby, but only if that's what you want."

Sven met his eyes, then nodded. "I'm pretty sure that's my decision. Will you help me?"

Grayson leaned in and kissed his forehead. "Always, with whatever you need. We'll raise this baby together, I promise."

"Thank you," Sven whispered.

A noise made Grayson look up and there stood a freshly showered Lars, his eyes wide open and his face pale. Oh god.

"A baby?" the beta said, then louder. "A baby? You're pregnant and didn't tell me?"

"No, Lars, it's not like that. You don't understand..." Sven said, and Grayson could hear his voice choke up with tears. No wonder, Lars looked like he was about to breathe fire at them both. Grayson could handle it, though it stung to see the beta so hurt, but for Sven, this had to be heartbreaking.

"And now you're raising it together, the two of you. How could you do this to me? You know what? I hope you two have a happy life together," Lars said, and his voice, too, sounded like it was about to break.

He whipped around and was halfway to the door when Grayson rose and planted Sven on his feet. "No. Lars, you're not walking away."

"Watch me," Lars bit back without facing him.

"No. You're staying." Grayson kept his alpha back who was champing at the bit to show who was boss.

Lars turned around, and Grayson's stomach turned when he saw the tears streaming down the beta's face. "Or what? You're gonna hurt me even more than you already did?"

LARS HAD ALWAYS TOLD himself that people who spoke of heartbreak were exaggerating a little. Sure, it would hurt when people you loved rejected you, but to compare it to a physical break seemed a tad dramatic. But right now, his heart shattered into a million pieces, obliterated by a rejection so profound he could barely breathe. His head was spinning, dark spots dancing before his eyes, even as he desperately tried to suck in air.

Grayson said something, but Lars didn't listen as he stumbled away, through the kitchen, into the hallway. He would never listen to him again. That lying, backstabbing alpha-asshole. He'd pretended to like Lars, to love him even, reeling him in with his daddy-care, when all that time, he'd been stealing Sven from him.

His Sven. His sweet, sexy Sven.

And his Daddy, the man he'd come to completely trust. And love.

God, they'd betrayed him, both of them. Planning a baby together behind his back. It was unimaginable, and yet that was exactly what had happened.

He stumbled, surprised when his legs gave out and he fell, more tears forming in his eyes as his kneecaps bruised on impact.

"Hey, are you okay?"

The voice pierced through the brain fog and he looked up to find his brother looking at him with concern. His older brother, the one who betrayed him once as well. If he thought about that now, it seemed laughable, what Enar had done.

"He's pregnant," he heard himself say, but as soon as the words left his mouth, he realized something. "You knew. Did everyone know but me?" He let out a bitter laugh. "God, the glee you guys must have had when you all knew and kept it from me."

Enar stepped back as if he'd slapped him. "Lars, I can't discuss any patients with you or anyone else. I may operate in some definite gray areas, but I never break patient confidentiality."

For some reason, that got through to him and managed to overrule his emotions. Enar was right. No matter what you could say about his brother, no one could ever deny how serious he took his job. He would have never told anyone else about Sven's pregnancy, and he wouldn't have plotted against Lars behind his back. That meant it was just Grayson and Sven, which still hurt him like a knife, but at least his brother wasn't involved.

"No, you wouldn't," he admitted. "I'm just hurting."

Lars sagged with his back against the wall, cradling his head in his hands. "Sven is pregnant," he said again, his tone much milder now. "And Grayson knew, and they're planning to raise it together, and they didn't bother to tell me."

"Oh, Lars," Enar sighed with a profound sadness, and he sat down on the floor right next to Lars.

Lars's heart softened as his brother offered him a shoulder, and he allowed himself to lean against him. Enar didn't say anything else, which Lars appreciated. No empty words here, no clichés that would fall on deaf ears.

"I walked in on them talking about it," he said after a while. "Sven was all beaming with happiness and Grayson was saying how they would raise the baby together." His throat choked up at the memory. "Why would they do this to me?" he whispered. "I thought we were happy together. Am I that much of a brat they don't want me anymore?"

"How the hell can you think that, let alone say it?" Grayson's voice exploded, and it made Lars freeze in shock. How long had he stood there, listening in? He tensed up, gearing up for a fight, when Enar squeezed his shoulder, then rose.

"I think you need to leave, Grayson," he said, his voice calm. "Lars needs time to cool off, and you do as well."

Grayson crossed his arms, looking pissed as hell. And hot as fuck, Lars thought, cursing himself for the reaction. "He's my mate. You gonna tell me to stay away from my own mate?"

Lars felt incredibly grateful Enar was standing up for him. It was the first time his brother had been there for him, or at least the first time he remembered. And for Enar it might be a small thing, but to Lars it meant everything.

Then Grayson's words registered. They were *mates*. Lars hadn't even thought of that, hadn't even let the worrying implications sink in. If they cast him out, he'd be lost, bound as he was to Grayson. He'd wither away, and as awful as that sounded, he still preferred it over watching Grayson and Sven be happy together without him.

Grayson's eyes narrowed, and the look he gave Enar was anything but friendly. "Stay out of this," he told Enar in a tone that left little room for discussion. "This has nothing to do with you. This is between me and my mates."

Enar would have to back off now. There was no way the guy would stand up to Grayson, right? Not when he was in full alpha mode. Hell, even Lars himself felt compelled to obey him, and he was used to Grayson going all alpha male dominant on him. But it seemed he had pegged his brother wrong. Instead, Enar rose to his full height, and his voice was more commanding than Lars had ever heard it.

"No, Grayson, that's where you're wrong. This has everything to do with me. First of all, your omega mate is my patient, and if I feel you are in any way curbing his freedom to make his own choices, I will be so far up your ass you won't know what hit you. Second, both of your mates are my brothers. That makes it my business. And third and not least, this is a pack. I am the pack alpha's mate, and we both know damn well I outrank you. I have never, ever used my position, but I will if you keep up this ridiculous alpha posturing. Back the fuck down, Grayson. Cool off. Lars will come to you when he's good and ready."

Lars wanted to cheer, but realized in time that would not be good form. He would've loved to see Grayson's face as he did, though, but he'd better not push his luck. Grayson was beyond pissed off, so not the best time to push his buttons.

Much to his surprise, Grayson's expression softened. "You're absolutely right, and I apologize, Enar. I was way out of line. I hope you'll understand that this was my emotions speaking."

"Grayson, I understand, believe me. But I'm glad you realize it too."

Grayson nodded, then turned toward Lars. "I will leave you alone, and Enar was right that you deserve the time to cool off. I want you to know that I love you more than anything and so does Sven. This whole situation is not what you think. I hope you'll come to that realization yourself, and when you do, or you want to talk, we will be there, waiting for you."

Lars watched him walk away, and something in his heart shifted. What did Grayson mean that this situation wasn't what he thought? Was it possible he had misunderstood something? He replayed the scene he had walked in on in his head. There was no other explanation than that Sven was pregnant. Enar hadn't denied it either.

No, he hadn't misunderstood. Not the pregnant part, at least. And he was sure he'd heard Grayson say it, that he and Sven would raise the baby together. Those had been his literal words, right? He went over them in his head, trying to look at them in a different way.

"Do you think he's right?" he asked Enar, who had sat down next to him again. "Did I misunderstand them?"

Enar's look at him was soft and kind. "I wasn't in the room, so I don't know what you overheard. But maybe the question is not what they said and whether you interpreted it correctly. Maybe you should ask yourself if the conclusion you came to fits what you have learned about their characters over the last few months. You've known Sven for such a long time, is this something he would do? You know he loves you. And so does Grayson. Lars, I see the way he looks at you, like you're his sun, moon, everything. You and Sven, there's nothing he wouldn't do for you. He's been such a good Daddy to the both of you, do you really think that what you accuse him of fits his character and behavior?"

Enar's words hit him like a sledgehammer, breaking through his conflicted emotions and cutting straight to the core. One of the reasons why it had hurt so much was that he couldn't believe they would do this to him. Enar was right, it didn't fit their characters, neither of them.

Sven would never do something like this behind his back. They had made every decision together over the last few years, and even now when he struggled with something, it was often Lars he came to first, something that frustrated Grayson sometimes. And Grayson was far too honorable to go behind his back like this, he realized. Sure, they butted heads sometimes, especially when he needed something from him but wasn't ready to admit it. Grayson had a way of getting under his skin, of pushing unrelentingly until Lars caved. But not once had he done anything that went against Lars's will. He had always respected Lars's "no."

"It doesn't fit their character," he said to Enar. "It doesn't make sense at all."

"You should ask questions, then, instead of drawing conclusions," his brother advised him, his tone understanding. "It's hard when something hurts this much to keep your emotions at bay and allow yourself to rationally look at the situation, but that's your best option right now. If you walk away in anger now, Lars, you may destroy something that can never be healed again."

Lars bumped his shoulder against his brother's. "You're pretty smart, even for a doctor," he joked.

Enar bumped him right back, a grin on his lips. "Wait till you get my bill for this psychiatric consult," he teased, and Lars smiled.

They sat for a few minutes in silence, their shoulders companionably rubbing against each other, and Lars felt himself cool off. The whirlwind of emotions in his head and body slowed down, and he knew he had to talk to his mates right away. "Thank you," he told Enar. "You said things I needed to hear. And thanks for getting Grayson off my back."

"You're welcome on both counts. And for what it's worth, Lars, you guys will get through this. It may not be easy for a while, but the most valuable things in life never are. If there's one thing I have learned, it's that. Everything beautiful and wonderful in my life has taken struggle and tears to achieve or acquire."

Lars thought about that, the concept of his brother struggling in life. It didn't take him long to realize that he was right. There was the obvious issue of him struggling with his alpha identity, but there was so much more than that. Being in a relationship with another alpha, constantly submitting to someone else, that couldn't be easy for him, no matter if he identified as a beta or not. And then to see that other alpha conceive an alpha heir with their omega, that too had to hurt. Lars had never realized that he and Enar shared that hurt, of always being second choice, or in Enar's case, even third.

He rose to his feet, then extended his hand to his brother and pulled him up. He hesitated for a second and then pulled him closer for a hug. "Thank you, bro."

He found Grayson and Sven waiting for him in their room, as Grayson had indicated. Sven's face was red and swollen with the evidence of a serious crying fit that had lasted for a while. Whereas Sven usually would've stormed right at him and hugged and kissed him till they both ran out of breath, there was now a hesitation that had never been there before. The truth of what Enar had said hit Lars. If he did this wrong, if they did this wrong, they could break something that couldn't so easily be patched together again.

"Enar said I should ask questions instead of drawing conclusions," he said softly. "So I'm here to ask questions."

"We'll answer them," Grayson promised him, and even his voice was choked with emotion, Lars noted.

"Are...are you pregnant?" Lars asked Sven.

The omega's eyes filled up with tears again as he nodded. "Yes. I'm about seven weeks pregnant. Enar confirmed it."

"And you're okay? I mean, you and the baby are healthy?" Lars asked, suddenly worried there was something wrong.

It earned him a grateful look from Sven and one from Grayson that beamed approval. "Yes. I'm just tired, that's it. We haven't done an ultrasound yet because..." He bit his lip.

"Because you needed to decide what you wanted to do first," Lars said in realization.

"Yes. Enar said it was my choice."

"It is," Lars confirmed. "D-do you want to keep it?" He forced himself to keep asking questions rather than to listen to the voice in his head that insisted that he knew the truth already and had every right to lash out in anger.

Sven nodded. "I do. I know it's soon and unexpected and that I'm young, but I want it, Lars. I want it so much."

A single tear meandered down his cheek, and Lars pushed down the desire to kiss it away. "Is that why you talked to Grayson? And not to me?"

A quiet sob flew from Sven's lips. "I didn't talk to him. You have to believe me! I didn't go behind your back. We wanted to tell you, but—"

"If you didn't talk to him, then how come he knew and I didn't? How come I walked in on you discussing raising a baby together I knew nothing about?" His anger bubbled up again, and he reined himself in when he saw the devastated look on Sven's face. "Please, baby," he pleaded, the sweet word falling off his lips. "Help me understand why."

"Will you permit me to explain?" Grayson asked, and it was as much aimed at Lars as at Sven.

Lars mentally braced himself, then nodded.

"I recognized he was pregnant," Grayson said quietly. "I have three kids, Lars, I know what a pregnant omega looks like. He was off the last few days, different, and it clicked for me. He didn't tell me until I guessed it, and we both agreed to tell you right away."

Some of the tightness in his chest released. "But you made the decision to keep the baby together, the two of you," he said. "Why wasn't I involved in that?"

"We didn't make that decision," Grayson said. "Sven did."

Lars's eyebrows shot up. "Are you seriously trying to tell me you didn't weigh in on that?"

"I needed to know he wouldn't be angry with me," Sven said, and that stopped Lars in his thoughts.

"Why would he be? *Oh.*"

"He already has three kids. I wasn't sure if he wanted to be a dad again. And I can't do this without him, but not without you either. I want this baby more than anything, but I need both of you."

His bottom lip quivered and Lars lost his last bit of willpower. He rushed over, pulling Sven into a tight embrace. "I'm sorry, so sorry. I'm here, okay? I'm here."

He felt his own eyes water as Sven sought shelter against his shoulder, his sobs turning into wails. "Don't be angry with me, baby, please!"

"I'm not angry anymore. I'm so sorry, baby. I misunderstood. I thought you didn't want me anymore, that you wanted to be with Grayson."

Lars would have given everything right then and there to turn back time, to not jump to conclusions, because as much as he'd felt rejected and hurt, he was only now grasping how much he had wounded Sven. And Grayson.

His eyes found the alpha's over Sven's head, expecting to see anger or disappointment, but there was something he didn't expect. A profound sadness.

12

He hadn't slept this well in ages, Ruari thought as he woke up. Jax was still asleep next to him, making soft little smacking sounds that shot straight to Ruari's heart. He'd never known how much you could love another person until his son had been born. Ruari had never considered himself the paternal type, maybe because he'd had such a bad example in his own father, but he couldn't deny that Jax had changed him. He loved him, wholly and completely, and there was nothing he wouldn't do to keep his son safe and happy.

Jax had slept peacefully as well, only waking up twice that night. No wonder, it was so quiet on the ranch, so calm and peaceful. The air was fresh, unlike the stale, moldy air in his apartment that had him so worried about Jax's little lungs. Here, everything was fresh, clean, the whole room where he was staying brand-spanking new. And the sense of peace he experienced wasn't just the absence of noise, but rather something that hung in the air. Ruari couldn't explain it, but it felt like coming home.

Of course, that made zero sense. It had to be his imagination. This couldn't be his home, not in the long term, anyway. He was beyond grateful to Enar for giving him a chance to stay, but there was no way he could stay any longer than a few weeks. His presence here endangered everyone on the ranch. If his father ever found out he was staying here, Ruari had no idea what the man would do, but it wouldn't be pretty.

His father was capable of violence. He'd seen it himself growing up, and he caught enough snippets of conversations to understand the man could be ruthless toward his enemies. Hell, Ruari had even overheard part of a conversation about an attack he had ordered on some group whose ideas he didn't agree with. Ruari had never mentioned it to anyone. He wasn't that stupid. When you grew up with a father like his, you learned to be blind, deaf, and mute. It was the only way you could survive.

And after what he had learned about the ranch, about the pack, these people had to be on his father's shitlist already. If he ever found out Lidon could shift, that the wolf shifters had returned? He would burn this place to the ground. He would make it his life's mission to destroy each and every person here. The thought made his blood run cold in his veins.

No, Ruari couldn't stay here permanently, but he would enjoy it while it lasted. It would give him the opportunity to figure out his next steps.

After making sure Jax couldn't roll out of the bed in any way, Ruari took a quick shower. He laughed at himself as he got out, because it was one other aspect where his life had changed a lot. He used to enjoy long, luxurious showers. Now he was lucky to get three minutes in, if that. When you were on your own with a baby, long showers were not possible, he had discovered.

Even now, he heard Jax stir, soft little cries drifting in from the bedroom. The baby wasn't angry yet, but that wouldn't last long if Ruari didn't come get him. He got dressed quickly, then picked up his son and after changing his diaper, dressed him as well. He'd have to feed him in the main house, where Kean had told him to go for breakfast to meet everyone else.

With Jax in the sling, he made his way over to the main house, amazed at how busy the ranch was even at this time of day. Various men were working on finishing up another building, greeting him with respectful nods as he walked by. Had they all been informed of his presence yet? Most of them were betas, but he did see one big alpha at work, and much to his surprise, there was an omega among the men as well. Apparently, Kean had been right when he told Ruari that the pack didn't care much for status and looked at talents foremost.

He caught a glimpse of Kean, on his way to the big stable with the cows. He wanted to raise his hand and greet him, but Kean never looked up. Maybe he would have the chance to talk to him later. His heart did a little jump at the thought.

He hesitated for a few seconds when he heard voices in the kitchen. Kean had shown him where everything was, but he had only met one of the people who lived in the main house: Grayson, an older but handsome alpha. He'd been super nice to Ruari, who had felt comfortable in the man's presence, despite what he knew from Kean about his prolific sex life.

He took a deep breath and walked into the kitchen, where several people were sitting at the table while an omega was making breakfast. A beta standing near the fridge was the one who spotted Ruari first, and he turned around to greet him with a big smile.

"You must be Ruari," he said. "Enar told us that you would be staying here for a while. I'm Palani, one of Enar's mates."

Ruari nodded. "Yes, thank you. This is my son, Jax."

Palani walked up close. "Oh, he is adorable. How old is he?"

"He's almost twelve weeks," Ruari said, as always filled with pride whenever someone admired to his son. It was another one of those strange emotions he'd never experienced before.

"That's close in age to our son, Hakon. He's eight weeks old," Palani said with the same pride in his voice. Right, the alpha heir, Ruari remembered. How lovely that Palani referred to him as "our son," even when the baby wasn't his biologically.

The other men in the room rose, he noticed, and he turned toward them, bracing himself.

"Let me introduce you to the others," Palani said, then pointed them out one by one. "This is Grayson, but I think you two met already yesterday. That's Sven in the kitchen, one of his boys. Lars, his other, is already at work outside. Then we have Sando, who is our main researcher into the Melloni gene, and that's Lucan, one of Grayson's sons, who you may have met in the clinic as he's the office manager there. Grayson's oldest son is the head of security here, Bray. Have you met him yet?"

Ruari tried to hide his shock at hearing that Sando, an omega, was doing scientific research. What kind of place *was* this? "Erm, thank you. No, I haven't met Bray yet, but I remember you from the clinic, Lucan." He did a little wave with his hand. "I'm Ruari and this is Jax. Nice to meet you all."

There was a round of friendly greetings, and then Sven,

the omega in the kitchen, asked, "What would you like for breakfast?"

"I need to feed Jax first, if that's okay. Can I please use a microwave to heat water for his formula?" Ruari asked.

"Absolutely. There is purified water in the fridge. Grab whatever you need, and ask me if there's anything you can't find. When you're done, I'd be happy to cook you breakfast," the other omega answered.

Ruari couldn't believe how friendly and welcoming they were, and it made him feel even more guilty about his father. If these people knew, would they still have welcomed him? Would they still have been as friendly? He doubted it, and he couldn't even blame them.

He quickly grabbed the things he needed for Jax's bottle from the diaper bag he'd brought, then measured water and formula. He'd done it so many times by now, he didn't even need to think. When the water was done, he added the formula and shook it well, then tested it on the inside of his wrist.

It seemed he had gotten it right as the bottle was the perfect temperature. It was also perfect timing, as Jax whimpered and made noises that would soon become a full-fledged wail if he didn't get something to eat.

He was just about to sit down at the table when Kean walked in, looking all male and sweaty. "Good morning," Ruari said self-consciously, aware that there were many people watching.

"Hey," the beta replied, his face lighting up when he saw Ruari. "I was hoping to catch you here."

Without hesitation, he stepped closer and looked at Jax, whose volume was increasing. "A little impatient for your breakfast, young man?"

Ruari smiled, his heart doing strange little flips at Kean's tender tone with his son. "Yeah, I'd better feed him, or he'll break out the sirens."

"Can I do it?" Sven asked a bit shy.

Ruari wasn't sure what to say. He didn't want to turn him down, not in front of everyone, but he wasn't comfortable handing his son over to a stranger, even if it was another omega. Sven looked as young as Ruari himself was, so did he even have any experience with babies?

"He's great with babies," Kean said, his voice kind. "He takes care of Hakon a lot."

Ruari hesitated for a few seconds more, then decided it couldn't hurt, not with him right there. If Sven did anything he didn't like or trust, he could always step in.

"You don't have to, if you're not comfortable with it," Sven said. "But I thought you might like to have a relaxed breakfast. And Kean is right, I love babies."

Grayson rose from his chair, then walked over to Sven and pressed a soft but claiming kiss on the omega's lips. "I'm heading to my room to work, honey. I love you so much."

He kissed him again, a much longer kiss this time, and Ruari watched with amazement as Sven melted against the alpha, apparently not caring there were a bunch of other people in the room.

Kean cleared his throat rather loudly. "Guys, let's not scare away our new arrival right away, shall we?"

The others left as Grayson pulled away, smacking Sven on his ass. "We'll have to continue this later. Come find me when you're done with your morning chores."

"Yes, Daddy," Sven said, and Ruari understood their relationship a lot better after that simple word, including Palani's words when he introduced Grayson and his boys. All right, then. Grayson was their Daddy. All good with him.

Jax had started crying for real now, no longer content

with being rocked. Sven washed his hands, and Ruari was surprised to see him practice the same hygiene that Kean had before. Someone had trained these guys well. Enar, he guessed.

Sven sat himself down at the kitchen table, then held out his hands to take Jax. Ruari watched as he cradled him in his arm, relieved when he noticed he got it right, and when Sven got his son to drink right away, Ruari's worries were gone. Sven looked up and smiled at him. "Grab yourself some breakfast. Kean can show you where everything is."

With quick greetings, the others filed out of the kitchen, leaving the three of them. "What would you like?" Kean asked. "We have all kinds of cereal, oatmeal, I can make you some bacon and eggs or pancakes, whatever you want."

Ruari's eyebrows shot up. "You would cook for me?"

He hoped it didn't come off as an insult, but he was surprised that a beta would cook for him, especially one like Kean who had a full-time job.

"Sure, I can make a mean omelet," Kean said. "We grew up with parents who believed in raising independent sons, so even though Palani and I are betas and our youngest brother Rhene is an alpha, my mom taught all of us to cook."

How about that? Ruari could barely keep his mouth from dropping open. "Oatmeal is fine, thank you. If you have it, could I please make it with milk instead of water?" God knew he could use the extra calories, as well as the vitamin D and calcium the milk offered.

"Absolutely. But I'll make it for you. You sit down and enjoy a bit of downtime," Kean said.

Ruari caught Sven looking from Kean to him and back, a soft smile playing on his lips as if he was privy to something

Ruari didn't know. Was this not normal behavior for Kean? Ruari pondered that as he sat down at the table, watching as Kean made oatmeal for him.

It was a bit of a coincidence, wasn't it, that Kean had come into the kitchen when Ruari was there? Had he timed it like that? His words had betrayed a little bit, indicating he was hoping to run into Ruari. He couldn't deny his attraction to the beta, but did this mean that Kean was feeling the same thing?

God, this would make things complicated. The man had no idea what he was getting into. Well, truth be told, he knew more than anyone else, having overheard Ruari's entire conversation with Enar. That should make Ruari nervous, he figured, or even embarrassed or ashamed, but it didn't. For some reason, it was comforting to know he wouldn't have to explain that part.

So many people jumped to conclusions when they met a single omega with a baby, and most of them weren't good. Ruari had endured more demeaning proposals over the last few months than he'd had in his entire life before.

But Kean was different. The man knew of his past, at least the sexual part, and he didn't seem to care. Not that that cleared the way for them to be anything more than friends, Ruari thought with sadness. There was still the insurmountable issue of his father, and the threat that kept looming over his head. No, they could be friends, but anything more was all but impossible.

Still, as Sven fed Jax, then made him burp and cuddled with him, Ruari and Kean spent a good twenty minutes chatting at the breakfast table. It was the longest conversation Ruari had had with another adult in months, and his soul rejoiced in being seen and feeling heard.

If only it could last.

THEY HAD all gone to bed the previous evening without more talking, and though Grayson knew it had been the right thing to do with Sven being too exhausted, it didn't sit right with him that they hadn't talked things out. There was an emotional distance between them, a lack of intimacy that had never been there before. It reminded him of their first weeks, when they had still been struggling to find how they fit together. There had been no sweet words, no morning sex for him, and he hadn't dared approach them either, too scared of forcing something they weren't ready for it. But it left him unsatisfied, yearning to gain back what they had lost. If only he could figure out how.

It bothered him deeply, and he knew it would bother Sven even more. The omega was so sensitive to tension, and now that he was pregnant, Grayson really wanted to avoid that.

So after writing for an hour or two, he ventured outside, into the far fields where Lars was working. The beta looked shocked when Grayson showed up.

"Hi," he said, and a stab of regret pierced Grayson's heart.

Would he ever hear him say the word "Daddy" again? They had lost trust yesterday, he realized all over again, setting them back months. And it wasn't just Lars. He found himself craving the intimacy that had been so easy and normal before. How could they get back to that? Maybe honesty was the best way.

"I figured it would be good if we talked," he said. "I am struggling with what happened, and I'm sure you must be too."

"Now?" Lars asked.

It wasn't an unreasonable reaction, Grayson told himself. Technically, Lars was at work, even if that was a little different here on the ranch.

"I wanted to try to talk things through before lunch," he explained.

Lars's eyes lit up with understanding. "You don't want to involve Sven in this."

"He's pregnant, Lars. I think he needs to be protected, don't you agree?"

Lars pointed toward a shack where he stored some of his tools. "Let's find shade behind the shed."

They found a spot in the shade with their backs against the shed, and they sat for a few minutes, neither of them speaking.

"Are you still angry with me?" Lars then asked.

That question only reinforced Grayson's decision to talk things through. "No, but you have every right to still be angry with me."

Lars's head shot sideways. "What do you mean?"

Grayson took a deep, fortifying breath. "I failed you yesterday, Lars, when I was angry with you, shouting at you, when I should've understood why you acted the way you did."

"I should've known you guys wouldn't go behind my back," Lars said, and it was easy to hear the remorse in his voice.

"That's why I was so angry with you," Grayson said.

"I don't understand."

There was a slight hesitation at the end of that sentence, as if Lars had wanted to tag something on, the term of endearment Grayson missed so much. Even if it had been out of habit, hope flared up in Grayson's heart that they would be able to get past this.

"Lars, sweetheart, I'm sorry for what happened yesterday. I can't apologize for you walking in on us, because there was nothing else we could've done. I swear we weren't talking about Sven's pregnancy for long before you walked in."

"I believe you."

"But I need to apologize for the way I reacted when I overheard what you said to Enar."

"You were so angry with me," Lars said, his voice sounding small.

"I was," Grayson confirmed. "Though I'm sure you were pleasantly surprised by how Enar stood up to me."

Much to his relief, Lars let out a smile. "That was badass," he said.

"I was wrong to get so angry with you over a gut reaction. And the fact that you came back to us, willing to talk things out, only proves it. I didn't give you the time to get past your initial reaction, and for that, I'm truly sorry."

They sat in silence for a bit before Lars reacted. "I hurt you by thinking you were capable of doing this," he said.

"Yes, but I should've recognized where you were coming from. I didn't consider the depth of your insecurities last night, and I blame myself for that."

He didn't want to say more, because this was not something they had ever talked about openly. It was always present beneath the surface, these insecurities, and all three of them had them. Sven, who was always worried either of them would be displeased with him. Lars, who even after spending months together, still wasn't convinced he was worthy to be loved, always waiting for the other shoe to drop. And Grayson, who, if he was honest with himself, still felt like an outsider sometimes when he was reminded of how much Sven and Lars were in tune with each other.

"In my head, I know that you would never do that," Lars said, his voice a hoarse whisper.

"But in moments like yesterday, when your emotions take over, it's hard to remind yourself of that." Grayson understood.

"I wish I could feel differently. I was so angry—"

"Don't be," Grayson interrupted him. "Don't blame yourself for this. Give it time, sweetheart. I promise you, it will diminish over time."

Again, it took a long time before Lars reacted. "Are you sure you have the patience to wait for that? What if something like this happens again and I freak out again?"

"Then I can only hope I'll have had time to learn from my mistakes as well and react with more understanding. The kind of understanding I should've given you yesterday instead of getting angry. This was on me, not on you. There's room for you to grow."

"Does that mean we're okay now?" Lars asked, and there was a meaning behind that question Grayson couldn't decipher.

"Yes, sweetheart, we are more than okay as far as I'm concerned, unless there's something else you think we should talk about."

A choked sob flew from his boy's lips. "Then why are you not calling me your boy? What do I need to do to make it really okay, to make you love me again?"

Grayson had never acted so fast as when he yanked Lars to drag him onto his lap, the air leaving the boy's lungs with a whoosh.

"You'll always be my boy, baby, even when I'm angry and upset with you. Nothing you could ever do could make me stop loving you. Do you hear me?"

Lars clung to him, sobbing, and it was so unusual for

him to break down like that that Grayson felt every tear in his heart.

"You didn't even spank me this morning, Daddy, and I needed you. I needed to feel that you still loved me."

And Grayson understood that by keeping his distance, he had fueled the boy's insecurities rather than helping him. He could explain it to Lars, and he was sure he could make him understand, but the bottom line was that Lars needed more than words right now. He needed his Daddy. Without a second's hesitation, he flipped him over and pushed him down on his lap, dragging his pants and underwear down with a rough move.

His hand came down hard, the slap mingling with Lars's cry, "Daddy!"

He spanked him hard and long, until the beta was a blubbering mess on his lap, his ass all red and angry, his mouth making sounds Grayson had never heard from him before. When he was done, he carried him inside, not caring that everyone saw, and caring even less that Lars's pants remained outside, his red ass on full display. They could look away if they didn't want to see it. Right now, his boys needed him.

He deposited Lars in a hot bath, then interrupted an omega-meeting in Vieno's bedroom, where Vieno and Sven were hanging out with the new kid. He kindly requested Sven's presence, and his sweet pup didn't hesitate a second before joining him. Grayson fucked him hard and fast over the bathroom sink, while Lars watched from the tub with hungry eyes, then sent him back with a butt plug and a cock ring, so he could do it all over again later that day.

They needed each other, he understood now, so he had to set the tone and show they were okay. For Sven, that meant being used, as the boy had developed a deep affinity for being used as a little cum hole. As if to prove it, Sven beamed as Grayson sent him off, despite being denied an orgasm, his lips still swollen from Grayson's demanding kisses and his ass smarting from their rough fuck and the rather sizable butt plug inside him.

But Lars? Lars needed something else. Lars needed his time, his care, his love. And so he tenderly dried him off, then rimmed his boy until he saw stars, gave him the blow job of his life, and fucked him for a long time, all the while forbidding him to come. By the time he finally gave permission, Lars was beyond talking, a pleading, shaking mess who exploded in an orgasm that left him trembling for a long time, after which the boy fell asleep in Grayson's arms.

It was, Grayson felt, worthy make-up sex and a well-spent morning.

13

K ean mentally braced himself before he walked into the living room, where he had agreed to meet with his brother. Or rather, his brother had agreed to meet with him, because after that morning's breakfast in the kitchen, Kean knew he had to take the next step. He wasn't sure if it would go anywhere. But before he could even try, he had to follow the rules.

Palani was already waiting for him, tapping away on the keyboard of his laptop, which perched on his lap as he sat cross-legged on the couch. He looked up when Kean walked in. "Hey bro, what's up?"

It took one look at Kean's face to put his laptop away and lean forward. "Okay, I can see something is going on. Talk to me."

It was funny, the dynamic they had. Kean was older than him by a year, and yet it felt like Palani was his older brother. He was an old soul, somehow, mature and wise beyond his years. He always had been. Kean wasn't exactly a party animal either, but Palani was in a whole other category.

Kean lowered himself on a chair across from his brother. He decided to skip the pleasantries and go straight for what he wanted. "I would like your permission to approach Ruari and see if he would be interested in more between us," he said.

Palani looked at him thoughtfully. "Enar told me he thought you two had a connection. It's pretty fast."

"I'm not saying I want to marry him," Kean said defensively. "I'm asking for permission to approach him and see if he's even open to the idea, so we can see if there's something between us."

"Kean, I understand. I hate to bring him up, but what about Bray?"

And that, right there, was the conversation Kean had hoped not to have with his brother. He had never told him about him and Bray hooking up. There had been no need as neither of them was an omega. But of course, Palani had found out anyway. There was little that escaped his attention. And it wasn't that Kean was uncomfortable with his brother knowing who he slept with or hooked up with. It was more that he might be forced to explain something he couldn't even explain himself, like his weird attraction to Bray.

"You know, huh?" he sighed.

"Would you like to talk about it?"

Kean considered it. Out of everyone on the ranch, Palani might understand this better than anyone, considering his complicated relationship with Vieno, Lidon, and Enar before the four of them had figured out what they were to each other. Plus, Palani was a good listener and might shed some light. Then, of course, there was the whole fated mates thing that Kean was still conflicted about, especially after what Bray had said, and he knew for a fact Palani would have opinions on that.

"Do you believe in fated mates?" he asked.

Palani looked at him quizzically, but replied, "Yes, absolutely. I never knew something could hurt as much as being separated from Vieno after he married Lidon. That wasn't mere heartbreak, you know? That was real pain, and he was feeling the same thing. He was withering without me, and if nothing else, that convinced me of the truth. The four of us, there's no other way to explain how we function than that of us being fated mates."

This was another thing Kean appreciated about his brother. Palani didn't immediately fill a silence with more words, but gave you time to think. And Kean did a lot of thinking as he pondered Palani's statement. "Bray doesn't believe in fated mates," he finally offered.

"But you do," Palani said as a statement, not a question.

"I do, but I'm not sure how it works. Like, can one person feel he is meant for someone else, but that other person not feel it at all? Is that even possible?"

Palani sent him a sad smile. "I assume we're still talking about Bray?"

It would be the first time Kean admitted his feelings to anyone else, maybe even including himself. But he was tired of lying to himself, and even more tired of pretending.

"Yes," he said quietly. "Remember that first time Rhene and I visited here? When I saw Bray, it felt like being shocked with a taser. I was certain it had to mean something, and I'll be honest that it was one of the reasons why I decided to move here. But I don't think he felt that, back then, and whatever he feels for me right now is not on the same level. So I don't know what to do with that, and with Ruari entering the picture, I'm even more confused."

"Hmm," Palani said. "And do you have any idea how Ruari feels about you? Do you think he's open to you pursuing him?"

Kean shrugged, letting out a soft sigh. "He likes me, of that I'm sure. Other than that, I couldn't tell you. That whole thing with Bray has me super confused and doubting my ability to interpret situations correctly."

"Did Bray ever tell you he wanted more when you guys started seeing each other?"

Kean grimaced. "Hell no, he made it crystal clear that this was super casual. Hooking up, that's it. Scratching a sexual itch, caused by the shifting."

"You had hoped he'd develop more feelings for you," Palani understood.

Kean shrugged again, unsure of what else to say. "I hoped, but I guess I was wrong."

"So does that make Ruari second choice? Because that's a hell of a wrong way to start a relationship, if I may be so frank."

Kean's first reaction was to get angry for even suggesting it, but then he realized Palani was right. Or rather, he wasn't wrong. The attraction with Ruari was there, for sure, but could he really forget about Bray? He would have to if he wanted a shot with Ruari. He couldn't start dating him, not even approach him, until he had broken things off with Bray. That thought saddened him, but he had no choice. If Bray didn't want him, and all the signals pointed to that conclusion, then Kean had to walk away before his heart got even more involved.

"No, he's not second choice. But I'll admit it may take me a while to let go of the idea of me and Bray together. But I promise you, I will break things off with him. I have no intention of deceiving Ruari, and even if it turns out he's not interested in me that way, I still need to end things with Bray. I'm too good to continue this. If he doesn't want me, then I need to draw my conclusions and walk away."

Palani's eyes were filled with sympathy as he nodded. "I was hoping you would come to that conclusion. I like Bray, I really do, but there's no denying the man has issues. All we can do is hope he'll work through them, but it may be too late for you and him by then."

A strange image filled Kean's mind, a picture of Bray, him, and Ruari together. An alpha, a beta, and an omega. It had the potential to be the perfect combination, but he realized the futility of even considering it. Bray wanted an omega, not a beta. Even if, and that was the biggest "if" ever considering those two hadn't even met, but even if Bray and Ruari connected by some miracle, Kean would always be the third wheel in that relationship. Bray would never accept him as a suitable mate, not when his heart was set on, how had he put it? *A sweet, pliant omega.*

Kean scoffed. Those were three things he would and could never be. So no, he had to forget about Bray and focus on Ruari instead, hoping that the connection he'd felt with him was enough to convince the omega to give them a shot.

But first, he had bad news to deliver to a certain alpha. That should be fun.

BRAY WAS surprised when Kean approached him while he was inspecting the new guardhouse near the main entrance. Jawon and his men had done a good job building it to Bray's specifications, and he made a mental note to tell him so. He had just finished writing down the few improvements he wanted to suggest when Kean walked in.

"Hey," the beta said, and something in his tone put Bray on edge. He wasn't sure why Kean was here, but he was certain he wasn't gonna like it.

"What brings you here?" he asked, skipping the niceties.

Kean dragged his hand through his hair, and that's when Bray knew his suspicions were correct. This couldn't be good.

"Can we talk?"

Bray sighed, that simple line giving him a good indication of where this conversation was headed. "Sure. I'm assuming you have something to tell me?"

For the first time since he walked in, Kean met his eyes head on. "Yes, I do. I wanted to tell you that I can't see you anymore."

Bray pushed down the flash of anger that rose at those words. "I didn't realize we were serious enough to warrant an official break up," he said.

Kean's eyes sparked. "That's exactly the problem," he said.

Bray frowned. What was Kean referring to? "I'm not following."

Kean rolled his eyes. "No, you're not, and that's the whole problem. Look, we agreed to keep things casual, and that may be working out for you quite well, but I have come to the conclusion that this is not providing me with what I need or want in the long term. It's—"

"Who said anything about long term?" Bray said, his frown intensifying.

"You're interrupting me. Again," Kean said quietly.

Oh my God, was he going on that tour again? Bray held up his hands. "I'm sorry, okay? Let's not do the whole 'you interrupted me' drama again."

"And that, right there, is the second reason I'm ending

this," Kean said, his voice louder than before. Bray opened his mouth to say something, but Kean lifted a finger and Bray shut it again. "No, you do not speak while I'm talking. You can at least have the decency to let me speak without interrupting when I'm ending things with you, you hear me?"

Bray could barely repress the urge to roll his eyes. Kean could be so super sensitive about things like this. Everybody interrupted others when they were in a conversation. It was the normal dynamic of any conversation. It had nothing to do with being rude or whatever, you just had to talk a little louder if you wanted to be heard. Once people realized you were serious with what you were saying, they would let you finish without interrupting. But apparently, this was something Kean had never learned, so Bray decided he could be magnanimous and let him talk. Maybe when Kean got all the drama off his chest, Bray could talk some sense into him.

"You said you wanted something casual, and I went along with that. The truth is that I am looking for a long-term relationship, but not with you," Kean said.

Bray frowned. Not that he was interested in anything serious, but what was wrong with him that Kean didn't see him as a suitable long-term partner? He could do worse than an alpha like Bray.

"You've made your wishes for a future partner crystal clear," Kean continued. "And we both know that nothing on your list applies to me. I'm not an omega, I'm not sweet and submissive, and I sure as hell won't take care of you or wipe your ass the rest of your life, as you seem to demand from your future mate. You've been honest about that, and while I think it's ridiculous and you're wrong, I can't fault you for your honesty. But it does mean that this is where our ways part."

For reasons Bray couldn't explain, his frustration with this conversation was growing. Why did Kean make it sound like his vision for a future mate was ridiculous? Hell, his own father had done the same, stating that if Bray ever found someone like that, he would be bored out of his mind. Why did other people think they knew better than himself who suited him? And come to that, who the hell was Kean that he thought he could tell Bray anything anyway?

"Okay, so you've come to the same conclusion I have, that we're not a good match in the long term. What the hell does that have to do with us hooking up? Why can't we continue to have fun until you meet someone else?"

One look at Kean's face, and Bray's stomach dropped, taking his self-confidence with it. Kean had already met someone else, that truth was painted on his face.

"You already have, haven't you?" Bray asked, a lot more subdued now.

Kean slowly nodded. "Yes, there's a new omega who arrived yesterday and who may be staying for a while. His name is Ruari. I already met him a few weeks ago in the clinic, and we connected. He has a baby, a three-month-old, and it has made me realize that is what I want. I don't want to hook up and be casual, Bray. I want a mate, a family."

Bray inhaled deeply, trying to ignore the strange way his heart behaved. "Well, if that's what you want. I mean, you're pretty damn young to settle down, but whatever."

Kean raised his head, his chin tilting up in that stubborn way that alerted more trouble was coming. "There's one more thing I want to say," Kean said. "I'm not sure I could've continued with you even if I hadn't met Ruari."

"Why? I thought we were good together in bed. You certainly seem to appreciate the way I fuck you," Bray said.

"I do, but I want more than just a good fuck, even for a

casual relationship. I want someone who sees me as his equal, and the truth is that you don't. Not in bed, not in conversations, not in any social situation. You are the alpha, and you always let me feel that. And I've decided that I'm worth more than that. I'm looking at my brother, and I can see what I could achieve in a relationship where I am taken seriously, where I am an equal partner. And I want that for myself. I deserve that. And I can't bring myself to settle any longer for someone who only sees me as a good fuck."

Kean looked him right in the eyes, until Bray averted his own. There was something in the beta's eyes that pierced straight through his armor, that came dangerously close to wounding him. It was bullshit, of course, what he was saying, the ramblings of an oversensitive beta who probably secretly yearned to be an alpha. And yet, as Kean's words sank in, Bray felt a shiver inch down his spine.

It couldn't be true, right? People respected him, they respected his position. That wouldn't be the case if he treated them the way Kean just described. There needed to be some kind of hierarchy, even in a pack. Hell, especially in a pack. Wasn't that why there was a pack alpha, whose command everyone was supposed to follow?

But there was also a second-in-command, he thought with a confusing clarity. A second-in-command who was a beta, and who was still in charge, even of Bray and the other alphas. He'd been uneasy with that decision from the start, even though he could acknowledge no alpha would've done a better job than Palani. That didn't mean he wasn't a tad uncomfortable with a beta being placed in a position over him.

But that was different. That was pack business, not a relationship or as Kean had put it, social situations. The fact that Bray might be a tad old-fashioned in some aspects didn't mean you couldn't treat people equally. He did. It was just that some people, and all evidence pointed toward Kean being one of them, were overly sensitive about this.

"Look, I don't know where you got the impression I only think of you as a good fuck, because I genuinely like you. But you're a tad oversensitive here. You're seeing things that are not true, though I am sorry you experienced it that way. I've worked hard to get to where I am, so if you think that everything's been handed to me just because I'm an alpha, you're wrong. I struggled when I started this business, because older alphas wouldn't give me a fair chance. But I learned to adapt and become the kind of alpha and business owner people take seriously. So I understand what it's like to be overlooked, but you have to position yourself better, to be more dominant and present, and then people will respond to you in a different way."

Kean stared at him for what had to be close to ten seconds before he slowly shook his head. "That has to be the biggest load of alpha-privileged crap I have ever heard in my life. You haven't listened to a word I said, Bray. But I'm done explaining this to you. It was fun while it lasted, but I'm hoping to have a shot with Ruari. I've already asked Palani for permission to pursue him, and he's granted me that."

A wave of anger rolled through Bray at that dismissal. "Well, of course, you've gotten permission. He *is* your brother after all," he snapped.

Kean's eyes narrowed. "If you think that's why he gave permission, you don't know Palani at all. But it doesn't matter. I don't owe any explanation to you, and neither does he."

He turned to walk away, and for some reason, that enraged Bray even more. To be dumped was one thing, especially when it was a casual relationship in the first place, but to be dismissed like that, like his voice and opinion didn't matter at all, that would not stand.

"You'd better hope that omega is satisfied with just one child, because you'll never be able to give him more."

He regretted the words as soon as they left his mouth, a cheap and low shot that he should've never made.

Kean turned around, and the look of devastation on his face hit Bray deep. If there had been any chance of them ever hooking up again, he had just ruined it.

"Not everyone prioritizes the way you do, Bray," Kean said, and much to Bray's surprise, his voice sounded sad rather than angry. "Love really does conquer all. But I guess you don't believe in that either. I feel sorry for you, Bray, because with that attitude, I doubt you'll ever find that kind of love in the first place."

Bray watched as Kean walked away without looking back again. He had deserved that last parting shot, he admitted to himself. He'd gone for a kill shot, and he'd hit his target, but it had been a low blow. He was better than that, even if the thought had crossed his mind that the omega might be better off with an alpha if he ever wanted more children. Then again, if he had a child now, someone must have sired it, so maybe he could ask that same alpha to be a sperm donor.

As he leaned against the wall, contemplating that whole conversation with Kean, a heaviness settled in his heart. He wasn't sure why, but this break up felt like a massive failure, much more than its casual status should've warranted. Why was that? Why were Kean's words still playing in his head, like some kind of bad but catchy ear worm?

It was a long time before he stepped outside, and when he did, his mood hadn't improved.

14

This was the weirdest day ever, Ruari decided. Ever since he found out he was pregnant, his life had been filled to the brim with stress. First, there had been pure panic when he'd tested positive, knowing what his father's reaction would be like. Then he'd gone through a few weeks of coming up with every imaginable plan to keep himself safe. After that, once he'd made his escape, he'd worried about making sure the baby was okay, about eating enough, getting his vitamins in. Then there had been the delivery, which thankfully, had gone easy. But man, once Jax had been born, a whole new level of stress had arrived. No, it was safe to say that he'd never had as much stress in his life as the last nine months.

But today, today was about as relaxed as he'd ever been. Jax was sleeping in the cutest little crib, right next to another gorgeous baby. Ruari had been introduced to Vieno, who turned out to be a lovely person who had apologized profusely for not being there that morning. He explained he was struggling with depression after giving birth and often felt the most blue and down early in the morning. Ruari understood now why Sven took care of baby Hakon so much, and he was grateful that Vieno had someone to help him.

They had hung out the entire morning, Sven disappearing for a while when Grayson came to get him, which promptly resulted in the undeniable sounds of sex drifting in. Vieno shrugged, not even looking embarrassed.

"I think they had a fight yesterday, those three," he said. "They were all tense this morning, and Sven didn't get his morning fuck, so I'm glad to see them make up."

Ruari wasn't sure he wanted to know, but he asked anyway. "Morning fuck? You're saying it like it's a routine."

"Oh, it is, trust me. They have one every day, about mid-morning. That's when Grayson comes up for air after writing for a bit and needs to blow off steam, and trust me, Sven is more than happy to accommodate him. It usually doesn't last long."

"Huh," Ruari said, strangely fascinated.

"Those three thrive on things like that. They start every day with bathroom sex for Grayson and Sven, usually Sven blowing him, and then after, Lars gets his spanking. They eat breakfast in the main kitchen, but they always lunch together in their room, which often results in more sex. Then when Lars is done with work, he and Grayson will take a shower, followed by either more sex or a spanking if Lars has misbehaved."

Ruari couldn't help but snicker at the casual way in which Vieno delivered this news. He brought it like facts, describing the rituals as if they were completely innocent. And they were, Ruari thought. Others tended to blow daddy kink like this completely out of proportion, but while it wasn't his particular type of kink, he had no issues with it.

"Never a dull moment here, I see," he commented.

Vieno grinned. "You'd better get used to it if you want to stay here," he said. "We're pretty open about our sexual activities, but I'm sure you've discovered this by now. Someone must have told you."

"Yeah, Kean was clear in his warnings to stay out of the main house at certain times," Ruari laughed.

Vieno's laugh sobered. "Yeah, he's right. He was, anyway."

Ruari guessed it had something to do with Vieno's depression, but since he barely knew the man, he was hesitant to ask. He was saved when Sven returned, his usually pale cheeks blushed, and judging by the slight hesitation as he sat down, his ass had been well used. Good for him. It was easy to see how much Grayson loved him.

Sven made them lunch, joining them. It appeared Grayson and Lars were taking a nap together. No wonder, after the rather loud noises they'd overheard from those two. Make-up sex, Vieno had mouthed to Ruari, and they had giggled. Ruari loved getting to know these two omegas better, and it turned out they had more than enough to talk about.

"Vieno always takes a nap in the afternoon, while I watch Hakon," Sven said when he'd cleared the remnants of their lunch. "If you would like some time to yourself, I'm happy to watch Jax as well. I'll be staying right here where I can hear them, and if you want to, you can leave his bottle and everything with me so I can feed him. I'm not sure if you feed on demand or have a schedule?"

Ruari could have kissed him. It was one of the first times anyone had ever offered to help him, aside from Kean, and where he had his reservations earlier that morning, by now he trusted Sven to take care of Jax.

"He's on a four-hour schedule, and since I just fed him,

he should be good for a while. He usually sleeps for at least two, three hours in the afternoon. If you could watch him for me, that would be amazing. I can't remember the last time I had some time to myself."

Sven's smile split open his entire face, and it was easy to see the omega was pleased to do something for Ruari. "You're so welcome. I'm happy I get to help you out. I love babies, I've discovered since Hakon was born."

There was something more in his eyes, something that told Ruari the man wanted one of his own, but he didn't say anything. They had time to get to the more personal conversations.

Vieno yawned and stretched his arms above his head. "Yeah, it's time for me to catch some sleep. Why don't you go outside and see if you can find that beta who was drooling over you in the kitchen this morning, from what I've heard?" he said to Ruari.

Ruari's eyes widened, and he felt his cheeks grow warm. "Who told you that?"

Sven giggled. "I did. Watching the two of you make lovey-dovey eyes at each other was the most fun I've had in weeks. You can't tell me you weren't aware."

Ruari's blush grew deeper. He tried to feign indifference and shrugged. "He's nice."

That resulted in chuckles from the other two. "He's not nice, honey. He's hot, and I'm allowed to say it because he's the spitting image of his brother," Vieno said. Then his face sobered as he added, "He's a good man, Ruari, I'm telling you. Those two brothers, there are something special. I've never met anyone as strong as Palani, but Kean is a close second. They're like a rock you can lean on, a safe harbor in the storm. I've leaned hard on Palani over the last years, and he's never let me down. And Kean, he's the same."

It was touching, this heartfelt tribute to the two brothers, Ruari thought. He could see what Vieno meant about them being alike, because even in the few minutes when he'd met Palani that morning, he had liked him instantly, much like Kean. Still, not only was it premature to even talk about something more with Kean considering he had no indication that the beta was serious about pursuing him, but there was always the impossible complication of his family, his father specifically. Still, those were not concerns he could share with these two. Or anyone else, for that matter.

"I'm sure I can find something to entertain myself with," he said with a cheeky smile, leaving the option open he would seek Kean out.

That's how he found himself wandering outside, alone for the first time since Jax had been born. It was a strange sensation, one that would take getting used to, he decided. His chest felt empty without the sling he always used to carry Jax, and it was hard to relax instead of being constantly aware of his child.

But outside, the sun shone and he lifted his face to catch some extra rays. As he walked around, the ranch impressed him all over again in its size, but even more in its depth. Kean had mentioned the goal was to become self-sufficient, and while Ruari was no expert, he could see they were making great strides toward that.

Again, it was more than the sum of the buildings, or the fields, or the animals and the men working there that made the ranch such a vibrant place. It was something that hung in the air, something that was hard to describe but that made Ruari's heart feel at peace. Home. His mind settled once again on the same word he decided on earlier. The ranch felt like home, impossible as that was.

Without realizing it, he found himself looking for Kean

when he hit the area where the animals were. He didn't see him, but he did run into Lars, who sported a happy grin as he carried a large crate with what looked to be fresh vegetables. Apparently the make up sex and the nap had done him well.

"He's in the main house," Lars said, "Dropping off the fresh eggs and vegetables I harvested."

Ruari couldn't help but smile at the cheeky grin on the beta's face. Had everyone noticed the attraction between him and Kean? Because that wasn't awkward at all. Sigh.

"Thank you," he said, deciding that denying it was useless when everyone knew.

He made his way back to the main house, not sure if he should seek Kean out, considering what he knew about the harsh reality of their situation and the impossibility of anything more between them. But it was like his legs had a mind of their own—or his heart, he wasn't sure—and he found himself at the door to the main house before he realized it.

He ran into Kean in the hallway, his sun-kissed face lighting up when he spotted Ruari. It did something to him, this unashamed joy Kean showed. It had been a long time since anyone had shown such happiness at simply being in his presence. His parents had lost any pride in him a long time ago, even before he'd gotten pregnant. To see someone react to him this strongly made his heart sing.

"Hi," he said, then mentally cursed himself for his lackluster greeting.

"Hey you," Kean said. "Where is Jax?"

Oh man, if Ruari hadn't already liked him, that immediate concern for his son would seal the deal. "He's sleeping. Sven is babysitting, so I have a little time to myself."

That made Kean smile even wider. "That is awesome,"

he said. "Sven is a true sweetheart, and he's great with babies."

It was sweet, this repeated reassurance Kean gave him that he made the right decision to let Sven watch his kid. "I've seen him with Hakon, and the fact that Vieno trusts him means a lot as well."

Kean hesitated for a second, then asked, "Can I interest you in a little walk? Like, just on the ranch property?"

Ruari suppressed a smile. Kean was being so sweet, but he couldn't resist teasing him a little. "You want to give me another tour?"

A faint blush stained the beta's cheeks as he dragged a hand through his short hair and shifted his feet. "Right, erm, you want to do something else?"

"I'm teasing you, Kean. I'd love to go outside with you," Ruari said quickly. He didn't want Kean to feel uncomfortable or embarrassed in any way.

"Oh, okay. Awesome."

Kean held the door open for Ruari and they stepped back into the sunlight. "I haven't had time for myself in a long time," Ruari admitted. "Not since Jax was born."

Kean shot him a quick look sideways. "Would you rather spend it alone?" he asked. "Because you want the opportunity to just be by yourself?"

He was saying all the right things, and Ruari was losing the battle with himself over why this was such a bad idea. "No, but that's sweet of you to say. I'd love to spend time with you," he said, and the radiant smile on Kean's face crumbled his last resolve.

Kean liked him, Ruari had no doubt, and the feeling was mutual. He couldn't explain it, but he had this instant trust in this man. He was kind, gentle, and yet there was a core of steel in him, somehow. Ruari hesitated for a bit, then decided to take a little jump. He reached out his hand and bumped it against Kean's, whose head shot to the side. Once the beta realized it wasn't an accident, his bigger hand took Ruari's and laced their fingers together. Ruari's stomach exploded with butterflies. It was such an innocent gesture, and yet it meant so much.

They didn't say much as they left the buildings behind and walked all the way to the far fields, where Lars was still working, greeting them with a quick raise of his hand before he turned his attention back to the soil he was toiling.

"I wanted to talk to you about something," Kean said. He tugged at Ruari's hand until they both stood still, facing each other. "As I told you, omegas are protected within the pack. That means anyone wanting to date an omega has to have permission from Palani. I asked him for permission to pursue you, and he granted it."

Ruari smiled. "Did he now?" he asked.

Some of the tension on Kean's face disappeared, which proved the beta was adept at reading Ruari's body language.

"He did," Kean said. "But I don't have your permission yet."

Ruari's smile sobered, and he pulled his hand from Kean's, causing the beta to look worried. "I really like you, Kean, and I would love to give you permission, but there are things you need to know about me."

He bit his lip, trying to figure out what to say and how much to tell Kean. He deserved to know what he was getting into, but how could Ruari inform him without endangering him as well? If his father ever found out, Kean's life might be at stake, because the man didn't joke around.

"Ruari, sweetheart, you can tell me as much or as little as you want to, but I can guarantee you, it won't change my mind about you. If you're not ready to talk about whatever is bothering you, or whatever worries you have about us together, then take your time. I'm not going anywhere. I wanted to tell you how I feel and ask your permission to at least spend time with you."

It almost wasn't fair, the way Kean managed to break through his usual defenses. Ruari knew he was good-looking, attractive. He'd always been, and as a result, he'd encountered a lot of admirers, both alphas and betas. He was used to men approaching him, some super slick, some a little more clumsy, some offensive and sexual. He'd gotten skilled in handling those advances with snarky retorts, but this simple, honest way Kean approached him stripped him of all his usual words.

What did you say to someone who put himself out there in such a simple but straightforward way? Kean wasn't playing any games, didn't have an ulterior agenda. He wanted to tell Ruari how he felt and ask him for permission to pursue him. How the hell did you say no to that?

"You heard about my past in the clinic," he said. "And if you read between the lines, you understood that I'm in a complicated situation with my family. I don't know how to explain it to you in a way that won't put you at risk, but my family is dangerous. I shouldn't be in a relationship, Kean. It's not safe, not for me but especially not for the man I would be involved with. And I can't in good conscience start something with you without you knowing. I come with a warning label, or at least, I should."

He almost held his breath, waiting for Kean's reaction. The beta took both his hands, then pressed a kiss to one hand, then the other, a gesture that seemed from ages ago yet left Ruari trembling.

"Thank you for telling me. I figured something was going on with your family, like you said. I respect that you can't tell me more, but I hope you will once we get to know each other better. Because this is not a deterrent for me, Ruari. I can't explain it, but I want to get to know you, would love to get the chance to be there for you, maybe take care of you a little. If that's what you want."

Ruari looked into Kean's blue eyes, so steady and calm, and he had no trouble imagining a future with this man. That was crazy since they barely knew each other, but it was like his soul recognized Kean's on a level he couldn't put into words.

"Okay," he said, capitulating to the inevitable. "Let's get to know each other better."

The smile on Kean's face shone brighter than a lit Christmas tree, and Ruari smiled right back. "You're gorgeous when you smile," he told Kean.

"You're gorgeous even when you don't," Kean said, and they both grinned like high school students.

"I have one more thing to tell you," Kean said. "Because it will come up at some point, and I'd rather have you hear it from me directly."

Ruari frowned, wondering what Kean was talking about. It sounded rather ominous. What did the man have, a mistress on the side somewhere? A child with someone else? He almost laughed at his own thoughts, as they seemed ridiculous for a man of Kean's character. No, it had to be something innocent, something that the beta just wanted to get off his chest but that didn't mean anything.

"I was seeing someone else in the pack, but I broke things off this morning and told him I wanted to pursue you."

Ruari's frown intensified. This was not what he had been expecting, and he didn't like the sound of it at all. Kean had dumped another omega for him? That sounded like he was a player, and while that didn't fit what Ruari had learned about him so far, it was hard to come to another conclusion.

"Who was it?" he asked.

Kean shuffled his feet. "Bray, the head of security. It was all super casual," he quickly added. "Just hooking up. We didn't even tell anyone, but people knew, so I wanted you to be aware in case someone brings it up. But I talked to Bray this morning and made it clear that I was ending our *arrangement*, I guess you could call it."

An alpha. Kean was breaking up with an alpha for him. That changed things. "How did he react?" Ruari asked.

Kean looked a little embarrassed. "He didn't take it too well, but that might also be because we got into a little argument, and I provided some critical feedback on his character that he wasn't too happy about. He was the one who wanted to keep things casual. He doesn't want a family, or at least not now." His shoulders dropped, and something profoundly sad flashed over his face.

"It wasn't casual for you," Ruari said, understanding the situation. It should've hurt, discovering that Kean had feelings for someone else as well, but it didn't. If anything, it proved to Ruari the man was serious about relationships and not only looking for hook ups.

"He hurt me," Kean admitted. "He is a very traditional alpha, I guess you could say. He's a good guy at the core, he really is, but he has rather old-fashioned ideas about relationships and dynamics. He pictures himself with an omega, so nothing I could ever do would make me enough for him. And I got tired of trying to be enough, you know?"

Ruari did understand. He understood perfectly, but he still had to ask. "Where do I come in?" he asked softly. "Am I second choice? A rebound?"

Kean looked pained. "No, and I'm sorry if I made you

feel that way. I think it was more that meeting you made me realize that I wanted more from him than he would be ever able to give me. I want a family, Ruari, so very much. And that doesn't mean I'm only interested in you because of Jax, which Bray was maybe thinking. He's rather hung up on the fact that betas can't have kids. As if adoption wouldn't have been an option, or even a surrogate. I really like you, and I want to see if what we have is strong enough to last. God, I hope I'm explaining this right and not turning you off of me," he said, grimacing.

So much went on in Ruari's head and heart that it was difficult to find the words. Kean's pain was clear, but so was his honesty, and Ruari swore he'd never had a proposal quite that brutally honest. Kean wasn't playing games, wasn't trying to paint himself in a more flattering picture, wasn't even bothering to come up with excuses. He had just laid it out there, his whole, vulnerable truth. The contrast with his family who had made lying into the golden standard and who wouldn't know the truth if it hit them in the face was so big that Ruari couldn't even describe it.

He discovered they were still holding hands, a fact he'd forgotten about until now. So he pulled Kean's hand until the beta got the message and stepped closer. Then Ruari lifted his head, offering himself in a gesture that left little room for interpretation, he figured.

Kean's eyes widened in shock before he cupped Ruari's head and brought his mouth in for the sweetest of kisses. His lips were so soft, exploring, not putting any pressure on Ruari whatsoever. But Ruari opened up, wanting more of this man who had been hurt in a way that made him want to find that alpha and beat the crap out of him. Not that he ever could, but the thought was nice.

He stepped closer to Kean, letting go of his hand and

wrapping both his arms around the beta's waist. Kean responded by pulling him closer, and as their bodies discovered how well they fit together, their tongues did the same, chasing and meeting with a growing intensity. It might have started out as a sweet kiss, but it grew hard and deep, until Ruari's neck hurt with the effort of straining his head. He reluctantly pulled back and Kean let him go immediately.

"Wow," Kean said, and for some reason, that took away the last of Ruari's worries and objections.

"Wow indeed," he confirmed.

They smiled at each other, and Ruari was happy to see the sadness gone from Kean's face.

"Want to go inside?" Kean asked. "I could use a cold drink right now."

"I could use a cold shower," Ruari said, and the look on Kean's face was priceless.

When they walked into the kitchen, an alpha stood at the sink, washing his hands. Man, he was huge, Ruari thought. He could only see him from the back, but his upper body was built like a wall. It reminded him a little of the alpha from the club. Then the alpha turned around, and the bottom dropped out from under Ruari's feet.

They stared at each other for a few seconds, the alpha as much in shock as he, but Ruari recovered first. "What the hell are you doing here?" he gasped.

———

15

Bray stared at the omega in utter disbelief. He recognized him from the club, though he had changed a little, looked like he'd been sick, maybe. Thinner, definitely.

"I'm... I live here," he managed. "What are you doing here?"

"Wait, you two know each other?" Kean asked, and Bray dragged his eyes away from the omega to look at his ex-lover. Why was Kean here?

"How do you..." Bray started, and then it clicked in his head, like pieces of a puzzle that fell into the right place, providing a complete picture. "You're the Ruari he was talking about."

This was the omega Kean had broken up with him for, the one that would be staying at the ranch for a while. His blood froze in his veins. Kean had mentioned a baby, a three-month-old baby. An alpha-son. Math had never been Bray's strong point, but that calculation was so simple that he made it in seconds.

"Your son," he gasped. "He's mine."

Ruari took a step back, and Bray noticed his hands were shaking. "No," the omega said, first softly, but then louder. "No. He's not yours. He's mine."

Kean had paled and now looked from Ruari to Bray and back, obviously trying to make sense of it. "What is he talking about?" he asked Ruari.

Ruari crossed his arms in front of his chest. "Who is he?" he countered, jerking his head toward Bray.

"That's Bray, the Bray I was telling you about."

It was a simple sentence and there was no venom in Kean's voice, and yet Bray's stomach turned sour. What had Kean told the omega about him?

"Ruari, talk to me. I don't understand," Kean said.

Ruari lifted his chin. "It turns out your Bray is the alpha who helped me through my last heat. He's Jax's biological father."

A wave of relief flooded Bray that Ruari was coming to his senses, despite his earlier denial his son—Jax, his son was named Jax—was Bray's.

"I told you it was all anonymous, so I had no idea who he was," Ruari added.

"Are you okay?" Kean asked, and that question was so quintessential Kean that it took Bray a few moments to realize it was aimed at Ruari and not him.

Then Ruari uncrossed his arms and reached for Kean's hand, allowing himself to be pulled close and to lean against Kean for support. Bray told himself it couldn't hurt as much as it did, that what he was feeling was because Ruari had kept this from him, not because he was confronted with the fact that Kean chose someone else over him.

He cleared his throat, willing the tightness that made it

hard to swallow away. "I'm glad you acknowledge my parental rights," he told Ruari.

He was met with an icy stare. "I don't. I acknowledged you as the provider of the sperm that produced my son, not as his father. There's a big difference."

Bray swallowed again, this time because his stomach had revolted. "W-what do you mean?"

"You said Jax was yours. He's not. He's mine, and he always will be. Your name isn't listed on his birth certificate if only for the simple reason that I didn't know it. We both signed a contract, remember? You released all parental rights in case there would be a pregnancy."

He had. The contract was crystal clear that if the encounter resulted in a pregnancy, the alpha father had no legal rights. It had been contested a few times in court, with mixed outcomes, but even if Bray had wanted to take his chances under the current government, he never would do that to Ruari. But what did that mean? Was Ruari going to keep him from seeing his son?

"I understand. But can I at least see him?"

"Why?" Ruari's tone hadn't defrosted yet.

"Because he's my son?" Bray said, unsure of what Ruari was getting at. Of course he wanted to see his son, to get to know him. Why was that even a question?

"I thought you didn't want a family, that you weren't ready for that," the omega said.

Bray's eyes found Kean's, who didn't look away but met his accusing gaze head on. "I see someone talked," Bray said, letting the anger seep through in his voice.

"Yes, he did," Ruari said. "But I'll give you a chance to refute it. Was any of what he told me untrue? About him wanting more and you telling him you weren't ready for a family?"

Bray's heart clenched. "No, but that was because..." He stopped talking, unsure of how to finish that sentence.

"Because he's a beta? Yeah, I got that part, too. Real classy, by the way. So tell me, would you have been just as interested in getting to know your kid if it had been a girl? Or an omega? Or god forbid, a beta?"

Bray felt exposed, bleeding from the cuts that Ruari inflicted with his words. And the worst of it was that Bray had nothing to say in his defense. Everything he came up with came down to the same thing, and it didn't paint him in a good picture.

If only Kean had kept his mouth shut instead of blabbing about why they'd ended things. Well, why he had ended things, because that had been all him and not Bray. Bray had to admit he'd been fine continuing their...whatever it was they'd been. The sex had been great, and Kean was a good man, Bray had to admit. An honorable one, always letting the truth prevail.

"Does that mean you won't let me see him?" he asked.

"Not right now, 'cause he's sleeping, but no, not today. And not tomorrow either. I need to see you're good enough for him first, Bray."

"Good enough?" he repeated stupidly, not understanding.

Ruari straightened his shoulders and despite him being at least a head shorter than Bray, he felt small with the stare Ruari gave him. "You'll need to prove yourself worthy of being in my son's life, Bray. Kean assures me you're a good man, but I'll need to see for myself. I grew up with a horrific excuse for an alpha as a father, and I will not subject my son to the same. Prove to me you're not the alpha-asshole I think you are, and we'll talk."

The omega wasn't pulling any punches, and Bray felt

battered. "How do I prove that?" he asked, feeling infinitesimally small. The fact that Kean was standing there to witness his humiliation made it even worse.

"Honestly, I don't know. Give me some time to figure that out. This is as big a shock to me as it is to you."

Bray slowly nodded, then had to ask. "Are you two together now?"

He asked Kean, but it was Ruari who answered. "Yes, we are. But we need time to figure that out as well."

It took every ounce of willpower Bray had to not fall apart, and so he managed to send them a terse smile. "I'm happy for you two. Let me know what you expect from me, Ruari. I'll stay out of your way till then."

He'd barely made it into the hallway, when his father's voice rang out. "Bray, hold up one sec. We wanted to talk to you."

He ground his teeth as he turned around, the words "Not now, Dad" on his lips, until he saw Sven and Lars standing right behind his father, hand in hand. Sven looked worried while Lars's face resembled that of a soldier about to go into war. What was going on here? God, he really couldn't handle more surprises right now. Then his eyes traveled to his father's face, and something in his expression told him things were about to get a lot worse.

"What's up?" he asked, calling up his last reserves to stay as friendly as he could.

His father reached for Sven's hand and pulled him forward, and with one look at the omega's face, Bray knew.

"Sven is pregnant," his father said, confirming Bray's suspicions. "It's unexpected, but he's decided he wants to keep it."

There were more words, but Bray couldn't process them through the buzzing in his head. How the fuck was it possible to be forced to face this much irony in one day? It hurt, to see his father happy with his young boys, to see him have the family that Bray claimed he didn't want in the first place. Why did it hurt so much? If he didn't want this, why did he care?

"I'm happy for you, Sven." He forced the words out, demanding of himself to be the better man and not show this broke him. "You'll make a great daddy. Congratulations to all of you."

He nodded at his dad, hoping against hope it was enough to placate him, so Bray could go fall apart in private without anyone watching.

"Thank you. We were hoping you'd be happy to have a baby brother," his father said, and then it sank in, that this baby Sven was carrying would be Bray's half-brother, younger than his own son. And he couldn't figure out how he was supposed to feel about this, not when he was so hurt and rejected and broken.

"I can't..." he started, cursing himself when his voice broke. "Not right now, Dad, okay? Please. Not now."

He turned around, wanting to get away as quickly as possible, but the tears in his eyes made it hard to see. He was already outside when a strong hand grabbed his elbow and steadied him. "Bray, what's wrong?"

His father. The very last person he wanted to see, because if there was anyone he didn't want to witness his humiliation, it was him. He'd always looked up to him, this man who'd raised three sons single-handedly, who'd sacrificed everything for them, and who'd always put his kids above everything else.

That's how Bray had come to define fatherhood, that your kids came first and you denied your own needs. It's why he hadn't wanted a family yet, because he wasn't ready

to give up everything for his kids. Not until he knew he
could make his father proud and be the kind of alpha he
had been—until he'd chosen Sven and Lars over him and
Lucan and even Dane, though his youngest brother wasn't
even aware.

"Not now, Dad," he said, avoiding his eyes. "I can't do
this now."

His father put a finger under his chin and turned it
toward him, just like he'd done when Bray had been a little
boy. "Tell me what's wrong, son. What happened?"

The concern on his father's face was genuine, and it
broke his resistance.

"Are you that upset over our announcement?" his father
asked, and Bray had to think for a second what he was
talking about.

He shook himself loose from his father's grip and took a
shaking step back. "No. Well, it's a shock, for sure, but I
guess I should've seen it coming. He's young and he's got the
gene, so he's fertile. It makes sense."

"Then what is it?" His dad frowned, but Bray couldn't
deny he looked worried.

He looked like a dad, Bray realized, worried for his child,
and it hit him all over again. He, too, was a father, but he
might never get the chance to be a dad, because of... He
couldn't put it into words, the temptation to call it exaggera-
tion from Ruari, false accusations, even, but something held
him back. It hit a little too close to home, too similar to what
Kean had said, and before him his own father.

"Are you hoping for an alpha heir?" he asked, unsure of
why that was on his mind, but it was. Ruari's son was an
alpha, Bray's alpha heir. What if he never got to know him?
What if he'd fucked up so badly that he'd never be a part of
his son's life?

"Bray, no. I don't care at all. If it's healthy, I'll be the luck-iest man on the planet," his father said, and Bray thought of his youngest brother. His father had experienced once what it was like to have a baby not be born healthy.

"I figured you might want an alpha, that's all," he said.

His father put two hands on his shoulders. "Bray, I have an alpha heir. You're my oldest, my son, my heir, and nothing and no one will ever replace you, do you not under-stand that?"

It wasn't until he heard those words that Bray realized that's exactly how he had felt, like he'd been replaced. First by Lars and Sven, and now by the baby, even before it was born.

"Dad," he said, and he couldn't stop the tears anymore. "I fucked up badly."

Bray hadn't known how much he needed his father's support until his dad's arms came around him and the man pulled him close. Bray put his hand on his dad's shoulder and let go of the tight hold he'd had on his emotions.

"Oh, Bray," his dad said, his voice filled with compas-sion. "What's wrong? What happened? Talk to me, son."

"I have a son," Bray managed, his voice muffled against his father's shoulder.

"You have a *what*?"

"I helped an omega through his heat and he got preg-nant. I just found out I have a son, an alpha heir." Bray couldn't keep the sadness out of his voice.

His father pushed him back to look him in the eye. "I don't understand. Why are you upset about this? Is it because you didn't want kids?"

Even his father knew he hadn't wanted kids, Bray real-ized with sickening frustration. Everybody had known. No wonder Ruari didn't want him anywhere near his son. Their son. He had no reason to believe Bray was genuinely interested in the kid, did he?

"His daddy won't let me see him," Bray started. "I released all parental rights in the contract we made," he added when his father's face turned angry. "It turns out he's the omega who just moved in, Ruari."

"Ruari? Jax is your son?" his father asked.

Bray's head shot up as he took a step back. "You've seen him? The baby, I mean?"

His father's strong hands clamped his shoulders with a reassuring grip. "I have, and he is gorgeous."

Bray's eyes filled with tears all over again at those words. He couldn't believe his father had met him.

"I have to say Ruari doesn't strike me as the type of person who would keep a father from his son, though. Are you sure there isn't more to this?" his father asked.

Bray sighed. Of course there was more to this, but that would mean embarrassing himself even more. Well, he might as well now, considering he'd already spilled enough for his father to figure out the rest, anyway.

"It's a little more complicated than that. Kean broke up with me because... Well, there were multiple reasons, but one of them was that he had met Ruari and they had a connection, and he wanted to pursue a relationship with him. But he told Ruari about me, not knowing I was the alpha Ruari had been with, so now Ruari thinks I'm a total alpha-asshole. His words."

His father raised an eyebrow. "Why would Kean speak negatively about you to Ruari? I thought what you guys had worked for the both of you."

Oh, there really was no end to this humiliation, was there? "That's what I figured, but Kean wanted more than I was able to give him. And he has an issue with the way I treat him. Or, people in general, I should say, as he subjected me to a scathing review of my social skills as a departure gift."

His father's eyes filled with something that hurt Bray even more than Ruari's words had. "Oh Bray," he said again, and Bray felt like a little boy again.

"I'm sorry to disappoint you," he said stiffly.

"It's not me you're disappointing, it's yourself. You're better than this, Bray, but for some reason, you're stuck in a certain way of thinking, and you can't seem to move past that. I can't figure out where it's coming from, though. It's not something I've taught you.

Bray shook his head. "I can't do this right now, Dad. Not today. I've had a lot to process, with first Kean confronting me and then Ruari. Please, don't add to it. Not today."

"I'm sorry you're hurting," his dad said. "I hope you will believe me when I say that. Did Ruari say you could never see Jax?"

Bray shrugged. "No, he wants to think about what he wants from me. Something about me proving that I'm worthy to be in his life or something. I don't understand what he wants from me, I honestly don't."

"Maybe he wants to make sure you'll be a good influence on his son. That wouldn't be unreasonable, right?"

Bray shrugged again. "And how do I prove that when he and Kean are convinced already I won't be? I've got things going against me, like the fact that I went on record to say I didn't want kids yet. I get that. But not wanting kids is a different thing than not wanting one that's already been born. Of course, I want to know my son. How could I not? But how do I prove that to them, how do I show that I'm not the asshole they think?"

"I can't imagine Kean thinks you're an asshole," his

father stated with a conviction that Bray didn't share. "If he told you he wanted more, that doesn't make sense. He wouldn't want more with you if he legit thought you were an asshole. Doesn't mean he can't have concerns about you or your behavior."

Bray rolled his eyes. "And we're back to this. You know what, why don't you say what you want to say. You might as well. It's been a pretty fucking crappy day already, so pile it on, would you?"

Before his father could say anything, Bray held up his hand to stop him. "I should've known you would take their side. Nothing I do ever seems to be good enough for you. I don't understand what I have to do to make you proud of me."

16

Grayson stared at Bray in utter disbelief, struggling to make sense of what his son had just said. Somewhere along the way, something had gone horribly wrong, and a deep sense of anger filled him. Not anger at Bray, but at himself, that he had somehow missed this.

How could Bray think Grayson wasn't proud of him? How could he feel nothing he ever did was good enough? Where had he gone wrong with his kid to make him experience that rejection? He knew Bray still struggled with his relationship with Lars and Sven, but this wasn't about that. This was not something that had developed over the last few weeks or even months. This was an attitude, a hurt, maybe even a trauma that had been fostered over a long period. How the hell had he missed this?

"Your silence is speaking volumes, Dad," Bray said. "Is it that hard for you to tell me the truth?"

"Bray, I don't know what to say, but not for the reason you assume. I'm shocked you think I'm not proud of you, that you're not good enough, somehow. I never meant for you to feel that way, and I am racking my brain right now to figure out where I went wrong."

Bray's shoulders dropped even further as he let out a long sigh that reached deep inside Grayson and squeezed his heart painfully. "Forget about it, Dad. You have enough on your plate right now."

This veiled reference to Lars and Sven made Grayson even more sad. "Just because I'm in a new relationship doesn't mean I don't have time for you anymore," he said.

"Really? You could've fooled me."

Bray's voice was dripping with sarcasm and Grayson had to bite back his irritation at that attitude. "Come on Bray, that's not true."

Bray's head shot up from the ground, his eyes blazing. "What do you mean it's not true? As soon as you met those two, it was like Lucan and I didn't even exist anymore. Do you realize we haven't hung out once since you started dating them?"

Grayson opened his mouth to deny it, because that couldn't be true. Surely they had spent time together, hadn't they? Hell, they saw each other almost every day, what with living on the ranch.

"Seriously, Dad, when was the last time we hung out? You and me, or with Lucan?"

"But we make the trip to the city twice a week to see Dane," Grayson protested, citing the first thing he could think of, the uneasy feeling in his stomach rising.

Bray scoffed. "That's not hanging out, Dad. That's visiting our brother. That's you multitasking, combining something you need to do with something else you need to do. That's you assuaging your guilt and pretending you're spending time with your children."

His son's words were sharp like daggers, and Grayson

wanted to lash out in defense, except that he tried to remember the last time he and Bray had hung out like they used to, drinking a beer and watching football or something like that, and he couldn't. He couldn't remember the last time he'd spent time with his son alone outside of visiting Dane or doing stuff for the pack. He'd been so swept up in his relationship with Lars and Sven, and making sure his boys were okay, that he'd neglected to check on his children.

Visiting Dane, that was routine, and there was so little else he could do for his youngest son, aside from making sure he had the best care available to him. But when had he spent deliberate time with Bray or Lucan, just the two or three of them? God, he had failed them.

Dammit, he was making an unholy mess of things. First with Lars, flying off the handle when he should've understood how wounded the beta was by what he thought Grayson and Sven had done behind his back. And now Bray, and possibly Lucan as well.

"Why don't you just come out and admit that you've replaced us?" Bray said bitterly.

"I haven't, but..." Grayson held up a hand when Bray wanted to interrupt him. "But I admit that you have every reason to feel like that's the case. I am sorry, Bray. I was so convinced you were jealous that I didn't even consider there was truth to your criticism."

They stared at each other, and it was easy for Grayson to see the emotions flash through his son's brown eyes, the same eyes that he saw in the mirror every morning. And after seeing Jax, if he had to take a guess, that gorgeous baby boy would end up with those same eyes.

"It feels like you replaced us, or I should say replaced me, 'cause I don't know how Lucan feels about this."

"He seems to be more accepting of my relationship," Grayson admitted.

"Sure, but that doesn't mean he doesn't feel neglected as well. Are you even aware he's involved with someone?" Bray asked.

Grayson's eyes widened in shock. "Lucan? Lucan is seeing someone?"

Bray let out an annoyed huff. "Yeah, this just proves my point that you really don't know shit about what's going on in our lives."

As much as Grayson wanted to deny that, he couldn't. How had he missed his son seeing someone? It had to be one of the pack, so it would have happened right under his nose, and he had missed it. Bray was right, that did speak volumes as to how little attention he had paid to anything but Lars and Sven.

"I'm sorry, Bray," he said again. "I never meant to."

Silence hung heavy and uncomfortable between them.

"Maybe it would've been different if you had been more accepting of the relationship in the first place," Grayson said.

"Oh, so it's my fault? Is that what you're saying? That if I had been all happy and supportive of you seeing two boys younger than me, you wouldn't have ignored me?"

Grayson cringed. He had meant it like that, but he had to agree it didn't sound good. "That didn't come out right," he admitted. "I don't understand why you are so dead set against them, Bray. It may not have been what you expected of me, or wanted for me, and I understand that. But I can't help but wonder if you would have reacted the same way if I had found happiness with someone my own age, if you would've felt replaced then as well."

"If you had ignored me like you were doing now, I sure

as hell would've," Bray said, and Grayson felt the truth in his words.

That stung, the realization that this wasn't about Lars and Sven, about Bray's objections to him seeing two men so much younger, but about Grayson prioritizing his new relationship over his own children. It was a hard pill to swallow, but he couldn't deny Bray was right.

"I never meant to replace you," he said. "I never meant to ignore the two of you. I don't know why it happened, but it did. I need to do better."

A little of the tension in Bray's frame disappeared as he jammed his hands into his pockets. "I appreciate you saying that, Dad, but we both know it's not gonna happen. Not with Sven being pregnant and you becoming a dad all over again. A few months from now, Dad, you'll have a new baby, and he's going to take up whatever time you have left after taking care of your boys."

Grayson felt deeply ashamed. He had walked out here with Bray, convinced he was about to show his son some hard truths. In reality, he was the one who had to face some painful truths. God, he had failed his kids. That didn't bode well for his role in the new baby's life, he thought with sobering clarity.

"It's gonna be a challenge," he admitted. "But I need to do better, Bray. I want to do better, can you accept that truth from me?"

After a slight hesitation, Bray nodded. "I do struggle with your relationship," he said. "But I will try to be more accepting, okay?" Something flashed over his face, and he winced. "Kean called me out on it as well, said he was surprised I had such a struggle with this, especially since I was a club member."

It was the first time Bray had admitted to what they both

knew, that he was part of a club Grayson had visited in the past as well. Grayson wasn't sure why his son was opening up about this now, but he valued his openness.

"I would appreciate you trying to accept this relationship, son, because it's not going anywhere. I love them. I deeply, deeply love them, and it would mean the world to me to see my children accept this."

Bray's mouth pulled up in the tiniest of smiles. "If you think I'm calling either one of those brats my step-dad, you're sorely mistaken."

Grayson returned his smile. "Duly noted."

DATING WAS WEIRD, Kean decided. It was uncomfortable and awkward under the best of circumstances, but it was downright absurd when you lived in a pack. Two days after asking Palani for permission, everyone knew he was dating Ruari. Or he should say, they were dating each other. And that meant everyone had an opinion as well. Now, all of those opinions had been positive, so Kean wasn't complaining about that, but most of the people who had expressed an opinion had also deemed it necessary to hand out advice. That's where things had gotten weird fast.

It was one thing for people to tell him congratulations or something similar, though he wasn't sure what they were congratulating him for, since he and Ruari were in the beginning stages of trying to figure things out. But when people had started handing out unsolicited advice, telling him to bring chocolate—where the hell was he supposed to get chocolate without leaving the ranch?—flowers, which were equally impossible, and gave him tips on what to do—

romantic walks were mentioned a few times—Kean got mighty frustrated.

He thought dating Ruari would be a matter of hanging out, chatting, and getting to know each other better, but it seemed he had missed a few memos on the whole dating scene. That wasn't surprising, as he was new at this, but he hadn't expected it to be so complicated.

Still, he didn't want to get it wrong, so when he showed up to the main house where he and Ruari had agreed to meet to spend the evening together—and wasn't that awkward with everyone knowing about it?—he held a bouquet of wildflowers in his hand. *Bouquet* was to charitable a word, but he done his best to pick some wildflowers for Ruari and he'd tied them into a nice little gift with a leftover ribbon from a birthday present.

Vieno's eyes went big when he spotted Kean with the bouquet, and then a big smile spread across his face. "Bringing out the big guns," he teased.

Kean shrugged, feeling his cheeks heat up. "Someone told me I had to make an effort," he mumbled. Then he got worried. "Did I get it wrong?" he asked Vieno. "Is it too much?"

Vieno put a calming hand on his arm. "Dude, chill. Flowers are never too much. He's in the kitchen. But I have to warn you, so is everyone else, because apparently, they all knew about this and are horribly curious to see it go down in person."

Kean rolled his eyes. "We need to get cable or something, so these guys have something better to do," he complained, but Vieno merely grinned.

Kean straightened his shoulders. He could do this. He only hoped Bray wouldn't be in the kitchen, because that would be majorly awkward. For all three of them. He didn't regret being honest about his relationship with Bray to Ruari, but after finding out he was Jax's biological father, he couldn't deny it had become complicated. Who would've ever thought he would find himself in a kind of love triangle? It was the stuff of those romance books Vieno loved to read so much.

When he entered the kitchen, he couldn't hold back his smile. Vieno had been right. Pretty much everyone was there, including a flustered Ruari, who looked like he didn't know what to do with the attention either. The one person who was conspicuously absent was Bray, and for that, Kean was grateful. He tried to ignore everyone else as he walked up to Ruari, who rose from his chair at the kitchen table where he had been sitting.

"Hi," Ruari said, and then he noticed the flowers Kean was holding out. "You brought me flowers?"

Any doubt Kean had had about the flowers evaporated when he saw the stunned expression on Ruari's face. "I picked them myself," he said proudly.

Ruari took the flowers from him, and after a second's hesitation, leaned in, rose on his tiptoes and pressed a soft kiss on Kean's cheek. "Thank you. They're lovely."

Maybe dating wasn't so hard after all, Kean thought. That being said, they needed to get away from the group of men who were watching their every move, commenting to each other in soft whispers and with meaningful smiles.

"Do you want to go for a little walk?" he asked. "There's a trail at the south border of the property we could follow for a bit."

Ruari looked at him with an apologetic smile. "Sven promised to look after Jax, but he's been super fussy tonight and refuses to fall asleep. I don't want to leave until I'm sure he's sleeping."

"Why don't you put him in the baby carrier or whatever you call it and bring him? I'm sure he'll fall asleep when you walk," Kean said.

"Are you sure that would be okay? I didn't want to ruin your plans," Ruari said, his tone still apologetic.

Kean felt a little awkward playing this out in front of everyone, but he pushed through it, reasoning this was the price he had to pay for dating and being part of a pack. It would be worth it to be with Ruari.

"Look, Jax is a crucial part of your life, so leaving him out of everything we do seems impossible to me anyway. We might as well get used to getting creative if we want to spend any time together, right?"

A chorus of "aw" erupted from the men in the kitchen, but the only approval that mattered to him was the blinding smile on Ruari's face.

"For that," the omega said, "there will be a reward once we have a little more privacy."

Now that was a remark Kean didn't mind the others overhearing at all, and he beamed as they whistled and laughed.

It took a little while for Ruari to gather all the stuff needed for Jax, but once he had the baby strapped to his chest and had packed a backpack that Kean insisted on carrying, they left. Ruari slipped his hand into Kean's as soon as they were outside, and Kean's heart did a happy little gallop.

They chatted about Kean's work, the ranch, Jax, and all kinds of things as they made their way to the edge of the property, where a trail started that led to the mountains, which were fifteen miles or so away. Far too great a distance to walk, but the path was gorgeous, and since it ran through a designated wilderness area, he wasn't expecting any people there.

The air still hung heavy, the remnants of a hot and humid day, and the weather forecast promised more of the same in the days to come. Still, Kean was happy to be outside, as always. They had a good three hours until nightfall, so he would keep an eye on his watch to make sure they got back before dark.

They were just about to leave pack land when they heard footsteps and Bray appeared.

"I'm sorry, I didn't mean to disturb you. I heard noises and wasn't sure who it was," the alpha said stiffly.

Kean wasn't sure why, but his heart went out to the big man. This had to be awkward as fuck for him, if not painful.

"No problem," he said, keeping his voice light and friendly. "We were just going for a little stroll. But I'm surprised to catch you here. Didn't you pull a double shift yesterday as well?"

"Two of my men came down with a stomach bug," Bray said. "Which means I'm a little short on manpower."

"That sucks," Kean said. "If it lasts too long, let me know. I'm not as qualified as your guys, but I can take a shift if you need me to."

Bray looked surprised. "Thank you. That's nice of you to offer," he said, and it made Kean a little sad to realize they were talking to each other like strangers.

"I mean it, Bray. There's no need for you to do it all yourself," he added.

Bray's expression softened. "Thanks," he said, and his tone had changed into something that sounded like the Bray that Kean knew.

Jax let out a little cry, probably protesting that they were standing still. "He's a little fussy tonight," Ruari said, and it had to be for Bray's benefit, 'cause Kean already knew.

He realized then that Bray still hadn't seen his son, and he was tempted to ask Ruari if he could, when the omega spoke up.

"Would you like to see him?" he asked. "He's not at his best right now, but I thought you might like a peek?"

It was almost painful, the way Bray's face lit up. "Thank you," he said, and it drove home how thoroughly chastised the man must have felt about not being allowed to see his son.

He took a few careful steps closer and Ruari turned toward him, lifting the sling sideways so Bray could see Jax's face better. He was still awake, making soft sounds of protest they were standing still.

"Can I..." Bray asked and Ruari nodded.

Bray raised a single finger and touched the baby's cheek. On reflex, Jax's hand reached for it, and his tiny fingers curled around the alpha's index finger.

"He's strong," Bray whispered, his voice cracking.

"He is. He'll have your eyes. They're dark blue now, but they'll turn brown," Ruari said, and Kean had all these swirls in his stomach, his heart clenching painfully.

This was a tough position for the proud alpha to be in, and despite everything, Kean hoped Ruari would warm up to Bray soon and would allow him a role in his son's life. He didn't regret telling him about his own relationship with Bray, but if he had known Bray was Jax's biological father, he might have worded his opinion of the alpha a little differently. He worried that it had come across as if Bray was unsuitable to be a dad, and that was not what he had meant at all. It still hurt, Bray's easy dismissal of him because he wasn't an omega, but he still wanted the man to have a relationship with his son.

They stood like that for minutes, Bray connecting with his son, and there was something magical about it. Jax was showing his displeasure with an increased volume, and Bray pulled back his finger, regret painted on his face.

"You'd better continue walking," he said. "Because he likes it when you move around, right? That's what I've watched you do when he's crying," he added.

Ruari looked at Bray as if he didn't know what to think, which could be close to the truth. "He does like it when I keep moving," he finally said, rocking back and forth to keep Jax happy. "Thank you."

"No, Ruari, thank you," Bray said, and Kean could see the relief on his face. He wasn't entirely sure what the thank-yous had been for, but it did feel like some of the tension between the three of them had dissolved, so that was something to be grateful for, he guessed.

17

Ever since the elections, Palani had been waiting for George York to make contact. He wasn't sure how or when, but he was certain that the prime minister would contact him at some point. Their previous meeting had been loaded with double meanings, especially in hindsight.

That's why he wasn't surprised when he got a phone call from the man's scheduling secretary, asking for a private, off-the-record meeting with him. He had to admit that the second part of the request—that Lidon be present as well—did surprise him a little.

Of course, his relationship with his three men was not a secret. They had become open about it, and York had to have known even before that. After everything Palani had learned about the elections and the win of the CWP, he had no doubt that York had vetted him even before talking to him when he was still working for the newspaper. No, this man knew as much as he possibly could, which was why this meeting was a potentially dangerous situation.

"Do you think I should go?" Lidon asked when Palani

told him about the invite.

Palani leaned back on the couch, folding his hands behind his head. "I honestly don't know. I'm inclined to say you should, if only because I'd love to have you present there, but at the same time, I'll admit I'm worried about why he wants you there."

Lidon nodded thoughtfully. "Do you reckon the news about my shifting has reached him already?"

"I was wondering the same thing," Palani said. "It's only a matter of time before it becomes public knowledge since we haven't closed the pack and have admitted new members. We've talked about this, and we both agreed it was a risk we're willing to take."

"We made the right call there," Lidon assured him. "Look, there was no way we were going to keep this a secret for long, so we might as well be as open about it as possible without broadcasting it. So it's possible that York has heard about it, which is why I have to say I'm not comfortable sending you to meet with York by yourself."

"I was planning on taking security," Palani said.

Lidon shook his head. "That's not what I'm worried about. Well, it is, and you should take a few of Bray's men, but I'm more worried about you having to face the prime minister by yourself."

Palani smiled. "You're worried about me being able to stand up to him?"

Lidon's reaction was swift. "Hell no and you know it, too. I don't like you being with that man on your own. We're a pack, we do things together. So I should come with you."

Palani debated protesting more, then surrendered. To be honest, he liked the idea of Lidon coming with him. As much as he liked to pretend he was taken as seriously as an alpha-journalist, his beta status did play into how he was treated. Having a strong über-alpha like Lidon by his side couldn't hurt.

"If he asks about the shifting, what do we tell him?" he wanted to know.

Lidon took his time to answer, and Palani took the opportunity to study him. He had changed since the shift. The last few weeks of Vieno's pregnancy, Lidon had been restless, on edge. Now that his body had made the shift, he radiated his usual calmness, though it felt to Palani like his power had tripled.

He'd always been aware of Lidon, from the day they had met. It was impossible not to feel him when you were in a room with him. But since he had shifted, that had increased. Palani could sometimes feel him walking into the house, like a swell of power rolling over him whenever Lidon approached. He wasn't sure if it was just him, or if Enar and Vieno experienced the same. He hadn't had a chance to ask them yet.

It had made him wonder, this perceived increase in power. If the three of them could manage to tap into his powers, like Vieno had done during delivery, would they be able to shift as well? It was a question as intriguing as it was scary. And there was no way of finding out until it happened. Or not. It seemed like a lot of what they were doing now was on a trial-and-error basis.

"I say we tell him the truth," Lidon said. "Their methods are questionable, not in the last place the election fraud. But they are our best allies right now. If the public finds out about the pack and about my powers, there will be a media frenzy to say the least, and the AWC will come for us for sure. Having the prime minister on our side could be beneficial then."

He was right. Palani didn't fear the media frenzy so

much, certain that Bray's men could keep reporters out. It was the reaction of other parties he was far more concerned about, the AWC foremost. There was no predicting how they would respond to the undeniable proof the shifters were back.

"They've been quiet publicly," he commented.

"The AWC? Yeah, I noticed," Lidon said.

"Their militant wing is growing, though, according to one of my sources. They're getting a lot of new members since the new government, mostly older alphas who resist the challenge to the status quo."

"I'm not surprised."

"They're not only growing in numbers but radicalizing. Their leader is a guy named Bennett Wyndham, calls himself a business man, but there's a euphemism if I've ever heard one. He's kind of like the unofficial mob guy from the south side."

"Big Bennett?" Lidon asked, dragging a hand through his hair. "I shouldn't be surprised. He's got quite the empire, all right. We butted heads with him multiple times, but we never could make a charge against him stick. A few of his underlings, yes, but never the big man himself."

Palani wasn't surprised Lidon knew him. From the little research he'd been able to do into the guy's dealings, a lot of them were drug-related. "I think he's Watkins's client."

He'd spent quite some time trying to figure out the clues Watkins had given them and he'd stumbled across Wyndham's name. Turns out, the man had a son, an omega, though Palani hadn't been able to find out much more than his name. James Wyndham. It sounded like some kind of earl or duke, he'd thought wryly, but he doubted the boy's life had been much fun with a father like that.

Lidon's eyes widened, then closed as he shook his head.

"Dammit. Of course, he is. It fits."

"It does. And it makes Watkins's info on Melloni even more reliable."

"What would they have him work on?" Lidon wondered.

Palani had considered that. "My guess? Reversing the effects of the gene. They don't want wolf shifters."

"Isn't it crazy how it all crosses? Our enemy is kidnapping Melloni to basically do the same thing we want, to reverse the gene, while the people who claim to support us are the ones behind it," Lidon said with a sigh, rubbing his temples. "I swear, it gets harder and harder to tell who the good guys are anymore."

They hadn't told Sando about Watkins's suspicion. They had debated it long and hard, but had decided not to say anything until they had hard proof it was Melloni. The kid had been through hell and giving him false hope would be cruel. They'd waited for Watkins to contact them with more info, but he'd gone quiet after their meeting. Palani was almost at the point where he was getting worried, but there was little they could do.

"Let me assure you that Wyndham is definitely not a good guy, not even close. He's now branching out into anti-government militia," Palani said. "One of my former colleagues from the paper told me they're stocking up on all the guns they can get their hands on."

"The prime minister should investigate that."

"They've done nothing illegal. Yet."

"Not that anyone can prove," Lidon said. "But if Watkins is correct, they were behind the attack on the ranch."

"Not something the prime minister can use without going against the official police report, now can he?" Palani countered. "Or something he can investigate without us giving him access to the pack, which we don't want to do."

Lidon let out a frustrated sigh. "I hate it when you're right."

Palani grinned. "You must hate me a lot, then."

Lidon laughed, a full laugh, and Palani realized how long it had been since he'd heard that sound. He acted on impulse and slid off his chair, crawling toward his alpha on his knees. "Maybe I can do something to get into your good graces again?" he asked with a sly smile, reaching for Lidon's belt.

Much to his surprise, Lidon bent over, grabbed his head with both hands and kissed him hard. "I couldn't possibly love you more than I already do."

Palani beamed, his lips tingling from the kiss. "Does that mean you don't want the blow job?"

Lidon unbuckled his belt himself, then unzipped and whipped out his cock, which was already growing hard. "I wouldn't go quite that far."

LIDON WAS nervous for the meeting with York. Something about the man made him uncomfortable. Maybe it was the knowledge of what he had been involved in, the many shady practices tied to his name.

There was the Melloni gene, first of all, and while they possessed no concrete evidence York was involved, he'd had knowledge of it and certainly hadn't spoken out against it. More damning by far was the election fraud. The man was prime minister and his party had won the elections, but not by a democratic process. They had rigged the election, not just the pre-election polls.

"It's because you don't know what to expect," Palani told

him in the car. "You don't like to go into a situation blind, and that's exactly what this is."

Lidon pondered that for a bit. "You may be right. I don't like that we don't know why he wants to meet with us."

Palani smiled. "Of course, I'm right. Didn't we establish that two days ago when I sucked you off like a champ?" he teased.

Lidon snorted. "And so humble, too."

"You know you love me."

Lidon's face softened. "That, I do. Very much, in fact."

Since they were stopped at a traffic light, he leaned in for a quick kiss. He wasn't usually this mushy, but the whole thing with Vieno had hit him hard. His mates needed to feel and hear how much he loved them, and even though it didn't come easy for him, he'd vowed to do a better job showing them.

He wasn't sure why he had expected York to meet them with his whole entourage, but it was just him and one other guy, who he introduced as his personal assistant. Lidon and Palani shared a quick look at that introduction, as the small gestures of intimacy between the two men betrayed they were a lot more than coworkers. Lidon tried to remember if he'd seen anything in the news about the prime minister being married, but he couldn't recall. He would have to ask Palani afterward.

"I'm sure you're wondering why I asked for this meeting," York said.

"We are," Palani said, and how Lidon loved him for blatantly disrespecting protocol and speaking out as a beta rather than letting his alpha speak for him.

York didn't react other than his mouth pulling up a little into a hint of a smile. "Before we get into that, I wanted to assure you that this conversation is off the record," he said.

Again, it was Palani who reacted. "Off the record from your side or from ours?" he asked.

York's smile widened. "I do admire your sharp mind, Mr. Hightower," he said. "Let's say that you are guaranteed this is off the record from our side, and we hope you would extend us the same privilege."

That was not a call Lidon was prepared to make at this point, not when he had no idea what the topic was they would be discussing. He was sure Palani felt the same way. "We'll need to hear what you have to say first, before we can make any guarantees or promises," he said coolly. "Your track record so far shows you have little appreciation for the truth, so we're not exactly embracing you as our ally."

"Fair enough. I can see how you would come to that conclusion. I do hope that over time, you will see I do have the best interests of our species at heart."

"That's debatable statement," Palani said. "I think what you mean is that you have the best interests of the alphas at heart."

York's eyes sparked with anger before he got himself under control again. "How can you say that? No one has done more for omegas than we have in the last few months. Have you not seen all the new legislation that gives them more power to make their own decisions?"

"Oh, trust me, I've seen it. But don't you agree it's a tad hypocritical to talk about giving omegas power when you condone an alteration to their genetic makeup that takes away all their power. An alteration to which they never consented, which they weren't aware of, and which may have repercussions for generations to come. I don't qualify that as being in their best interest."

Palani stayed calm, which Lidon appreciated. He wasn't sure if he would've picked up on the prime minister's condescending tone a year earlier, but he sure did now. He had learned a lot from Palani about how subtly alphas could exert their dominance over betas and omegas. It only fueled the rage already flaring up inside him.

"Yes, I can see how you would interpret it that way, but I see it as a sacrifice that had to be made for the greater good of our species. And it worked, didn't it? We brought back the shifters."

There was one word in York's answer that stood out to Lidon. *We.* The man had used the word "we" when he spoke about bringing back the shifters. That meant he not only had been aware of the ultimate goal and strategy behind the gene, but he approved it, was part of it. They had suspected it from the start, but here was his own admission. Maiitsoh, Lukos, York, they all were connected. It was one big conspiracy.

"The greater good, right. That's been the excuse and rationale behind many wars, hasn't it? It was for the greater good. Meanwhile, the people who made the sacrifice were not consulted or informed, let alone asked for their consent. These women went into this blind, trusting their doctor, and you violated that trust in the worst way possible. You decided that this was a reasonable sacrifice, but those who actually made it didn't have a choice. What about all the omegas who committed suicide? What about all the omegas who were raped or sexually assaulted because of the gene? How can you say that's a sacrifice you're willing to make? It was never yours to make in the first place," Palani railed, his voice strong.

"You don't understand how heavy that weighs on those who created the gene, the suffering they unintentionally caused. They weren't aware of the side effects of the gene."

"Because it was never properly tested! How the hell

could they use this on unsuspecting women when they weren't even sure what it would do to their babies?" Palani exploded, and Lidon loved him for his fierce and passionate defense on behalf of Vieno, Sven, Ruari, and all the others they had met or heard about. They could not have asked for a better advocate than Palani Hightower, and it made Lidon proud all over again that this man was his mate. Fate had chosen well.

Lidon had to admit that York appeared genuinely sad and conflicted. "I'll be the first to admit that mistakes were made," he said softly.

"No, don't give me that," Palani said, his voice still tight with anger. "This is not a case of 'mistakes were made.' This was a deliberate violation of core principles of our society. How can you not see that with all your rants against how badly omegas were treated before that what you did to these women and their offspring was ten times worse? They had no idea. And there's still a lot you have more information about but you're not willing to share. That's not 'mistakes were made.' That's alpha men deciding what they think will be in everyone's best interest. That's dictatorship."

Lidon reached for Palani's hand, but it wasn't to calm him down. He was in pure awe of the beta's passionate words, every syllable dripping with his fury over the injustice of it all.

York took maybe half a minute to visibly calm himself, getting up from the table and pacing, sharing a poignant look with his assistant. Then he sat down again and, much more in control, leaned forward. "Perhaps I can convince you of my good intentions by sharing classified intel with you."

Lidon leaned forward, curious what the man was about to bring up.

"We have information that the AWC is growing militant," York said.

"We have that same information," Palani shot back. "And we already know they were behind the attack on our ranch."

York looked taken aback, as if he'd expected to wow them with this and had gotten cheated out of it. "Okay, then," he said, glancing sideways at his assistant before focusing on them again. "Then you also know they're awfully interested in your pack."

That was news to Lidon, though it didn't surprise him. "Interested how?"

"Interested as in an informant within their organization says they're gearing up for another attack."

Lidon swallowed back the fear that rose inside him. "On our ranch?"

York nodded slowly.

"And what do you plan on doing to stop them?" Palani asked, only the tightness in his voice betraying his emotions.

York held up his hands in a helpless gesture. "They've done nothing illegal yet, unless we officially reopen the investigation into the first attack. I'm fully open to that idea, but we'd need full access to your ranch and your pack."

There it was, the catch-22. "Why are you so interested in my pack?"

York leaned forward, dropping his voice. "Because you know something that's eluding us. The gene was supposed to enable the offspring of these omegas to shift, not this generation, but somehow, you managed. We want to know how. We're well aware your bloodline is strong, but there's an element we're missing that you've discovered that's enabling you to shift, and we want to find out what it is."

The polyamorous dynamic, Lidon realized. That was the piece of the puzzle they were missing. They hadn't realized it was because of his three mates that his powers had gotten so strong, that they were able to share those powers.

"So what you're saying is that you're blackmailing us," Palani said calmly.

"Blackmail is an ugly word," York protested.

"How else do you want me to call it when there will be an attack against us but you refuse to stop it unless we give you certain information? That, to me, is a classic blackmail scenario."

"I think of it more as helping each other out. Tell us how you managed to shift, and we'll help you defend yourself."

Rage bubbled inside Lidon, red and dangerous. He couldn't show it, couldn't let this man witness the depths of his anger. He did allow his eyes to change, something he recognized now when it happened. York gasped as he witnessed it, then shrunk back visibly, as did his assistant.

"I'm not comfortable discussing this topic with you," Lidon said, leaning back in his chair, his fingernails digging in his palm to keep his temper in check. He despised this, this political game of cat and mouse, this pretense. He'd play it, but he told himself he didn't have to like it.

"I had hoped we could have a reasonable discussion," York said, his voice tight and controlled. "But I can see you've made up your mind that we are the villains in this story."

Lidon squeezed Palani's hand as he answered. "To be honest, I'm not sure if there are good guys anymore. It seems to me that between you and the AWC, we're stuck between a rock and a hard place."

"Is that why you didn't act on the information you had about election fraud?" York asked.

Lidon shouldn't be surprised that the man knew, and yet

it amazed him, the sources this guy had, the amount of information he had to be sitting on.

"Yes. Well, one of the reasons anyway. It was kind of like the least evil of two choices, So I wouldn't take it as a compliment," Lidon said.

"After Mr. Hightower's rant, there's no risk of me interpreting anything you say as a compliment," York said.

"Good," Lidon said amicably. "Because I wouldn't want you to think for a second that we support you, your party, or your methods."

"Not even when those methods gave you back the power to shift?"

"No. And I'm sure you think I'm lying, but I am not." Lidon considered it for a second, then decided that he might as well admit what York knew to be true anyway. "There's incredible power in being able to shift, and I won't deny that." York's eyes widened at Lidon's admission, and he shared another look with his companion, who had been silent the whole time.

"And you may think I would value that power more than anything else, but I don't. If I could trade it to see not just my mate be rid of this gene that has wrecked his life in so many ways, but the other gene carriers as well, I would do it in a heartbeat. You may not understand, but nothing compares to their suffering. Every time I shift..."

He surprised himself by choking up, not something he was accustomed to and especially not in front of strangers. He closed his eyes for a second, willed himself to calm down and swallow back his emotions.

"Every time I shift, I'm aware of what Vieno had to suffer in order for me to do it, and I can tell you, it wasn't worth it."

18

It was time for another pack meeting. Palani tried to hold these bi-weekly now. Sometimes they ran as short as fifteen minutes, just a simple run-down of everything that was new. Other times, they ran for hours when there was more they needed to discuss. Bray appreciated them, valuing the open communication from the alpha and his second-in-command.

Of course, he knew most of what they shared already, but it was good to hear others react, especially when it was hard news, like tonight. Bray's own heart was heavy as he tried to assess how others would react. Kean would stay, he had no doubt, but what would Ruari do? He couldn't fault the omega for leaving after tonight, but what about his son? It would mean Bray would lose the opportunity to be in Jax's life.

"Guys, thank you all for coming," Palani started, and Bray settled down in the back, where he could see everyone.

Kean and Ruari weren't that far from him, the omega feeding Jax while Kean glanced sideways every now and then with hearts in his eyes. They looked good together, he had to admit, Kean's every action and gesture signaling his tender care for Ruari. He'd make a great dad for Jax. Better than Bray, and that thought made him look away and take a steadying breath.

"I'm afraid we've got some hard news to share, so I'm gonna start with that and we'll go from there." Palani looked at Lidon who quietly stood behind him as if to get his strength. The alpha reached out for Palani's hand, then pulled him close so he stood in front of him, his alpha literally behind him.

"We have credible evidence that a militant group is planning an attack on this ranch."

A loud wave of gasps ran through the pack.

"We don't know when and how, but it's aimed at us specifically. This group knows we're a pack, and they've found out Lidon can shift. They're determined to stop the wolf shifters before more will come."

Palani's voice cracked at those last words, and Bray felt it too, the deep emotion at the thought that people wanted to kill them simply because of who they were, of how they lived their lives.

"They're armed, they're training, and they're dangerous," Palani said. "And even though Prime Minister York knows, he's not inclined to stop them at this moment."

That resulted in some angry murmurs, and Palani wasn't even telling the whole story, which Bray had heard from him. The sheer balls of a prime minister to engage in blackmail was beyond comprehension, and Bray respected the hell out of Lidon and Palani for refusing to give in to a man who was more than comfortable playing with the lives of his constituents to further his own cause.

"We wanted you all to know this, so you can make a decision. You are free to leave the ranch at any time, and we will not blame you for doing so. This is a credible threat, and everyone should decide for themselves if they're willing to risk it. Again, we won't fault anyone for leaving," Palani said.

"No one should stay if they don't want to," Lidon spoke up. "I want to make that absolutely clear. If you decide to leave, no hard feelings."

"Does leaving mean leaving the pack as well?" Kean asked, and Bray's heart sank.

Was the beta considering leaving? Had he misjudged him? Did that mean Ruari was leaving as well? His chest stabbed at the thought.

"Yes," Lidon said. "We completely understand if people leave because they didn't expect this. But if you leave, you leave the pack. You can't be a part of the pack if you're not willing to face this threat together. That's also because we'll be shutting down all traffic in and out of the ranch as much as we can for security reasons. We won't allow commutes anymore."

"What about Maz and Rhene? They're in the pack but live in the city half the time," Urien said. "No offense, but I want to know what the rules are."

Palani nodded. "We've informed both ahead of this meeting. They have a choice to move in full-time or leave the pack."

Bray sat with bated breath, awaiting how many the pack would have left. He was staying, not even a doubt, but he didn't have much to lose. For others, that was different. He wasn't even sure what his own father would do, now that Sven was pregnant.

"Lidon, alpha, I'm sorry, but I can't stay. I have my daughter to consider, and I can't endanger her."

That was Urien, sounding deeply apologetic. What a

hard spot for him to be in, losing his job and his place to live. Still, Bray had expected this from him, and his guess was there would be more.

Urien hesitantly walked up to Lidon, who hugged him hard. "I understand, cousin. Be well."

Jawon, Servas, and Ori were whispering with each other, and others started doing the same.

"I'm staying," Rhene said.

"But what about finishing your degree?" Palani asked, clearly stunned.

"That can wait. I'm not leaving both of my brothers and my nephew," the alpha spoke, sounding more mature than he ever had before.

"I'm staying as well."

"Maz!" Enar gasped, jumping up. "You can't—"

Maz cut him off by raising his hand. "Doc, stop. My place is here, now more than ever. I'm staying."

That was unexpected, Bray thought, but man, was he happy to not only have another alpha join them, but a doctor at that.

"We're staying," Grayson said, and Bray's heart was a little lighter. "We've successfully fought off the previous attack, and I have every confidence we'll do it again."

"Previous attack?" Ruari asked.

Right, the omega was new, so he hadn't heard they'd been attacked before.

"About a year ago, a small group of men attacked the ranch when many of us were out. Grayson and Vieno hid, while Bray and his men were able to fight off the attackers," Palani said.

He'd lost one of his men that day, Bray thought, which still upset him after all this time. He still made monthly payments to the man's mother to supplement her meager pension now that her only alpha son was dead, and he knew Lidon did the same. It wasn't enough, and it didn't bring him back, but at least she was taken care of.

He'd missed Ruari's reaction to Palani's words, too lost in thought to pay attention, but he spotted the omega walk out a minute later, Kean staring after him with a look of bewilderment. Maybe he needed time to think? Bray couldn't blame him, not with a young baby he was putting at risk, but the thought of Ruari leaving left him shaken. He needed more time with him, time to prove that he could be a good influence on his son, that he was worthy to be in his life.

At the end of the meeting, they'd only lost Urien. Everyone else had decided to stay, including Lidon's cousins. Everyone, except Ruari, who had never returned after he'd walked out. Bray was elated with that result, having expected to lose more people.

"What was up with Ruari?" he asked Kean when the meeting had ended.

"I don't know. He went pale and said he had to leave. Maybe he wasn't feeling well? I texted him but he didn't reply, so I was about to check up on him."

Something tightened in Bray's stomach, something that felt an awful lot like worry. "Can you let me know if he's okay?" he asked.

Kean studied him for a second or two, then nodded. "I will."

RUARI WASN'T EVEN sure what excuse he had made up to get away. All he had known it was that he had to get out of there, because he couldn't breathe. He knew his departure had been conspicuous, he'd caught the weird glances from

Kean, but he had to go. Ever since, he'd been pacing his room, Jax blissfully asleep in his little crib.

It had clicked, all the snippets he'd heard, when Palani had told about the previous attack. Ruari's stomach had heaved as he realized he knew who was behind it.

His father.

Months ago, right before he'd found out he was pregnant, he'd overheard a conversation. He'd escaped to go to the club for his second heat, and when he came back, the punishment had been severe. He'd been locked in his room again, but this time without daily trips outside. His father had been livid, and Ruari hadn't understood why exactly. What was the difference between an alpha shoved into his room to fuck the living daylights out of him and an alpha in a club? But then that one day, his mother had forgotten to lock the door behind her after visiting him, and he'd snuck downstairs for a bit of fresh air.

He'd tiptoed past his father's office and he'd been talking to someone Ruari didn't know, someone whose face he hadn't even seen. His father had left the door open, very unusual for him, but that was maybe because he assumed Ruari was safely locked up.

Ruari had caught only snippets of the conversation, but it had been enough to determine his father had authorized some kind of attack on a ranch. It had been unsuccessful, Ruari had deduced from the two minutes he'd listened in, his shock rising with every word he'd caught. What the hell was his father involved in?

He'd always known the man was a massive asshole, and it had been no surprise to him he was capable of violence, but to find out he had flat out ordered an attack that had killed people? It had left him shaking. It also made him wonder what else his father had been involved in, because if he had done this once...

A few days later, he'd found out he was pregnant, and that was what had made him leave, the knowledge that his father was more than capable of killing. He'd done it before and had planned to do it again.

"We underestimated them," his father had said. "We'll regroup and get them next time."

Apparently, that time had now come. How had he not made the connection that it was the pack, this ranch his father wanted dead more than anything or anyone else? He'd known of his father's intense hatred for the CWP, for anyone promoting change, especially those who wanted to better the position of omegas. His father was more old school than the staunchest traditionalists, determined to keep the old rigid structures and hierarchies in place. And the return of the wolf shifters? That was pure horror to him.

Ruari should've known, should've deduced the pack was the target, but he hadn't until he'd learned about the previous attack. And now his father was gearing up for another attempt.

Could he keep this a secret from the men, that it was his father who was behind this? They knew who it was, he'd gathered from Palani's words, but what if they found out it was his father? Would they kick him out? He'd only been here for a little over two weeks, not long enough for them to get to know him well. They'd look at him differently, and he couldn't blame them. It was his father who had caused them so much pain already and was about to do it all over again.

Maybe he should leave on his own, before they found out. His thoughts went to his own son. If there was another attack, Jax might be at risk. Should he leave? They'd be safer, wouldn't they? Yet the thought of leaving sent him almost into a panic.

He didn't want to leave. He wasn't sure what had happened that he had gotten attached to this place, to these men so soon, but he didn't want to go. There was Kean and their special connection, which had given Ruari hope for a future. He wasn't sure how it was possible that he and Kean had gotten so close so fast, but they had. They'd only had a few dates, but Ruari found himself dreaming of a future with him, the happy ever after he'd thought he'd lost forever.

But it was more than that. It was the friendship with Vieno and Sven. It was the safe place he had for himself and for Jax. And if he was honest, it was also Bray. He wasn't sure how the alpha fit into his life, but he couldn't shake the feeling it would be good for Jax to have his biological father in his life. It was all of this, plus the peace in his soul of feeling safe and loved and at home. He didn't want to lose that, but could he keep this horrible secret from them?

No, Ruari couldn't do it. He couldn't keep this from them. No matter how scared he was for their reaction, he had to tell them. What a horrible coincidence he had ended up here, that the place he'd grown to love was the very place his father hated so much.

He'd had no idea this was the group of men his father had been so opposed to. No, opposed wasn't the right word. Opposed assumed somewhat civil methods, a political disagreement rather than taking matters into your own hands and sending armed men to...to what exactly? He wasn't even sure what his father's objective had been when he had his men attack the ranch for the first time.

From the little information Palani had shared, Ruari understood that Palani, Lidon, and Enar hadn't even been home during the attack. It had been Vieno, with Grayson. Bray and his men, one of whom had been killed, Kean had whispered to him.

Had they been after Vieno? It made sense. His father's strategy had always been to go after the weakest link, and he must have thought that getting to Vieno, probably kidnapping the omega, would ensure compliance from the other three. It was how his father fought and operated, and it made Ruari sick. He had to share this with the pack, had to come clean not only for himself, but also to protect the pack. Any and all information he could give about his father's strategies could help them.

His mind made up, he texted Sven to ask if he could watch Jax and as soon as the omega arrived, Ruari headed out to find Palani. He'd decided that would be the best person to talk to, as he didn't want to skip ranks and go for the pack alpha himself.

Palani closed his laptop when Ruari asked if they could talk and after a few minutes of chitchat about how Ruari was settling in, the omega decided it was time to come out with the truth.

"I have something to tell you."

He took a deep breath, grateful for the quiet way the beta was listening to him, allowing him time to voice his thoughts. Palani listened to him without interrupting, then asked a series of questions that left Ruari impressed with how sharp his mind was. He told him everything he could remember, everything he'd ever overheard, everything about how his father worked and operated.

Ruari had no qualms about being open and honest with him. He had no loyalty to his father anymore, not after what the man had done to him, but also not after what he had done to the pack. This was his pack now, Ruari realized with a rush. These were his people, his brothers. God, he hoped they'd let him stay. He'd never wanted anything more in his life.

"Ruari, I can't thank you enough for telling me this. I realize how hard this must be for you, considering this is your father."

Ruari let out a breath he'd been holding, releasing his fear over how Palani would react. It had been nothing but support and understanding, and he could've wept with gratitude.

"He never was a good father to me," he confessed. "And I swear I didn't know when I came here. I had no idea why my father had attacked this ranch, back when I overheard that conversation. All I knew was that he considered them enemies, but not why. It wasn't until I heard you guys talk about the attack that I realized this was the place. And of course, it makes total sense."

Palani gave him a look filled with compassion. "He must not have been happy his firstborn was an omega."

Ruari shook his head. "No, he wasn't. He wasn't aware at the time my mother consulted a fertility specialist behind his back, which turned out to be the very reason why I am an omega. But yeah, he made his disappointment in me clear from a very young age, so you can imagine what his reaction would've been like if I had told him I was pregnant."

"He doesn't know?"

"I didn't tell him. I ran away from home, but I'm sure he's figured it out by now. My father has a way of finding things out. I'm sure he ordered an investigation when I disappeared, so he must've discovered by now. But he hasn't contacted me so far, so we'll consider that good news."

"He's hired a PI to find you," Palani said.

Ruari's eyes went big. How did the beta know this? Had he known all along?

"And no, we didn't know it was you he was looking for. I can't tell you more than this to protect others, but he's still looking for you, Ruari. I just wanted you to know."

"Thank you. I'm not surprised he's trying to find me, but it's not because he misses me or longs for a tearful reunion or some shit."

"Jax?" Palani asked.

Ruari had to remind himself to keep breathing, because every time he thought about something happening to Jax, he got light-headed. "I'm afraid of what he'll do to him, knowing that I have the gene," he whispered.

"Oh, Ruari, I'm so sorry. What a horrible thing to fear. I hope you'll stay with us."

Ruari's heart skipped a beat. "I can stay?"

"Of course you can stay. We won't hold you responsible for what your father did or does, that's not how it works. You're a pack member now, one of us. Plus, my brother would kill me if I sent you away," he teased.

Ruari smiled. "He's a good man. I really like him."

"Rightfully so. He's one of the good ones, Kean is. Loyal till the bitter end."

There was a layer to that statement that Ruari didn't quite grasp, but he let it go. "Thank you for everything. This place truly feels like home to me."

Palani smiled back. "We are so happy to have you here. You fit in wonderfully well. But Ruari, I need to tell Lidon about this, as you can imagine. Bray needs to be informed as well."

Bray. Ruari hadn't considered it, but Palani would want to inform their head of security about the threat against them. "Can you tell him without revealing your source? I don't want him to know who my father is."

"Yeah, no problem. He needs to know what you told me, not who told me. Bray will be curious, I imagine, but as a journalist, I'm used to protecting my sources. And I can imagine things are complicated enough between the two of you already to add this to the mix."

Ruari breathed out with relief that Palani would not only keep his identity secret, but understood.

"Can I ask you something?" he said, still hesitant if this was the right thing to do.

Palani cocked his head, then smiled. "Let me guess, you want to ask me about Bray."

Damn, he really was smart. "Yes. If you don't mind."

"Look, Ruari, you must've gotten mixed messages about him and maybe even from him. The fact that you and Kean are close makes me suspect Kean has shared some of his experiences with Bray, and I'm sure those painted a certain picture of him. I'm not saying Kean is wrong, because Bray does have a tendency to put on his alpha act rather thickly, but... It's hard to explain, but he's a good man, Ruari. He wouldn't be here if he wasn't. My guess is that he's still struggling with his identity, weird as that may sound. He hasn't figured out who he is and how he's supposed to behave, so sometimes he puts on this mask, this act of how he thinks he's supposed to act. It's not him. If you give him some time, he will surprise you."

Ruari bit his lip. Interestingly enough, Palani's words confirmed his own gut feeling. Bray might be an ass at times, but still Ruari instinctively trusted him. But was he wrong in that trust? "What about what happened between him and Sven?" he asked. "I hate to bring this up, but I understood he attacked him."

Palani let out a deep sigh, his face sobering. "Yes, he did, and it was horrible. If Grayson hadn't been there, I don't know what would've happened. But the thing is that we can't fully hold him responsible for it. Sven's smell got to him, and it overwhelmed him. He would've never done that otherwise. I swear, I've investigated this gene, and I've heard too many stories that sounded similar, men who would never otherwise attack omegas." He stopped talking, his eyes narrowing. "Not to get too personal, but didn't he react the same way when he helped you through his heat? I mean, you have the gene, so you must've smelled irresistible to him as well."

Ruari's mouth dropped open a little in shock. That thought hadn't even crossed his mind, not even after everything he learned and heard about the effects of that gene. Sure, the sex between him and Bray had been explosive and heated, and Bray had certainly been into it to the point where he had surprised Ruari with his stamina, but he hadn't attacked him. Bray had been able to go into the room and at least control himself long enough to sign the damn contract. How was that possible? Why had Bray not reacted the same way to him as he had to Sven? That didn't make sense at all.

"No, he didn't. We didn't start right away, as he had to sign a contract, and he never was as overwhelmed as the alpha who assisted me through my first heat."

Palani's eyes widened, and a series of emotions flashed over his face, too fast for Ruari to interpret. Then Palani smiled at him, a smile that meant something, but Ruari wasn't sure what.

"Huh," the beta said, his smile widening. "That is interesting."

Interesting? What the hell did he mean with that?

19
_____

Something was off with Ruari, and Kean was worried. Physically, he was looking better every day, his too-pale skin making way for a healthy glow from spending more time outside, from sleeping better and eating proper food. He hadn't been dizzy anymore either, he'd told Kean, courtesy of taking better care of himself and the iron supplements Enar had prescribed.

No, it was something else, and it had started at that last pack meeting three days ago. At first, Kean had thought the omega was scared, and he couldn't blame him. It was scary shit, to think about another attack. Kean hadn't been here during the first one, but he'd talked about it both with his brother and with Bray. Palani had choked up as he explained how worried they had been for Vieno, and Bray's voice had cracked as he recounted losing one of his men.

The idea of something like that happening again was enough to scare anyone, let alone an omega like Ruari who would have a hard time defending himself, and who had a son. Man, Kean only had to think of something happening to Jax to get all teared up. They couldn't let anyone near those precious babies. So it made sense for Ruari to be scared.

And yet, that wasn't it. He'd asked Ruari if he was sure he wanted to stay, and his answer had been definitive, leaving no room for doubt. So what was going on? Kean kept mulling it over as he worked and even during a security drill Bray had them perform right after lunch. He studied Ruari as they did the drill, and the omega was closed off. Hell, he was even avoiding Kean a bit and more than anything, that made Kean worry.

After dinner, which had consisted of monosyllabic answers from Ruari, Kean confronted him in the hall away. "Wanna go for a walk?" he asked him.

Ruari looked at the floor. "I'm tired."

"We won't go far."

"Bray said we shouldn't venture outside the gates at night."

"We won't."

When Ruari still stubbornly refused to look at him, Kean gently lifted his chin with his finger. "Ruari, are you having doubts about me, about us?"

He had to ask, even though he feared his heart couldn't take another rejection after Bray. Was it possible he made the same mistake twice, thinking someone was his mate when he wasn't? It would be too crazy to even consider, but he had to ask. They couldn't continue like this, with Ruari avoiding him.

Ruari's eyes filled with tears. "No! Please, no, don't think that."

Sweet relief took away the tightness in Kean's chest, though the worry was still there. "Then what's going on, baby? What's got you so down?"

Ruari bit his lip as more tears filled his eyes, a few trickling down his cheeks. Kean balled his fists to keep himself from touching him, from kissing those tears away.

"I have something to tell you, something horrible, and I'm so scared you won't like me anymore."

It sounded ominous and dramatic, and yet Kean only had to see the despair on Ruari's face to understand the omega meant every word. "Does this have something to do with your family?" he guessed, thinking back on their previous conversation and how Ruari had wanted to protect him by not saying too much.

Ruari nodded slowly.

"With your father?" Kean guessed again, reasoning that was the most likely problem.

Another slow nod.

"I'm guessing your father is not a good man?"

This time, Ruari's head went side to side, but the omega's eyes found his, and Kean thought that a good sign.

"Baby, I would never hold you responsible for what your father did or does. It doesn't change how I see you, how I feel about you."

Something changed in Ruari's eyes, in his face. It was the smallest of changes, his lips that curled up just a little, the tightness that relaxed, the hint of a sparkle returning to his eyes. Encouraged, Kean pressed forward.

"You have to know by now I'm crazy about you," he said, his body tingling when Ruari sent him the sweetest smile in response.

"I'm crazy about you too. I know it's soon, but..."

"But it feels right," Kean answered, his heart dancing in his chest after Ruari's admission. He hadn't been mistaken then. This was it, his chance at happiness. He would not fuck this up.

"It does," Ruari admitted.

Kean cupped his cheek. "You can tell me or not, it's your choice, but I promise you, baby, that it won't change how I feel about you."

Something seemed to lift off Ruari's shoulders. "I'd rather not tell you until I have to," he said. "But I told Palani 'cause I wanted him and Lidon to know."

Kean fought hard to keep the surprise at that remark off his face. Ruari had talked to Palani about his father? That meant that...the pack meeting where Ruari had walked out after learning about the first attack... Kean connected the dots in his head, and a picture emerged. Ruari's father had to be connected to the attacks on the ranch. Well, that explained a lot, including his reluctance to tell Kean and why he had told Palani.

"Then we're all good, baby. Nothing more to worry about."

Ruari stepped close and Kean's arms snuggled around him as the omega rose on his toes and offered his mouth for a sweet kiss.

"Thank you," Ruari whispered, then kissed him again.

Kean opened his mouth, desperate for a full taste of him. He didn't dare think it out of fear it would elude him again. Soft lips pressed against his, then a tongue slid into his mouth with boldness, like only Ruari could do. He recognized his taste already, that sweet, spicy mix that was uniquely his, as his hands reached around Ruari's waist to pull him closer, that lithe body fitting perfectly against his.

Ruari wasn't shy about holding onto him, one hand sneaking around him to grab his ass, kneading it. Kean let out a low rumble into Ruari's mouth, sliding his own tongue against his. He angled his head to get more, sinking his tongue in deeper, exploring every inch of his mouth.

Ruari's teeth scraped Kean's bottom lip in a rough caress,

and he moaned into the omega's mouth. "You like that, huh?" Ruari whispered, his voice low and seductive.

"I like everything you do to me, but yes, I do," Kean managed, before diving back in, Ruari's lips curling against his in a smile.

Their bodies pressed together and there was no hiding that Ruari was as hard as he was. He ground against him a little, just to see how he would respond. They hadn't moved past kissing yet, which was fine with Kean if Ruari wanted to take things slow, but he couldn't help test the waters a little.

Ruari pushed right back and Kean walked them backward until he had his own back against the wall, Ruari pulled tight against him, their mouths fused together. Then Ruari's hand slipped between them, and Kean drew in a sharp breath when the omega's hand grabbed his cock over the cotton of his shorts and put pressure on it.

"How do you like that?" he whispered, his grip intensifying a notch, making Kean gasp.

"Oh god, yes..."

Ruari's tongue continued its erotic dance with his as his hand started making slow, hard circles against his dick. Sweat broke out on his back and a flush of pleasure crept up his neck. "Ruari," he breathed.

The omega kept up his slow torture, bringing Kean closer and closer to the brink, his cock leaking and his breathing labored. "Ruari," he grunted again, as much in a plea as a warning.

Ruari's hand clinched hard around his cock, sending a shock through Kean. He hissed, and when the omega repeated the move, he lost the fight and came with a raw noise, clenching his eyes shut even as Ruari's mouth caught his sounds.

He kept rubbing him until he'd stopped trembling, then

pulled back, shooting Kean a sexy smile that made him want to kiss his swollen, red lips all over again. "That was... ungh," he managed.

"Good?"

"So good."

He pressed a soft kiss on those kissable lips. "Thank you."

A sound made them both look sideways. Bray stood in the hallway, his cheeks flushed and his eyes blazing with something Kean couldn't decipher.

"You two need to get a room," the alpha said, his voice low and husky, before stalking off.

Kean watched him until he was out of sight. Was it his imagination or had Bray looked jealous?

Ruari didn't need a doctor to tell him what was about to happen. He could feel it in his body, the awakening of something that had lain dormant since the pregnancy. It worried him, and that was an understatement. After everything he had learned about the gene, he didn't think he would feel relaxed about being in heat ever again.

Being on the ranch offered him some kind of protection as he would be safe in the omega bunkhouse. But even then, he wasn't guaranteed a positive experience. He'd discussed it with Enar, and the doctor had assured him he could help Ruari find an alpha to help him through his heat. That had been before he'd started dating Kean, before he'd discovered Jax's biological father was here.

Kean's and Bray's presence made it a hell of a lot more complicated. He would've asked Kean to help him, knowing they were headed to more intimacy anyway—god, that make-out session two days ago in the hallway had been hot; he'd almost come himself from pleasuring Kean—but he remembered Enar's little speech about the importance of an alpha. Not just that, but an alpha taking him without a condom. The condom hadn't worked last time, and now he would have to trust going bare with just Enar's birth control methods to prevent another pregnancy.

And not only that, but he also remembered from his research into the gene that gene carriers were far more fertile. That made going through a heat incredibly risky. You only had to look at Sven to see what could happen, and he was in a committed relationship, so it wasn't that big of a deal for him. For Ruari, that was different, so what did he do now?

The weird thing was that it didn't even scare him so much to become pregnant again, though it would be hell on his body this soon. No, it wasn't that, nor the idea of raising children on his own. He hadn't known how strong he was until he had no choice, and now there was little that fazed him.

No, what had him worried was once again risking legal implications and complications if he ended up pregnant. If he had the bad luck of encountering an alpha who was hell-bent on getting access to his child, he'd be fucked. Bray had proven to be honorable, only asking to meet his son and not once mentioning legal strategies to realize his goal, but not all alphas were like that.

Maybe he was overthinking things and the risk of a pregnancy wasn't as big as he made it out to be, but he couldn't help worrying. Enar had told him all alphas on the ranch were good men, but he had a hard time imagining himself with anyone. Anyone but Kean, that was, and he wasn't an alpha, so where did that leave Ruari?

His thoughts went to Bray once again. They had experienced good sexual chemistry, he mused, even if Bray hadn't been able to fully satisfy that desperate craving inside him during his heat. At first, he'd blamed Bray for that, but with what he had learned since, he'd realized it was because of the gene. If Bray had not used condoms, the outcome might have been different.

And in every other sense, they had been a good match. God, the man had a glorious dick, thick and long and perfect to take him hard, exactly the way he liked it. He had never been one to have a lot of one-night stands, but he'd done his fair share of experimenting before his first heat, and his experience had been that a lot of alphas were more careful with him than he'd like them to be. He got that many omegas were fragile, but he wasn't. At least, not during his heat.

But it wasn't like he could ask Bray, right? That would be majorly awkward not just for himself, but also for Kean. Kind of an insult to the beta, asking his alpha ex-boyfriend instead of him. No, Ruari couldn't do that to him and it would be awkward for himself and Bray, not to mention he would lose all credibility if he wouldn't allow Bray full access to his own child but then asked him to help him through his heat. That would be hypocritical, and Ruari couldn't stand that. No, Bray wasn't an option, so why did his mind keep returning to him?

"Ruari, can I talk to you for a sec?" Kean asked.

Ruari had been so deep in thought, he hadn't even realized Kean had walked into the kitchen.

"Hi," he said, almost automatically raising his head for a kiss, and Kean didn't disappoint him. He leaned in and covered Ruari his mouth with his, taking his time for a deep, sensual kiss that left them both panting.

"Mmm, you're such a good kisser," Ruari sighed.

Kean set himself down at the table next to him and sent him a soft smile. "I could say the same about you, baby."

"What did you want to talk to me about?" Ruari asked.

Kean averted his eyes, looking at the table, and Ruari's adrenaline spiked. This was not the look of someone who had something innocent to ask. This was the look of someone who had to bring up something that wasn't good. With bated breath, he awaited Kean's response.

"Two of the men have approached me to tell me that your scent is starting to affect them. You need to seclude yourself in the bunkhouse, baby. I hate to say this to you, but I don't want anything to happen to you."

Ruari didn't understand why, but tears formed in his eyes. He hated that he had this effect on people without wanting to. It wasn't fair, not to the men and not to him. This was the part about the gene he hated most. In creating it, these men—these monsters—had made him into a seducer, something and someone he didn't want to be.

"I know. I realized today that I could feel my heat coming," he said softly. It had to be hard for Kean, not just knowing that others could smell him, but being unable to help Ruari through this. "Can you smell me?" he wondered.

Kean slowly raised his eyes to meet his gaze. "No, not as they are describing it."

Ruari frowned. "How is that possible? Is it because you're a beta? I thought the smell affected everyone? Or is it not strong enough to get to you?" he asked, curious.

Kean's eyes dropped once again to the table, and Ruari's stomach swirled uneasily. "Kean, what are you not telling me? What do you know about this? It feels like you're hiding something from me."

Kean let out a deep sigh, then reached for Ruari's hand

and met his eyes. "You're right, I was keeping this from you, but not for any reason except that I didn't want to put pressure on you."

"I have no idea what you're talking about. What do you mean, pressure? What's going on?" Ruari asked.

"Vieno's smell didn't affect his men the same way it did others," Kean said carefully.

"Well, that's because they're together, right? Isn't that what happened, that they bonded with him and his smell changed? Because after he was alpha-claimed, no one could smell him anymore, right?"

Kean shook his head. "No, that came after. Even before Vieno was claimed, Lidon and Enar couldn't smell him in the same way others could. Palani neither, but they reasoned that was because he had gotten used to him over the years, growing up together and living together for a long time."

Something tickled Ruari's memory, something about this same topic. Who had he discussed this with? It wouldn't come to him, so he focused on Kean's words. "You said it wasn't because of the bonding, so what was it? What made those three react differently?"

And as soon as he had formulated his question, he knew. It was why Grayson had been able to help Sven through his first heat with such relative restraint, as the omega had told him, because they were mates. Not mates as in together, but mates as in fated mates. Grayson had reacted differently to Sven because they were supposed to be together.

"Fated mates," he whispered. "Because they were fated mates. And you think that's the same for us."

He didn't put it as a question, but as a statement. Their eyes were burning into each other's, Kean's filled with insecurity as he nodded. "I do, but I didn't want to tell you, because I don't want you to feel pressured into anything. I'm not even sure if you believe in this theory."

Ruari raised an eyebrow. "Why wouldn't I believe in it when the evidence is all around us here? I've heard the stories of the alpha and his men, and Sven has told me enough about him, Grayson, and Lars to know they're definitely meant to be as well. What's not to believe?"

"Bray doesn't," Kean said with a sigh. "He figures it's manipulative bullshit."

The moment his name was mentioned, Ruari remembered what his brain had tried to connect earlier, but had failed at. He had talked to Palani about his experience with Bray, and why Bray hadn't reacted as strongly to him and had been able to control himself enough to sign the contract first. What was it Palani had said? *Interesting*, he had called it.

Then it rushed through him, the deep sense of truth in the only conclusion he could draw.

"Oh my god," he whispered. "You, me, Bray...we're fated mates."

"Yes," Kean said, seeing no reason to pretend anymore.

It had weighed heavily on him, his discovery about the three of them and not telling either one of his supposed mates about it. Kean wasn't even sure when he had figured it out, but sometime that night after Bray had caught them making out, he had realized it. He wasn't Bray's mate or Ruari's mate. He was both. They were supposed to be together, the three of them.

Not telling Bray made total sense, considering the alpha's strong objections against the concept of mates, but it had killed Kean to not say anything to Ruari. He hadn't lied though; he had merely kept his mouth shut out of fear it would put pressure on the omega.

"But what does that mean for us?" Ruari asked, looking stunned.

"Honestly? I don't know."

"When did you realize it?" Ruari wanted to know.

"I've had my suspicions about me and Bray from the moment I met him, but when he didn't respond to me the same way, I reckoned I was wrong. And then when we broke up and he was pretty mean, I decided I'd been mistaken, because I figured the man who was my intended mate would not talk to me like that. Then I met you and we had this weird connection, so I reasoned you might be the one, but I couldn't let go of Bray. But when he saw us kissing, he looked jealous, and that made me think about you and him, and I realized the truth."

Ruari slowly shook his head. "I don't see how that is going to happen with Bray refusing to accept the concept."

"That's your biggest concern? How about the fact that me and Bray have ended things and you and Bray were never a thing in the first place, and the two of us are still trying to figure out what we are?" Kean said, amazed at Ruari's acceptance of the whole thing.

Ruari sent him a sweet smile. "We can safely say we have answered that last question, wouldn't you say? Mates, that's what we are, you and me. But apparently, we're missing a third person, so the question is how we convince him he belongs with us."

"I can't believe how okay you are with this," Kean remarked. "I had kind of expected you to freak out about it, especially since it's Bray."

Ruari's smile widened and he got up from his chair, then without a second's doubt, parked himself on Kean's lap. "There are worse things than hearing you are supposed to be with not one but two super-hot guys, can I just point that out?" he teased.

Kean couldn't help but smile. "Bray is damn sexy," he admitted.

"Damn right he is. And his cock is a work of art," Ruari said, and that made Kean snicker.

Who would've ever thought he would be sitting with his

—well he guessed he could call Ruari his boyfriend now— on his lap, gushing over a mutual ex who was at the same time their intended third? It was almost too far-fetched to be true, and yet that was where they were.

"It is," he affirmed, getting hard at the thought of that fat cock in his ass.

Ruari leaned his head against his shoulder, and Kean held him close. "How do you want to proceed?" he asked Ruari after they'd been sitting like that for a while. "Because if we tell Bray, he'll balk. The harder we try to convince him, the faster he will run."

"I'll admit it's gonna take some time for me to switch my perception of Bray from not even a friend to my mate," Ruari admitted. "I mean, it is a big change, even for us. We can't fault Bray for not believing us if we tell him we want to be with him when you broke up with him and I told him to prove himself worthy of my friendship."

Ruari had a good point there, Kean admitted to himself. If he hadn't seen his brother's reaction to being separated from Vieno, if he hadn't realized the dynamics between the alpha and his three men as well as Grayson and his boys, Kean would've felt differently about the realization that he belonged with Ruari and Bray. So yes, Ruari had a point that it might be hard for Bray to take it seriously, especially with their history.

"So we don't tell him," he said. "We build a friendship with him and let it develop naturally."

He played with Ruari's hair as he waited for the omega to speak. "Under different circumstances, I would've agreed that's a good strategy," Ruari said. "But you're forgetting one major complication: my heat. I have maybe a week before it starts, and I'm gonna need to ask an alpha for help. Do you really think I should ask anyone else but Bray with what we know now?"

Kean was not a jealous person by nature, but the thought of Ruari with anyone else but him or Bray made his vision grow red. He hadn't realized it till then, how familiar the idea of Ruari and Bray together felt. If nothing else, that convinced him of the fact that they were meant to be together.

"You're right," he said. "You can't ask anyone else but him."

"Both of you." Ruari leaned back so he could meet Kean's eyes. "I want it to be both of you, not just him."

A rush of pleasure surged through Kean. "Are you sure? It's him you need, not me."

Ruari shifted on his lap so he straddled him, and then he grabbed Kean's face with both his hands. "I do need you. I don't even think I realize how much I need you, but I do."

They both leaned forward for a soft kiss, and the comfort of that gesture made Kean's beta deeply content.

"There's a lot about this we have to figure out," Ruari said. "But I only have to sense my soul's peace with all of this to know it's the right thing. My omega has accepted the both of you as mates, even if Bray isn't quite there yet."

"Same here," Kean said. "I've never been more sure of anything in my life. I belong with the both of you, and while it terrifies me considering the circumstances, I know it's right."

Ruari let his forehead rest against Kean's, and they sat like that for a little while. "What if we don't tell him?" Ruari asked. "What if I approach him for my heat and don't explain anything other than I want it to be the two of you? Would he go for that?"

Kean considered it. It felt a tad dishonest, though they wouldn't be lying. But would Bray go for it?

"Maybe you should try to make him offer," he thought out loud. "He's a good guy, and if he felt you were in a pickle, he would offer to help you out. I mean, I'm sure he wants to anyway, but he'd be scared to offer out of fear you'd reject him, I'm sure."

Ruari chuckled. "That's a pretty passive-aggressive approach," he said. "I like it. But I would have to do it soon, because as you said, I need to go into seclusion."

"So do it now. Tell him you are sequestering yourself and that you can't figure out who to ask because you don't know the others. I know he'll offer to help."

Ruari slowly nodded. "Okay. I'll find him. But Kean, when I'm done talking to Bray, can we meet in my room?"

"Sure. You want to talk some more?"

Ruari leaned in for another kiss, but this one was anything but soft. It was fiery, deep, and it left Kean wanting more.

"No. Talking is not what I had in mind."

BRAY WAS SO surprised when Ruari walked up to him that he dropped his phone. Luckily, it bounced on the grass without sustaining any damage, and he quickly picked it up again.

"Hi, Bray," Ruari said, and there was something in his voice that hadn't been there before, a friendliness and openness that had been absent so far.

"Hi," Bray said lamely, feeling like a blustering teenager on his first date. What was it about this omega that made him feel like he was back in high school?

"The time has come for me to sequester myself, in case you were wondering where I was the next week or so."

His heat was coming. Bray had to swallow at the thought, memories of their time together assaulting him. Maybe he'd romanticized it over time, but their first encounter had been almost magical. The single best sex of his life, though if he was honest, the sex with Kean had been damn spectacular as well. Maybe that was because he was a beta and that was new to Bray? He shook his head to clear his thoughts.

"H-have you found an alpha to help you?" he asked, then mentally slapped himself. That was absolutely none of his business, and he had no doubt Ruari would ream him out for even asking.

To his surprise, Ruari's shoulders dropped a little as he looked at the ground. "I don't know what to do. I want Kean to be there, but I don't know who to ask who would be okay with that. I need an alpha, Enar was crystal clear on that, but I don't want to exclude Kean."

Bray could barely breathe. Sex with Ruari and Kean at the same time? Being in a room with the two of them, naked, having permission to do everything dirty he wanted? That was like a dream come true. What alpha wouldn't go for that?

And yet, when he tried to imagine any of the single alphas on the ranch with those two, his mind not only blocked the image, but it sent a red-hot surge of anger through him. They didn't deserve them, none of them. No matter how honorable and good men like Adar and Isam were, they weren't good enough for him, nor for Kean. Bray knew what Kean liked, how the beta liked it rough and hard. And dammit, Ruari had been the same.

And god, watching them together in the hallway, that

kiss that had made him so hard he almost came on the spot, with Ruari's small hand grinding Kean's dick until he'd come in his pants. Bray had been so hard, so aroused, and so...*jealous?* He'd wanted in on the action, though that made zero sense.

But after watching that, his mind had kept imagining the two of them together, naked flesh slapping against naked flesh, Kean's sturdy frame against Ruari's much smaller one, Kean fucking Ruari again and again. Dammit, Bray's cock was throbbing in his shorts just thinking about it.

"I can do it," he heard himself say. "It may sound awkward and complicated, but Kean and I have a history, and we're a good match sexually. And so were you and I. We have our differences, I get that, but I respect your boundaries, and Kean would keep me in check. I would have no problem with him being there, would allow him to take care of you. I wouldn't be jealous like many other alphas, I guess is what I'm saying."

He stopped talking, abhorred by the speech that had fallen off his lips and convinced Ruari was about to laugh in his face. Instead, the omega canted his head and studied him. "You're serious about this? You're absolutely sure this wouldn't be a problem for you?"

Was he considering it? A rush of energy flowed through Bray. "Yes. One hundred percent serious. I would love to do this for you."

That sounded a little too altruistic. "It's not like it would be a hardship for me," he added. "Despite our differences, I loved being with Kean in the bedroom, and I had a wonderful time with you the first time. The idea of a repeat, but then with both of you with the same time, is really attractive."

He tried to word it as politely as he could while still

speaking the truth. He didn't know Ruari well enough to guess what the omega was used to or how much frankness he appreciated.

Ruari's mouth pulled up in a sly grin. "What you're saying is that the thought of the two of us naked makes you horny as fuck."

Well, that answered the question of what Ruari was used to, and considering he was hard as iron right now, Bray didn't see much use in denying it.

"Pretty much," Bray admitted, allowing himself to smile back since the omega didn't seem to have a problem with that concept. "Will you at least consider it?" Bray asked carefully.

"I don't need to. I would love to take you up on your offer."

Bray could barely prevent his mouth from dropping open. "You would? Are you sure?"

Ruari laughed. "Are you telling me there are reasons why I shouldn't? You should really take a course in sales techniques, Bray, because you suck at it."

He laughed back, because Ruari had a point. "I'm honored that you trust me with this, and I promise to make it a good experience for you."

Ruari reached out and put his hand on Bray's arm, sending a shock wave through him. "I know you will."

Bray swallowed. "What will you do with Jax?"

Ruari left his hand on Bray's arm as he answered. "He'll stay with me until my heat starts, and then Sven will take care of him until it's over, with Vieno as his back up."

Bray nodded. "You can trust those two to take care of him," he said. "They won't let anything happen to him."

Ruari's eyes seemed to soften as he squeezed Bray's arm before letting go. "I'm so grateful to have found a home on the ranch here. I don't know what I would've done if I hadn't made all these wonderful new friends."

It spoke volumes about how lonely the omega had been before coming to the ranch, Bray thought. He didn't know anything about Ruari's past, but this simple statement was so revealing.

"You know you can always talk to me, right?" he said, then jammed both of his hands in his pocket to hide how nervous and self-conscious he felt about even saying this. Of course, Ruari would not talk to him. Why would he? He had Kean, and he had new friends here on the ranch, friends who weren't the alpha-asshole who'd gotten him pregnant, he thought miserably.

Ruari took a long, hard look at him, then stepped in, reached up and pressed a soft kiss on Bray's cheek, leaving him trembling. Ruari shot him a last glance, then walked off.

"I'll send a message when my heat starts," he called out over his shoulder.

Bray stood there, watching the omega until he was out of his sight. Maybe he was making progress on that whole proving-to-be-worthy thing after all.

IT STILL FELT STRANGE, being without his son, Ruari thought. You would think that after two weeks on the ranch, he would be used to it, leaving Jax in Sven's capable hands, but it still felt weird. Especially now, when he was in his own room in the omega bunkhouse, not having Jax made him restless. He really had lost all sense of his previous life, when he was able to entertain himself, he thought wryly. Well, if everything went according to plan, the entertainment would soon show up, right?

Or maybe that restlessness was because of his coming heat, surely a plausible explanation as well. Not that he had much experience with it, considering this was only his third heat ever. Enar had said it could take anywhere between a few days to another two whole weeks, but not much longer. But he had warned this was the estimate for normal omegas after a pregnancy, not for gene carriers. They didn't have enough information for those yet.

He might not be in heat, but he was certainly looking forward to tonight. Not with the same crazy, desperate yearning he'd had during both his heats, but the thought of being with Kean didn't leave him unaffected; on the contrary, as he had taken a shower, he'd wondered how it would be between them. He had been with betas before his first heat, and it had been good. Not spectacular, but that was to be expected when he himself didn't have much experience yet and his partner hadn't either. It had been clumsy, adorable, and yet satisfying. But he had a sneaky suspicion his experience with Kean would be ten times better.

His body was perfect, he mused, all male and strong, yet somehow soft and cuddly at the same time. Whereas Bray made him feel weak, though in the best way, Kean made him feel protected.

He wondered how it would be, sex with both of them. It was almost too crazy to even consider, and yet here they were. Who would've ever thought he would find himself in a position where he would have not one, but two mates? And not any mates either, but both good, honorable, strong men.

He couldn't quite wrap his head around it, Bray especially. It was hard to reconcile, the deep knowledge that he was his mate while at the same time realizing he was far from perfect. Then again, the same could be said for Kean and for him, he realized. None of them were perfect, and they all made mistakes. Maybe the difference was that Bray's flaws had come to light earlier or in a more obvious way.

But it wasn't even Bray that Ruari was most worried about in their relationship, if he could even call it that yet when one of them wasn't even aware he was part of it. No, it was his father, his family, the biggest secret he was keeping from them. They needed to know. They deserved to know. He had to tell them, but selfishly, he didn't want to do it before his heat. He needed Bray and Kean both, and he wasn't risking the chance of them saying no after he told him about his father. After his heat, he'd tell them. After they'd had a chance to be together with the three of them, if only for a sexual encounter.

A knock on the front door interrupted his thoughts, and he jumped up from the bed he'd been lounging on. He checked through the peephole to make sure it was Kean, as he had been instructed, and his heart jumped up in his chest when he spotted him.

He smelled his shower gel as soon as he opened the door, the pine fragrance Kean always used that smelled like a forest, like freedom. Ruari stared at him for a few seconds before he gathered himself and let him in. He wasn't sure where Sando was, but it seemed they had the house to themselves for now, and he had every intention of making good use of that opportunity.

Kean closed the door behind them, and without saying a word, Ruari stepped in and offered his mouth. The kiss was slow, languid, a lazy, unhurried exploration. Ruari moaned a little into Kean's mouth, tingles dancing over his skin at the erotic dance their tongues did.

When his neck started to hurt, Kean lifted him effortlessly, and Ruari wrapped his legs around his waist, putting his head on the man's shoulder as he was carried to his bedroom. Kean lowered him on the bed, stretching out next to him, fusing their mouths together again.

It was magic they created, a song increasing in its intensity, every touch, every little moment, every slick move of Kean's tongue creating a new note.

"You're so beautiful," Kean whispered reverently, his hand slipping under Ruari's shirt, drawing slow circles on his stomach that made his skin break out in goosebumps.

He rolled on his back, pulling Ruari on top of him, and the omega loved being spread out on that sexy body. Kean's hands continued their journey on his back, gentle strokes, soft caresses, random patterns that set his skin on fire. He was meticulous, slow, and the best torture Ruari had ever endured.

The downside of his position was that it was hard to find Kean's naked skin, to touch him. So with regret, Ruari let go of his mouth, then slid down the man's body until he reached the hem of his shirt. He pulled it up with his teeth, which earned him a low moan from Kean, then found that smooth skin with his mouth.

He closed his eyes as he tasted, licked, savored. The pine fragrance was on his tongue now, mixing in with Kean's own smell and taste. He drew circles on his belly, pushing his shirt higher and higher as he made his way up.

"God, you have the perfect belly button," he said, admiring it with a soft feeling in his belly.

Kean chuckled, the vibration echoing through Ruari's body. "Thank you. I'm glad to hear it gets your seal of approval."

His laughter transformed into a grown as Ruari's tongue found the little valley. The man was sensitive there, Ruari discovered, which filled him with delight. He kissed it, sucked a little, then flat out tongued until Kean was squirming underneath him, his hands holding onto Ruari's head with quite the pressure. If he got this excited about Ruari's mouth on his belly button, Ruari wondered how he would feel when he sucked him off. Definitely something he wanted to try.

He took mercy on him and continued his journey north, only to discover that Kean's nipples were equally sensitive. Ruari scraped his teeth along the little bud, and Kean almost bucked him off.

"You're killing me," he moaned, but it didn't sound like a complaint.

Ruari smiled, then decided the other bud deserved equal treatment, and made Kean tremble all over again. Damn, the man was responsive, and Ruari was loving it. He didn't need to ask Kean to remove his shirt. When it was clear Ruari couldn't push it any further up, the beta rose up and pulled it off himself, then lowered back down again and pulled Ruari close.

"Give me a second to take something off as well," Ruari said with a laugh. "I want to feel your skin against mine."

Kean let him go, then watched with hungry eyes as Ruari took off more than just his shirt. Why bother with more interruptions when it was clear this was where they were headed?

"Ruari, baby, are you sure this is what you want?" Kean asked softly. "You know there's no pressure, right?"

Instead of answering him, Ruari kneeled and pulled off Kean's socks, his boots already on the floor where Kean had kicked them off before they had fallen on the bed. He unbuttoned Kean's shorts, when the beta's hands covered his.

"Ruari, baby, should we be doing this without Bray?"

Ruari had debated this long and hard with himself while

in the shower. Yes, he'd spent a long time there, enjoying the unbelievable luxury of a long, hot shower without having to worry his son would wake up. He didn't see why they would have to wait till Bray came to his senses. He and Kean were officially dating, everyone knew, they had permission, and dammit, he was dying to get back into it, the first time since his pregnancy.

Plus, Kean deserved it, didn't he, a one-on-one meeting with Ruari? He was such a sweetheart who'd been so kind and patient and perfect that he deserved to be treated special. Bray hadn't earned that yet, Ruari felt, no matter if they were mates or not. He'd get his turn when Ruari's heat started, but this round was between him and Bray.

He looked up, met Kean's concerned eyes that showed his struggle. The man was hard as iron and Ruari could smell his arousal, and yet he'd stopped him to make sure they were doing the right thing. "You love him," he said, filled with wonder. "You're in love with him."

One second of hesitation and then Kean nodded. "I am. He's had my heart from the moment I met him, and the fact that he didn't treat it with care doesn't change that."

"Oh, baby," Ruari said, his heart filling with the soft and fuzzies. He crawled on top of Kean again to hold him, letting his head rest on the man's chest. "Do you feel like this is cheating on him?" he asked when Kean's arms came around him and he let out a deep sigh.

"It doesn't make sense, right?" Kean said, frustration dripping from his voice. "I want you so much, and I can't believe we're here, together, about to make magic together... but I can't let that feeling go that we shouldn't."

"Can you explain it?"

"If we didn't know all three of us are mates, it would be different. But we do, and it feels like we're cheating on Bray, like we're excluding him. And it doesn't make sense at all, because he's not there yet and it could take a long time before he is, but as much as I want to be with you, I want him to be there as well. I don't want to have to tell him that we both knew and went behind his back."

Ruari wanted to argue with him, wanted to point out they didn't owe Bray anything when he was being a stubborn ass, but he knew Kean was right. It didn't make sense rationally, but until they were together, he and Kean couldn't do this.

"Well, this sucks," he said, rolling off Kean. "I was dying for a good pounding."

He pouted as Kean turned on his side to watch him. "Are you angry with me?" the beta asked.

"No. You're right. But can I say I admire your honor and hate you a little bit for it at the same time?"

Kean's lips pulled up in a smile. "I'm sorry?"

Ruari decided that if they weren't gonna have sex, they could at least snuggle and he scooted up the bed until he was nestled against Kean. "No, you're not. But it's okay. Let's snuggle for a bit, okay?"

Kean's arms around him tightened, pulling him closer until their bodies were melted together. "Snuggling is nice," the beta whispered.

Ruari closed his eyes, willing his body to calm down. "With you, it is."

21

Damn, he was tired. Knowing Ruari's heat was coming, Kean worked his ass off to make sure he'd be able to take two days off. Lars had been willing to take over for the basic stuff, like feeding the animals, milking, and gathering the eggs, but he didn't have time—or the skills—to do much more than that. Kean had made long days to make sure everything else was in tip-top shape. He'd gotten lucky the omega took longer than expected, so he'd checked off every item on his to-do list and felt confident Lars could manage. It had, however, reinforced his need for an assistant he could train.

It had also reinforced his need for more caffeine, which is why he was in the main kitchen for his sixth cup of the day. They each had a coffee machine in their bunkhouse, but it wasn't the same as the one in the main kitchen. Lidon had splurged there, and oh my god, it had been worth it. It was the single best coffee Kean had ever tasted, and he gladly walked over to the main kitchen a few times every day to get his fix. It wasn't like Lidon or anyone else minded. Lidon had made it crystal clear that the main house was accessible to everyone living on the ranch. Even if you lived in the bunkhouses, you could use the main kitchen at any time.

He really should cut back a little, he thought. That much caffeine wasn't healthy. But he'd needed it to keep his energy up when he worked fourteen-hour days. At least he'd be able to be there for Ruari and right now, nothing was more important than that.

God, he was infatuated with him. He could be sweet like Sven, but he was as strong as Vieno, if not stronger, and sassy as fuck. Kean loved it, loved that he was stubborn as hell and not afraid to get into a debate with Kean if he thought he was wrong.

And he was honorable. Even though his cock had cursed him for it, Kean stood by his decision to refrain from sex with Ruari until his heat, so their first time would be with Bray. Ruari had fully accepted Kean's viewpoint, hadn't tried to change his mind on that, and all they had done was snuggle—which had been the sweetest form of torture. And Kean hadn't wanted to jerk off, since he figured Ruari would need his stamina, so he was pretty sure that if Ruari's heat didn't start soon, his balls would explode.

"Nothing from Ruari yet?"

Bray's voice broke Kean out of his thoughts. He turned around, facing the alpha who looked at him with genuine concern.

"Shouldn't it have started by now? He told me it would be about a week," Bray said.

"I know. It's taking longer than he had expected, but Enar says that's normal for a first heat after a pregnancy."

Kean took a sip from his coffee, leaning against the kitchen counter.

"Oh, he's talked to Enar about this? That's good to know. I was getting worried."

Kean studied him, but everything in Bray's expression told him he was serious. Wasn't that something? He was genuinely concerned. Maybe the times were a-changing.

"Yeah, Enar went to check him yesterday. For obvious reasons, Ruari doesn't want to leave the bunkhouse anymore, so Enar went to him. He says everything is pointing toward his heat starting any day now."

Bray walked over to the counter and turned on the machine to make himself a cup of coffee.

"This coffee really is to die for," Bray said as if reading his mind from earlier.

Kean grinned. "Totally worth spending some time in the main house for."

As the coffee machine sprang to life, rattling and coughing as it produced a double espresso for Bray, they waited in companionable silence.

"He must be getting antsy by now," Bray said.

"He's stir-crazy," Kean confirmed.

The machine gave a last cough, and Bray shut it off and grabbed his coffee. To Kean's surprise, he didn't walk out of the kitchen, but leaned against the wall, opposite from him. They stared at each other for a bit, but it didn't feel weird, more like they were assessing each other, reconnecting, somehow.

"Are you okay with me helping Ruari?" Bray then asked.

When Kean didn't answer right away, mostly because he was surprised by Bray's thoughtfulness, the alpha added, "I promise I'll take good care of him. And of you. I'll do what I can to make it a positive experience for the both of you."

Now what did he say to that? It was not what Kean had expected Bray to say. At all. It burned inside him, this knowing that they were supposed to be together, that this was how it was supposed to be, Bray, Ruari, and him, but he couldn't say it. Bray would never believe him and they'd lose him. No, he had to wait until the alpha saw himself, until he was willing to see the truth.

"Thank you," he said simply. "I appreciate that more than I can say."

Bray took a sip of his coffee, his brown eyes never leaving Kean's. "This must be hard for you," he said.

"Why?"

"Because he's your boyfriend? Because I'm Jax's father? Because I'm an alpha and you're not?"

"I don't have a problem with the fact that you're an alpha and I'm not," Kean said.

Bray lowered his cup of coffee. "You don't?"

Kean frowned, not understanding. "Why would you think I want to be an alpha?"

"I'm sorry, I must've misunderstood."

Kean saw Bray close down, saw him pull up the mental barriers and walls the alpha used to keep others out.

"I am not upset or angry, Bray. I'm just curious why you would think that."

With an abrupt gesture, Bray emptied his coffee cup and put it on the table next to him. "Forget I said anything."

"Bray, please, don't walk away," Kean pleaded.

"If I explain my line of thinking, you'll get angry or upset with me again, and we'll fight all over again. I don't want that, especially not when Ruari's heat is about to start."

It had taken Kean a little while to figure out what was going on, but then it hit him. "I hurt you," he said slowly. "When I broke things off with you and I explained why, I hurt you much deeper than I had realized."

Bray, who was already halfway to the hallway, stopped. "I

don't understand why you would want to be with me in the first place if you hate me so much," he said without turning around.

He had missed this, Kean realized. He had not understood how deeply he had cut Bray, unintentionally, but still. His goal had been to give the alpha a wake-up call, but not to hurt him to the point where it affected his self-esteem, as it had clearly done.

That was something else he had misjudged, the alpha's self-confidence. He'd thought Bray was arrogant, thinking too highly of himself, but he had been wrong. How had he not seen it was a defense mechanism, a way to hide how insecure he was on the inside? His belly weakened as he reassessed the situation.

"I don't hate you, Bray. I never could. Quite the opposite, in fact."

That was as close as he could come without blurting out the truth. Bray turned around slowly. "You don't?"

There was a hope in his voice, and more than anything, that told Kean how wrong he had been about this man.

"No, I don't. I promise you, Bray, I don't hate you at all. I just wanted you to see some things, but I went about it the wrong way. I shouldn't have said it when I was still emotional myself, because breaking things off with you hurt."

"But you had Ruari," Bray said.

The man had no idea of the depths of Kean's feelings, he realized all over again. "I didn't have him at all at that point, but even if I did, it still would've hurt. It pained me to break things off with you, Bray. A lot. It wasn't what I wanted."

Bray stood there for a long time, but Kean waited patiently. Finally, the alpha took a seat at the kitchen table.

"I talked to my dad about this, about you and what you said."

Wow, that was not what Kean had expected him to say. The man was full of surprises today. "What did he say about it?"

"I think he agreed with you."

"You think?"

Bray let out a sigh, a long one. "I was pretty upset and emotional, so I'm not sure I understood everything correctly. But my recollection is that he shares your assessment that I'm an alpha-asshole."

The pain of those words hung in the air, and Kean's heart broke a little for this proud alpha. He took a spot opposite from him.

"We went about this wrong," he said quietly. "Or at least, I did. Because you hurt me, I confronted you with something in a way that made you hurt as well, and for that, I'm sorry."

"My remark about you not being able to give Ruari more kids was horrible," Bray said.

"It was," Kean agreed. "We both said things we shouldn't have."

Bray bit his lip, a gesture that was so uncharacteristic for the alpha that Kean wanted to tell him to stop. It made him uncomfortable, seeing Bray so insecure. Instead, he waited, giving Bray the time to formulate his thoughts.

"I don't understand what you're all trying to tell me," Bray said, avoiding his eyes. "But I want to. I don't like it, this idea that I'm seen as some arrogant asshole. I want to be a part of my son's life, Kean, and I want to be respected here on the ranch, within the pack. The idea that I'm not, that I'm just tolerated, it's..."

His voice cracked at the end, and the alpha closed his

eyes for a few seconds, before he opened them again, still studiously avoiding Kean's.

"What am I missing? What am I doing wrong that I am not the person I think I am? The person that I want to be, that I thought I was? Why is everyone else seeing someone I don't?"

If Kean acted on what he wanted to do most, he would walk right over to that big guy and hold him, try to take away some of the pain that hung so thick in the air. But he couldn't. Even though he knew Ruari would have no problem with it, Bray wouldn't understand. He would see it as cheating, and Kean knew the alpha had strict standards on that one.

"If you really want to know, if you really want to learn and are open to trying to see things from another perspective, I will help you. We will help you."

When Bray did lift his gaze to meet Kean's, his brown eyes looked suspiciously moist. "You will?"

Kean nodded. "Gladly. And I promise you I will have more patience with you, Bray. I was wrong to expect you to get it instantly. Let me try again, okay?"

"Thank you."

Bray's voice was barely above a whisper, and it was layered with emotions.

"It's my pleasure. And Bray, just so we're clear, I do like you. We like you. Everyone here on the ranch likes you. We may have issues with your attitude and behavior at times, but no one here hates you. I want you to know that."

If he'd had any doubts left about the depths of Bray's insecurity, the alpha's first reaction sealed it. "They don't?"

How was it possible that a man his size could look like a puppy that had just been kicked? Kean's heart filled with love.

He got up from the table, rinsed his coffee cup, and placed it in the dishwasher. When he turned around, Bray was still sitting at the table, following his every move with anxious eyes. Kean walked over, and before the alpha could react, he leaned in and kissed him softly on his cheek. He forced himself to leave it at that, though every fiber of his being was calling out for more.

"No, alpha, we really don't."

22

Palani sat down with Sando about once a week to stay up-to-date on his progress. Granted, that progress was slow, much slower than they had hoped. Sando was working his way through the boxes of medical records from Dr. Baig's patients that Kaila Kelley had unearthed for them, but so far nothing had stood out to him to further investigate. They had debated bringing in another genetics expert to help him, but had decided against it for security reasons. Instead, Lucan had offered to go through the medical records first to see if there was anything he thought was of interest.

The beta was not an expert, but he had a good head on his shoulders and Sando had taught him some things to look out for. When he walked into Sando's office in the clinic, Palani had no trouble distinguishing between Sando's notes and Lucan's. The first were illegible scribbles full of formulas and medical jargon. The latter were neatly written, some even color-coded. Palani decided he liked Lucan more and more every day.

The two of them were hard at work, two heads bowed

together, so concentrated they hadn't even noticed him walking in. Their elbows were touching, Palani noticed, and he smiled. Was there something going on between the two of them? Lucan hadn't approached him yet for permission, but maybe he would soon enough. Then again, he would have to either break things off with the alpha he was seeing —seeing being a euphemism for rather passionate encounters—or the three of them would have to find a match together.

Palani considered those three, decided they had potential, then shook his head. No, they would have to figure it out themselves. He was not getting involved. He was leading a pack, not moonlighting as a matchmaker.

"Hey boys," he said. "How are we doing? Any news?"

Two heads turned around at the same time, and Palani only had to see their expressions to ascertain that yes, they did have something to tell him. He found a seat, after carefully removing a stack of papers and handing them to Lucan, who accepted them with a smile.

"Talk to me," Palani said, leaning forward.

Sando looked at Lucan, and that simple gesture told Palani a lot about their relationship. He suppressed a smile, not wanting to alert them he was onto them.

"Do you want to tell him?" Sando asked shyly.

Lucan shook his head. "No. This is your show. I'm only assisting you."

Oh yes, Palani really did like him.

"Remember that I took blood from every gene carrier who volunteered for this research?" Sando started.

Palani nodded. Of course he did. His blog post had brought almost a hundred omegas out of the woodwork, almost all from the city where they lived. Not all of them had tested positive, but Sando had found seventy omegas willing to come in for regular tests so he could research the gene further.

"When comparing all the test results, I found something interesting, I guess would be the right word. Disturbing? I'm not sure."

Palani picked up on the omega's stress. What had he found that had him so worried? "What did you discover?" he asked.

Sando and Lucan exchanged another long look, with the beta nodding at him for encouragement.

"One of the omegas I tested was Sven. As we all know, he was adopted, and he doesn't know who his birth parents are. Enar tried to discover who they were, but Sven's adoption records were sealed at the request of his birth mother."

Palani's stomach swirled. Oh my god. Had Sando found Sven's biological family?

"He's a genetic match with another omega I tested," Sando said quietly. "And it's someone you know."

"Who?" Palani asked, his mind rapidly considering every option.

He didn't know that many omegas with the gene personally. There was Vieno, but that seems unlikely as they have grown up together. Was it Ruari? Or Sando himself? That seemed even more far-fetched, considering they weren't even sure who Sando's biological parents were. His father had been a beta, so either his other parent had been a mother, or he had been adopted, somehow. Still, a biological connection between him and Sven didn't seem logical. What other omega had he met?

Then it hit him. He hadn't met them, but he'd written about them. There was only one other option, and it fit with what he had learned about them, keeping things from their husbands.

"Sven is a McCain?" he asked softly.

Sando nodded, a look of relief on his face that Palani had figured it out himself. "The two moms you talked about, two of their sons volunteered for the research, Michael and Matthew McCain."

"Abby McCain's son's," Palani remembered.

"Yes. They're a partial genetic match to Sven, leading me to believe he's their cousin."

Palani tried to process that information. "Abby and Rosalind were two sisters who had married two brothers or cousins, I can't remember. That's why they both had the last name McCain, but they were sisters. The third McCain woman wasn't, she was their sister-in-law. Would that help you determine whose son Sven would be?"

"Yes. I saw that in the files, and that helped me determine that Sven is in all likelihood a son of Gillian McCain, their sister-in-law."

"Oh my god," Palani said. "She's the one who lost two sons, Colton and Adam."

He remembered their stories. Hell, how could he forget? They had been the ones who started the whole research into the gene. Colton had been a stripper, a former patient of Enar's, who had committed suicide caused by a major depression. And Adam, his younger brother, had shot himself after three alphas had sexually assaulted him at the nursing home where he worked, then proceeded to blame him for it. They had been the ones who had started it all. Palani couldn't believe there was a surviving brother after all, a surviving son.

"We need to tell him," he decided.

"Palani, don't forget that Sven is pregnant. Is this the right time to tell him?" Lucan spoke up.

Palani blew out a slow breath. "Good point. Let me think

about this. I could tell Grayson, but I'd hate to put him in a position where he has to hide something from his boys. Maybe I'd better ask Enar for advice here."

He considered that, then decided that was the best option. "But thank you for telling me, Sando. That's something I never even expected."

"Imagine the reaction of that woman," Lucan said softly. "She lost two sons and may be getting one son back. And not just that, but she'll be a grandmother. Isn't that something? After everything she has lost, to bring her a message of life?"

The beta sounded emotional, and Palani couldn't blame him. He was feeling it himself, and even though he had never met her, he couldn't wait to tell her the good news. But first, he and Enar had to decide whether this was the right time to tell Sven.

"That's not everything," Sando said. "We've had a breakthrough in the actual research as well."

Palani leaned forward again. "Tell me."

"As I told you, my father's last notes let me to believe that the alpha-beta-omega relationship was crucial to the shifting process. I wasn't able to prove that theory until Lidon had shifted. I compared the tests I did on the four of you before and after Hakon was born, and then again after Lidon had shifted a few times. There are definite changes in your genetic sequences. The scientific explanation would bore you to tears, or so Lucan assured me, but the gist of it is that the proteins in all four of your bodies have changed. Lidon's most of all, but Vieno is a close second, with you and Enar following behind. I'm now confident in stating that an alpha-beta-omega relationship is crucial to shifting, though I can't tell you exactly how. All I can say is that the four of you are influencing each other, and both your blood work and your genetic code shows it. Your codes have become more alike, and what's most amazing, is that one spot where gene carriers have a bit of DNA in common with the wolves, is now present in all four of you. It's like it's contagious, somehow, like Vieno is transferring it to the three of you."

Palani forced a deep breath into his lungs, which were tight with tension after that explanation. He didn't need Sando to explain to him what the results would be. All three of them were moving toward being able to shift. Not merely Lidon, but the three of them as his mates. The longer they stayed together, the more their codes would become similar and would ultimately allow them to shift as well. It was mind-boggling and amazing and terrifying at the same time.

"What about Hakon?" he asked. "What does his genetic makeup look like?"

The look on Sando's face was pure wonder. "This is where it gets really interesting," he said.

Palani couldn't suppress a laugh. "Oh, because what you just said was normal? Holy fuck, man, you told me I'll be able to turn into a wolf!"

It took a second for Sando to realize Palani wasn't actually upset with him, and then he smiled. "Okay, I get your point. Those results were in line with what I was expecting, but Hakon is where I was stunned. In a good way," he added quickly when he saw Palani freeze with worry.

"Spit it out," Lucan said, bumping Sando's shoulder with his own. "You're scaring the crap out of him."

"Right, right, sorry. Erm, my guess is that you all expected Hakon to be Lidon's son biologically, right? He is the alpha heir, after all."

Palani's head got light and dizzy. "He is Enar's son?" he asked, jumping to the only other option.

Sando slowly shook his head. "No. He's all of yours."

Palani blinked, then blinked again, still not following. "I don't understand. What do you mean, all of ours?"

"I compared his DNA to all of yours, and like you, I expected it to be a mix of Lidon and Vieno. It is, for the most part, but there is DNA of you and Enar in there as well. It shouldn't be possible, and I've never, ever seen this or even heard of this, but I've checked my results five times, and there's no denying the truth. He has about ten percent of your DNA and ten percent of Enar's. Don't ask me how, but it's there."

Palani tried to process it, tried to force his brain to make sense of it, but he couldn't. "How is this even possible? I'm a beta. We can't produce children with omegas."

"You couldn't," Sando corrected him. "Not in our modern genetic makeup. But something is changing in your bodies that is causing more than the shifting. Don't you remember what my father told you, that in the old days, betas were able to produce children with omegas?"

He was right. Oh my god, he was right. Melloni had mentioned that, the first time he and Enar had visited him. And the man had been all excited about their foursome that second time. Had he known this? Had he not only anticipated the shifting, but this as well?

He couldn't wrap his head around the consequences. It would mean...it would mean he could have a child of his own with Vieno. No, not of his own, because that was not how it worked anymore. But like Lidon had donated most of the parental DNA with Hakon, Palani might be able to do it for a second child, or maybe a third, after Enar. Time would tell, but the idea that he could have biological offspring, it was... No, he corrected himself. Hakon *was* his biologically speaking. Ten percent was still ten percent. That baby had his blood, his DNA in him. God, his head was a mess.

"I don't know what to say. My mind is blown. Can I tell the others about this?"

Sando nodded. "Of course. I would never ask you to keep secrets from your mates, but a word of caution. I have no idea how this works, or if it only works for the four of you because of Lidon's blood and heritage, or if it's applicable to others."

Palani considered that. "We can test the theory with Sven's baby," he said. "Grayson, Lars, and Sven are in a similar relationship, so when their baby is born, we can see if he shows mixed DNA."

"It's a lot to take in," Lucan said, and Palani realized that they were in a similar position. As a beta, Lucan always had the disadvantage of not being able to have kids with an omega, but this could change that. He would need an alpha to make the alpha-beta-omega connection complete, but then it could be possible. Man, this changed everything. It meant Lucan and Kean could be dads too. How amazing was that?

"One more thing," Lucan said. "We're dumping a lot on you, but this is important."

Palani chuckled. "More? Have mercy, man. My brain can't take much more."

"This is of a different caliber," Lucan assured him. "Remember that I helped Sando apply for some research grants? Well, one of them was granted."

"That's great news! How much?"

Grayson's initial grand had helped Sando get started, but they were nowhere near done yet, and the omega needed continuous funding to keep going with his crucial research. Now that the news about the gene was public, they had decided he might as well go public with his research grant requests.

"It's for a hundred grand," Lucan said. "And before you get all excited about it, I think you should check it out. I looked up the foundation behind the money, and my alarm bells are going off. They're an unknown, completely new, barely any presence on the internet. I think you should look into it before we accept."

Man, Palani thought, they really had chosen their pack well. Or the pack had chosen itself, he wasn't sure. But even that chance encounter with Lucan, meeting Lidon during an arrest of all things, had proven to be so crucial to their pack. He couldn't even imagine them functioning without Lucan, without Grayson and Bray. They were such an integral part of their pack, of their family. And now Lucan proved he had the smarts to look out for the pack first.

"Thank you," Palani said. "Send me the info and I'll look into it."

Both men nodded and Palani rose. "Thank you so much for your hard work, you especially, Sando. I am in awe of what you have discovered so far, and your father would be so proud of you."

It killed him not to be able to say anything about Watkins's findings, but they still hadn't heard back from him, and Palani was fearing the worst by now. Before Sando could even react or say anything, Lucan's hand came down on his shoulder, another telling gesture.

"You get back to your research, Sando," Palani said. "Lucan, walk me out, would you please?"

His eyes met Lucan's, and he was pretty sure the beta had an idea what this would be about. He nodded and followed Palani to the hallway of the clinic.

"I meant what I said in there," Palani said. "The two of you are doing phenomenal work, and we're not only proud, but super grateful. That being said, I trust you'll come find me if you need to ask my permission for anything."

Lucan blushed, a pretty red glow that stained his cheeks and made him even cuter than he already was. "We're not there yet. He needs closure about his father first."

Palani cocked his head, studied him. "I also trust that when the time is there, you will either end things with the alpha you've been seeing or bring the three of you together."

The blush on the beta's face intensified. "You heard?" he mumbled, shuffling his feet.

"Here's a tip, Lucan. There's very little happening in this pack without me being aware. For your sake, in the future, assume that whatever you're doing, I'm aware of it. That will save us both a lot of trouble, don't you agree?"

Lucan only nodded, and Palani smiled as he walked out. His guess was he would see the beta again soon, asking for permission to woo a certain omega. He almost rubbed his hands. Maybe he *should* consider a career as a matchmaker after all.

23

Bray was doing his daily security briefing with Palani, going over every bit of news they could think of. He appreciated the daily briefing, learning as much information as he gave himself. Between him and Palani, he doubted there was anything happening on the ranch they were unaware of. And fuck knew they had to stay on top of things with this new threat looming over their heads.

He was content with how the security updates were functioning. He'd spent a lot of time developing a new security system for the whole ranch, letting Palani and Lidon chime in every step of the way, as well as his men. It was an approach he wasn't used to, as he usually decided things on his own, but this job was more complex than anything he'd done so far.

Part of it was also because Palani kept insisting things work differently in a pack. Getting everyone's input was of crucial importance not just to get them to accept the final outcome, he'd explained to Bray, but also because different people offered different views and together, they were smarter.

Bray had thought that a little idealistic, until a few of the men he'd consulted had pointed out flaws in his plan that he hadn't thought of. After that, he'd come to appreciate the input of the different men, even if they had no security background. Palani being a prime example, though the beta had studied up, as he did with everything.

"The front gate guard house is fully operational as of this morning," he told Palani. "There will be two guards on duty there twenty-four/seven, but as agreed, they won't be pack."

Palani blew out a slow breath. "Yeah, Lidon still isn't happy with that, but I don't think we have much of a choice."

"I agree. It's why we built that guard house outside the gate, so we can stick to the pack rule of not letting strangers inside the gate."

"It's a huge risk for them, though. They're our first line of defense."

"Yeah, and they're aware. We've been open with them, Palani. They signed up for this, and they're getting paid extremely well."

"I know. I don't like it, but it's the best we can do. All the extra security measures are tested and operational as well?"

Bray nodded. He had re-tested them himself earlier that morning. "Yes. We've installed hidden cameras and motion detectors all along the driveway to the main gate, so no one should be able to sneak up on the guard house unnoticed. We've done the same along the outside perimeter."

They both pulled up the app on their phone, and Bray showed Palani the live feed from the different cameras and the status of the motion sensors. "They're infrared, so they also work at night," he assured him.

He was just about to tell Palani about the changes and the security system for the main house, when his alpha stirred. He froze, sensing something he had never felt before. *Ruari.* He could feel his yearning, his desperation. He needed Bray, but how was it possible that Bray could feel this?

His phone buzzed, yanking him out of his head. He didn't need to check it, knew what it was. Still, when he saw Kean's short text, calling him over to Omega One, his heart rate tripled in speed. This wasn't possible.

"I have to go," he told Palani.

"Ruari?"

Bray had informed the beta. He needed to know why his head of security would be absent for two days. "Yes. It's started."

"You sensed it before that text came in."

It wasn't a question, but Bray didn't want to get into this now. "I need to go," he repeated.

Palani's smile widened. "Have fun," he called after him as Bray hurried out.

He ran all the way to Omega One, punching the access code into the security pad as quickly as he could, his hands trembling. This was his chance to redeem himself a little. He'd better not mess this up.

Bray smelled him as soon as he opened the door, that same, rich aroma he remembered from their first time. He inhaled it deeply, allowed it to fill him and fire up his blood. Then he heard him, a desperate low moan that gutted him.

He stumbled into the omega's room, his hands already on his belt, unbuckling it while kicking off his boots. He didn't look up until he was naked, and the sight his eyes found made him stumble.

Kean was sitting on the bed, his back against the headboard, that beautiful, strong body of his on full display. Ruari kneeled between his legs, sucking Kean's cock like he was being graded on it. It was the single most beautiful sight Bray had ever seen.

"He's here, baby," Kean said, shooting a look of gratitude in Bray's direction.

He shifted on the bed, ready to hand Ruari off, but the omega wasn't having it. "No, need you first," he said, his voice thick.

Bray's heart softened, even though it might be a rejection of him. Kean had chosen well, it seemed, if Ruari was already this loyal to him, even in the throes of his heat. And god, the boy was beautiful now, his whole body flushed, radiating sex and want.

Ruari crawled up, found Kean's lips for a sloppy, wet kiss that made Bray ache to get in on the action, and then he sat back, holding Kean's cock with one hand as he lowered himself. He didn't stop until he was fully seated, making Kean's eyes cross.

Ruari rocked a little, as if to loosen himself, then started rising and falling. Kean let out a moan, and his hands were on Ruari's slender hips as the omega fucked himself on his cock, his head thrown back and his eyes closed, a litany of moans falling from those full lips.

"Bray," Kean gasped, and Ruari stopped for a few seconds to shoot him a desperate wave that he should join them, then continued pleasuring himself.

How could he refuse that invite if they thought of him even in a moment like that? Bray took position behind them, pushing Kean's legs wider to make room for him. His cock was leaking already, dying to get inside Ruari, but he would wait. He would make true what he had promised Kean, to make it a good experience for them both.

He remembered from his first time with Ruari that he'd been rock hard for two days solid, even after coming too many times to count. There was no need to get impatient. He would get his turn.

His hands covered Kean's on Ruari's hips, the beta jerking in surprise. Then Bray started helping, lifting Ruari up and helping him slam down. His reward was a chorus of moans, and Bray smiled. He inched closer toward Ruari, pulling the omega's body flush against his, trapping his own cock in Ruari's crack.

"Oh fuck, yes," Ruari moaned, letting Bray maneuver him. He lifted him slowly, then pushed him down with force, the omega's crack creating the perfect friction for his own cock, while his hole swallowed Kean's. They were a tangle of limbs, the three of them, their already sweaty bodies touching each other everywhere. The sounds alone were almost enough to make him come, flesh slapping against flesh, the endless stream of erotic sounds falling from Ruari's lips, those little grunts Kean made that used to spur Bray on to make him peak even higher.

Ruari came with a shout, spurting all over Kean's chest. Kean was seconds behind him, jerking as he climaxed, his cheeks flushing with the telltale proof of his orgasm. They were both stunning. For a second or two, Bray wondered why he was even there.

Then Ruari collapsed against his chest, panting, and Bray held his trembling body. The omega was still sitting on Kean's dick, which hadn't softened. That didn't surprise Bray at all. They would both stay hard until they crashed with exhaustion.

He nuzzled Ruari's neck, gently biting his earlobe. "You catch your breath, honey, while I get rid of my first load. We'll take good care of you, I promise."

His eyes met Kean's, and the intensity of the emotion in the beta's gaze floored him. He couldn't drag his eyes away as he rutted against Ruari, his cock finding the perfect slick friction in Ruari's crack, his own big, full balls rubbing against someone else's flesh. Kean's, probably, and wasn't that an erotic thought?

It only took half a minute, maybe, and all that time his eyes were locked with Kean's, something happening between them Bray couldn't explain. He came hard, depositing his cum all over Ruari's back and ass.

It was a short relief, his cock filling up again instantly, urging him to continue. He ran his palm over the smooth skin of Ruari's chest, playing with his nipples until the omega was squirming.

"Bray," Ruari pleaded, though for what, he probably wasn't even sure. He was lost to his heat now, Bray realized, consumed by that indescribable need to be filled.

"Bray," Ruari whimpered again. "Please, please fuck me. I need you."

Even as it rushed through him, this unbelievable sensation of being wanted and needed, his eyes found Kean's again. The beta held them for a second and then nodded his approval.

Bray lifted Ruari off Kean's dick and settled him down on his own without having to change position. As he had expected, the omega took him with ease, his hole already stretched out and slick from his first round with Kean. He clung to Bray, leaning back with his full weight.

"Alpha," he whispered, circling his hands backward

around Bray's neck and gyrating his hips to get even more of Bray's cock inside him. "My alpha."

Bray was a goner.

～

RUARI'S HEAD WAS FOGGY, buzzing with that feverish need, that desperate urge. They were hours in now, and how different it felt this time. He was safe, wanted. Loved.

Kean hadn't said the words, but Ruari knew the beta had fallen in love with him, and that feeling was completely mutual. It was crazy fast, but he loved him, and now, it was time to conquer his alpha's heart. But first, he needed something else from him. Bray was fucking him with slow, deep strokes, but it wasn't enough. "Harder, Bray. I'm not gonna break."

Bray snapped his hips, driving hard inside him, and Ruari's breath whooshed out of his lungs. "Are you gonna start giving me orders again?" Bray said, laughter audible in his voice.

"If you don't fucking give me what I need, I sure will," Ruari promised him, his last word turning into a moan as Bray repeated his move.

Bray's hands gripped him tight as the alpha made them change position, dropping Ruari on his hands and knees, then yanking him backward on his cock.

"God, yes, like that!" Ruari encouraged him.

"As you wish," Bray growled near his ear, then slammed in hard, and again, picking up speed until all Ruari felt was that pressure inside him that built and built and built. Bray curled over him, his teeth sinking into Ruari's shoulder as he fucked every breath right out of his lungs until he was gasping, rattling, dying for that last push, that last...

With one massive last shove, Bray came, shooting his hot load inside him, and Ruari teared up, knowing what was to come, knowing this time would be different. Bray lowered them on their sides, spooning him, lifting Ruari's leg over his so he could push in deep.

With effort, he turned his head and found Kean sitting on the bed, watching him with loving eyes.

"Kean," he whimpered.

"He's gonna knot you, baby," Kean soothed him. "It's gonna feel so good."

"I need you too." He couldn't explain it, this deep need to feel them both, to touch Kean and know he was near.

"I'm right here, baby, I promise."

Inside him, it tingled with want, with need, and then Bray's cock started to swell, and Ruari was losing his mind. He could feel Bray's sweaty chest against his back, the alpha's heartbeat racing in a similar rhythm to his own, and that cock kept growing and swelling, filling that place inside like nothing else ever could.

He reached out for Kean because he needed him, too, needed to hold on to his sturdy body because otherwise he would shatter with the sheer pleasure of it. Kean stretched out in front of him and Ruari pulled his hand to indicate he should move in closer. And as Bray's knot widened, his mouth found Kean's. Finally.

His climax raced down his spine, his balls aching to come. He didn't realize he was crying until Kean's mouth moved from his lips to his cheeks, licking his tears away. "You're so beautiful, baby," he said.

Bray's knot completed and Ruari came with a soft cry, his cheek against Kean's. His brain turned to absolute mush, but he held on to Kean, the beta whispering words he couldn't even understand until he calmed down, until that frantic ecstasy waned off.

"How long will it take?" he heard Kean ask Bray.

"I don't know, but Enar said it could take over half an hour the first time," Bray said, his low baritone rumbling in his chest that still pressed against Ruari's back.

"You asked Enar?" Kean asked, and though Ruari's brain was slow as shit, he'd come to the same conclusion.

"I wanted to prepare myself this time, to make sure I'd be able to take care of him," Bray said softly. "With you," he added, and Ruari's heart tripped and fell.

He closed his eyes, too tired to stay awake, and he allowed himself to drift off.

When he woke up, Bray was no longer inside him, and his hole ached with emptiness. He stretched out, then opened his eyes and found Bray balls deep inside Kean, fucking him with feral intensity. Kean was flat on his stomach on the bed, legs spread wide, with Bray on top of him, his bigger body blanketing him. The alpha had his arm wrapped around Kean's neck, holding him in a tight grip, as his hips rolled and flexed in a rhythm that made the bed shake.

God, they were beautiful together, all power and male, smooth skin and strong muscles, grunts and labored breaths as their bodies joined in a brutal fashion. Kean took one hell of a pounding, Ruari thought, but considering the beta pushed back and took everything the alpha dished out, he was loving the fuck out of it.

"Ungh!" Bray grunted low and deep, and his body spasmed.

He dropped on top of Kean before rolling them both over on their sides. Kean's ass turned toward him, and Ruari could see the cum starting to drizzle out. What a waste, he thought, and before he realized it, he was on his knees behind him and dug in. He moaned when the rich taste of Bray's cum hit his mouth, impatiently yanking Kean back when he clenched his ass in shock.

"Ruari," the beta grunted, the surprise easy to hear. Then, "Oh god, Ruari..."

He loved rimming, always had, but nothing had ever tasted as good as this. Kean's hole was still fluttering from the pounding he'd took, and Ruari stuck his tongue in deep, licking and sucking until he'd taken every last drop.

He wanted more of that taste, more of Bray, so he crawled over Kean to find Bray's cock, smacking his lips when he found it. He licked the purple head, smiling as it quivered, then looked at Bray from under his lashes. The look Bray gave him made his stomach dance, the alpha's eyes smoldering as he watched Ruari lick his cock clean.

He was about to start begging for something, someone to fill the emptiness inside him, when he felt Kean move in behind him. "Can I..." he asked.

"You'd fucking better," Ruari said, before he took Bray in his mouth again.

He deep-throated him until his eyes watered. God, why did that feel so good? It was demeaning and yet he loved that sensation of being used, though Bray was more passive than he'd like him to be.

Thank fuck Kean wasn't, who merely chuckled as he slid in with a firm push, shoving Ruari down deeper on Bray's cock. It made him gag, but he fucking loved it. Why did everything feel differently during his heat? God, the things he wanted to try.

Kean's hands found his nipples, then pinched. The dirtiest sound left Ruari's lips. "That's..." he groaned.

"Yeah?" Kean asked.

"Hell, yeah."

He'd better keep his teeth away from Bray's dick, he thought, and he took him in again, gagging and moaning at the same time when Kean slammed in while pinching his other nipple. He wanted to buck, but had nowhere to go, since two pairs of hands now held him, Bray's on his head and Kean's on his hips.

Kean roasted him, fucking him fast and deep and pushing him onto Bray's cock until Ruari went light headed from barely getting oxygen. The beta stopped long enough for him to catch a breath, and then he was at it again. Ruari's ears buzzed, his senses overloading with his mouth full of Bray and his hole full of Kean.

Bray thrust in his mouth now with shallow, rapid thrusts that showed he was about to come again, and Kean seemed to keep pace with him, doing the same on the other end. It was filthy and perfect and exactly what Ruari needed and when both came at the same time, all he could think of was that he had hours more of this. It was fucking heaven.

RUARI LIKED A LITTLE PAIN, Kean concluded. And boy, was he a horny little shit during his heat. Kean loved it, loved how the omega was unafraid to take initiative and tell them exactly what he wanted. Right now, Bray was knotting him again, gently rocking Ruari on his dick, the omega half asleep.

He stole a glance at the clock. Twenty-four hours in, and not a sign he was slowing down. Then again, neither were he and Bray. He could feel it rush through his blood, the push of Ruari's heat, the drive to take care of him. It made his cock grow hard again and again, no matter how often he'd come.

"Are you okay?" Bray asked, interrupting his thoughts.

The question was so uncharacteristic for the alpha that Kean frowned. "Why wouldn't I be?"

"I wanted to make sure you didn't feel left out," Bray said, and Kean was floored that he cared.

Was Bray changing? He'd seen more tenderness from him than ever before. It made hope spring up in his heart.

"I'm good," he assured him, then said, "You're taking great care of him." He nodded at Ruari, who was deep asleep now, with Bray balls deep inside him.

"He's a firecracker in bed," Bray said, sounding surprised.

"I thought you'd know that from before," Kean commented.

Bray looked sheepish. "I may not have given him as much opportunity to voice his wants and needs back then."

Of course he hadn't. Kean suppressed a smile, because it was so classic Bray.

"What else does he like?" Bray then asked.

"How would I know?" Kean answered.

Bray looked puzzled. "I assumed you'd had slept together, before... No?"

"You know what they say about assuming."

Bray's eyebrows rose high. "Really?"

"Why does that surprise you so much?"

Bray scratched his chin. "I guess because I know you like sex, and Ruari was certainly into it our first time, so I guess I thought you'd be eager?"

Kean smiled. "Ruari wanted to wait until his heat," he answered.

Bray's frown was replaced by a much deeper look. "So

this was your first time? You had your first time in front of me?"

There were a lot of things Kean could say, but he held them all in. Ruari and he had agreed that they needed to let Bray set the pace. No pushing, no answering questions he wasn't asking.

"Yes, we did. And it was wonderful, as you saw."

"Huh," Bray said, and then he was quiet for a long time.

Kean closed his eyes, dozing off while he could to regain some strength. Just before he fell asleep, he heard Bray whisper, "Thank you for asking me."

24

A week after Ruari's heat, Bray still hadn't figured out what it all meant. It hadn't been mere sex. As much as Bray had tried to assure himself right after that it had been only sex, that notion was ridiculous. There was something much more, something far deeper going on than sex—though the sex had been phenomenal. Hell, he only had to think about it to get hard all over again.

But what did it mean? Ruari and Kean had made him feel part of it, not like they were a unit, a couple with him as a guest, but like an equal partner. But that was ridiculous because they were together and he wasn't part of that. Right?

But you want to be, his alpha told him. And Bray was right back where he'd been all week, trying to answer that question. Why couldn't he stop thinking about Kean and Ruari? As much as he wanted to convince himself he only wanted those two for the sex, he knew it was bullshit. With Ruari, he could tell himself it was because of Jax, because they shared a bond because of him, but that excuse sounded weak, even to his own ears. And Kean, that was the part he struggled with most.

He could've understood if it had been only Ruari he wanted, if his thoughts had been focused on the omega. Granted, he didn't fit the picture Bray had of his future partner, but he could adapt. They already had a child together, so that was a good start for a family, right?

But why the hell was his mind as fixated on Kean as it was on Ruari? Why did his stomach go all weak and mushy when he thought about how sweet and caring Kean had been with Ruari, how he had selflessly focused on him, putting the omega's pleasure first? Did he have feelings for Kean? Was that why he'd been angry when the beta had broken things off with him? He'd thought it was because his pride was wounded, because he'd been pushed aside—for an omega.

He didn't do *feelings*, or at least, he never had. Clearly, that had changed because fuck knew he had plenty of feelings now. Messed up feelings, complicated feelings, feelings he couldn't figure out, but they were there all right. Maybe he should talk to them, bring things out in the open?

He considered that as he did his morning rounds, checking in with all of his guys along the perimeter and making sure all systems were working as they should. It was scary as fuck, putting himself out there like that, admitting he wasn't sure what was going on. He hated not having the answers, but admitting that had to beat trying to figure it out on his own, because clearly, he sucked at that.

He was checking in with Adar on the south perimeter, close to the cottage where Urien had lived with his daughter, when his alpha stirred. At first, it was an uneasy feeling, the tiniest of tingles down his spine, but when it persisted, he checked in with Adar. "Are you feeling it too?" he asked.

Adar nodded. "My alpha is uneasy. What's going on?"

"I don't know, but we're going to find out. Check in with the main gate."

While Adar raised the main gate on his phone, Bray pulled up his and checked for any breaches of their security system. Everything looked green, and yet something told him they had a problem. He couldn't explain it, but after everything they had been through, he trusted his instincts enough to take it seriously.

He called Palani, who picked up almost right away. "Code orange," Bray said. "I don't know what's going on, but something is wrong. I'll get back to you with more details as soon as I can."

"On it," Palani said, and Bray was grateful that the beta trusted his assessment without questioning it.

They had practiced this enough times that Bray trusted the system to work. Before he could say anything else, his phone dinged, proof that Palani had put everyone on a code orange, as requested. Okay, now he needed to find out what was causing his alpha to be uneasy.

Seconds later, his phone beeped, and so did Adar's. Bray's adrenaline spiked and his stomach dropped. The motion sensors near the main gate were going off. He pulled up the camera feed and started shouting as soon as he saw figures moving on the live feed. At least five men, dressed in black. Armed.

"Code red, code red!" Bray called out to Palani, who was still on the line. "Lock down the main house! We're on our way."

Angry signals from his phone told him there were more breaches of their motion sensors, then Palani's code red came through, which should alert everyone.

"Bray, main gate is reporting gunfire!" Adar shouted. "They're not sure how long they can hold them off!"

This was it. This was what he had trained his men for, what they had prepared for. He hoped and prayed the drills and training he'd done with the pack would prove to be enough.

Bray grabbed his gun, taking the safety off. He didn't have to tell Adar what to do, both breaking out into a mad run toward the main house. That was the strategy they had decided on, he, his men, Palani and Lidon. If there was a code orange or red, everyone but Bray's men would hunker down in the main house, which was the easiest to defend. They might lose some of the other buildings, but they wouldn't lose people, and that was what mattered most.

As they ran, Bray scanned his surroundings and saw everyone running to the main house. Thank fuck the clinic was closed today, so they wouldn't have to worry about pregnant omegas getting to safety. He was most worried for Lars and Kean, whose workplace was farthest on the edge of the property. He couldn't remember if he'd seen Lars that morning, what field the guy was working on. He hoped he'd been close to the main house. And Kean, he'd seen him an hour ago, and he'd been in one of the far fields with the cows. What if he couldn't make it back to the house on time? He couldn't think about that now, not when he needed his head in the game.

He heard the gunfire when he had almost reached the main house, and he and Adar looked at each other with horror. *Oh god.*

"Do a headcount," Bray ordered Adar. "Inform me if anyone is missing. I'm heading to the main gate."

He was already running again when Adar called after him, "Be careful!"

He lifted his hand in acknowledgment but never broke pace. By the time he'd reached the main gate, the gunfire had stopped. His breath caught in his lungs when he saw the main gate was open. Oh fuck, this was not good. Not good at all. How many attackers had come in this way?

Seconds later, a gunshot rang out, sending fragments of asphalt flying into his body. It was close, too close. Should he keep running or to take cover?

He couldn't take cover, not here out in the open. Instead, he kept running but with irregular zig-zag movements so he would at least create a harder target. That decision turned out to be wise, as another shot rang out, again inches from hitting him. Dammit all to hell, who was shooting at him? Focus, he told himself. Stay alive.

He increased his speed and sprinted until he reached the guard house, which was quiet, too quiet. He didn't go in, but took position behind it first, scanning his surroundings. There were trees and bushes here, but not a lot, so it wouldn't be easy for attackers to hide.

At first, he didn't see anything or anyone, but after a few seconds, something rustled up high in the tree maybe thirty, forty feet away from him. He did a quick assessment and concluded the shot that had almost hit him had come from that direction. It made sense for the attackers to leave a sniper here to take out any men who would come to check in on the main gate—like him. Anyone hiding up in a tree right now was not one of his men, he reasoned. If they had been, they would've made themselves known to him.

He mentally cursed himself for not having a rifle while raising his gun and scanning the tree until he found what had caused the rustling sound. Not a professional sniper, then. The guy made way too much noise. He didn't hesitate but fired at the dark shadow in the tree. A muffled cry sounded and then a loud curse. Good. It meant he'd hit his target.

"Show yourself," he called out. "Or the next bullet will be in your brain."

Sure, that was a bluff since he could only see the shape in the shade and thick leaves of the tree, but he'd fire his gun into the damn tree until the clip was empty. He'd be sure to hit something vital, right?

Another curse, then a voice called out. "Don't shoot. I'm coming down."

Bray kept scanning his surroundings, not convinced he was dealing with only one shooter. He hadn't heard anything else, and his phone had stayed silent, but you never knew.

Wait.

His phone had stayed silent. He'd asked Adar to inform him when his head count was completed. Either he'd missed a notification, or Adar hadn't messaged him, and the latter meant that he hadn't had the opportunity, which meant shit was going down at the main house. Bray's stomach revolted at that thought. That was where the omegas were, where Ruari was and Vieno, Sven, the babies. Oh hell, the babies. His son was there. How many attackers were there? Would they be able to fight them off? It all depended now on whether the pack would be able to take a stand as they had practiced.

As he watched a man in black fatigues carefully climb and slide down the tree, favoring his right leg, Bray realized with a sickening clarity that the stakes had been raised far higher than before. There were babies in the house, and not just any babies. That was his *son*. Someone was attacking his son.

His vision went red, and he was on the guy before he

even reached the ground, pinning him against the tree with a smack that rattled the guy's teeth. Bray's gun pressed against his neck.

"Who the fuck are you, how many of you are there, and what's the objective?" he snapped.

When the guy didn't answer immediately, Bray grabbed his throat with his left hand. "Listen, fucker, I am not joking around here. I don't have time for games. Either you answer me, or I shoot. What's it going to be?"

He increased the pressure on the guy's throat with his hand, and apparently that was enough of a signal he meant business, because the guy started talking. Fast.

"The baby," he said, his voice quivering with fear. "We're after the baby."

His son? They were after Bray's son? His blood ran cold. "What do you want with him?"

"I don't know," the guy said, his voice almost whining. "They told us to grab the alpha's baby and get out."

It only took a second before the truth hit. It wasn't his son they were after, but Hakon. They were after Lidon's alpha heir.

"How many?"

"Twenty."

Bray pushed down the panic that rose up. Twenty? How the hell would they manage to fight all of them off? They'd counted on ten at the most.

He had so many questions for the guy, but they would have to wait until he was sure the threat was neutralized. He didn't hesitate but found the guy's carotid and pressed until he passed out, sagging against the tree. Bray would've loved to tie him down, but he had nothing to use and he wasn't wasting anymore time. If the main house was under attack, they needed him.

He took a moment to check his phone, and when he saw Adar hadn't texted, sent out an alert to all his guards to defend the main house. He sent up a quick prayer that Kean, Ruari, and Jax would be safe. God, he'd die before he let anyone hurt them.

The gunfire started just as he broke into a dead run.

KEAN WAS on his way back from checking on the cows when his phone beeped. He recognized the tone from the drills they had done. Code orange. That meant something was wrong, and they had to convene at the main house. After a moment of shock, Kean started running, which wasn't easy considering his heavy-duty work boots weren't made for sprinting.

This was it. This was the attack they had been fearing. What were they up against?

At least he was certain Ruari was in the main house. Now that his heat had passed, the omega spent his entire day there, hanging out with Vieno and Sven, helping wherever he could. He still slept in Omega One, but he only went there at night. That meant he had to be there right now, so at least Kean wouldn't have to worry about him.

Now Bray, that was a whole different matter. Kean's stomach clenched at the thought that the alpha would be in the thick of it, whatever was going on. It took his breath away, and he willed it down, knowing he couldn't afford to waste energy while making it to safety.

His phone beeped again, and his adrenaline spiked. Code red. Something serious was going down, and he increased his speed, his feet already hurting and his breathing labored. He caught up with Jawon, Ori, and

Servas as they closed in on the main house. When they turned the corner, they almost ran into four guys, dressed head to toe in black. Their leader let out a loud curse even as his men reached for their guns.

Oh god, this was not good. Kean didn't think, but jumped on the guy closest to him, wanting to incapacitate him before the guy had pulled his weapon. He managed to knock him down flat on his back with such force that the man was gasping for breath. One of the advantages of being on the heavier side for a beta, Kean thought, even as he rolled his full weight onto the guy's chest and tried to kick away the gun.

He got an elbow to his midriff, which hurt like a mother-fucker, then a knee to his thigh, which wasn't pleasant either. God, how he wished he had taken some kind of martial arts training. He rolled away to avoid the punches, getting a good kick in that hit the guy in his knee. His boots sure came in handy now. He couldn't look away, too scared to take his eyes off his opponent, but the surrounding sounds were all of fights. Fists meeting flesh, grunts, boots hitting, cries of pain.

Gunshots rang out from elsewhere, and Kean's heart stopped. That distraction cost him. He doubled over when the guy hit him full-on in his stomach, and even as he real-ized he needed to keep moving, another first to his cheek sent him flying. He crawled back up, determined not to give up just yet.

"Everybody freeze!" a voice called out. "You have three seconds to disengage, or I will shoot."

Kean didn't have to look to know it wasn't one of Bray's men. He didn't recognize the voice so that said enough.

"We can do this the hard way or the easy way, but no

matter what you guys will do, we will win. We will overtake this house."

If the man had stopped talking after his first warning, Kean might have obeyed, simply because he had no desire to get shot. But now that the guy had stated his objective, all bets were off. There was no way he would let him into the main house without a fight, not when the most vulnerable people were there. He would die to defend Ruari, Jax, Hakon.

"No," Jawon said, apparently feeling the same thing. "We will not give up this fight."

Kean pushed himself to his feet, standing up wobbly, but determined to fight. Before he could open his mouth to voice his agreement with Jawon's words, the man who had been speaking calmly turned around, pointed his gun at Jawon, and fired.

Kean screamed in horror, as did Servas and Ori. Oh my god, he had *shot* him. He had point-blank shot Jawon. Who the hell were these men? With a sickening clarity, Kean realized they meant business and whatever goal they had, it wouldn't be good.

Something rushed through him, a deep sense of justice, of pride, of being scared to death yet knowing this was when he had to take a stand. So he did, spreading his legs and inhaling as deeply as he could, despite the pain in his body. They couldn't give up, not when people's lives were at stake. Not when inside, two babies depended on their abilities to defend them.

He felt it again, that power, and he pulled it in, using it to feed his resolve, then pushed it back out. He didn't know how, only that he could and that he should. They were one, this pack. They would not surrender.

He took another deep breath, feeling his body grow

stronger. Then a massive wave of power rolled through him, and he knew what had happened. From the corner of his eye, he caught Ori and Servas jerking as well. Jawon was on the ground, still moving. Kean had no idea how bad he was. But they would win. These guys had no idea what was about to happen, but Kean did.

When the howl came, so loud that it made his ears hurt, he threw his head back and much to his own shock, joined in. All around him, howls sounded, from inside and outside the house.

And then, as one voice, they shouted. "Protect the pack! For Hakon!"

Kean's body jerked again, his skin breaking out in goose-bumps, his hair on end, his muscles itching and shaking. And then he appeared, behind them, but Kean didn't have to look. The pure horror on the faces of the four men attacking them told him everything. That humongous gray wolf rushed right past Kean, growling with a deafening noise before he attacked.

The assailants scrambled for their guns, which they had lost in fighting off Kean and the others. As the first shot rang out, Kean dove for the ground, where he encountered the guy had been wrestling with. He was done with this shit, Kean decided. The guy's eyes were glued to Lidon, who was ripping his teammate to shreds, a sight that was almost too satisfying to look away from, but Kean made good use of the distraction.

He pulled back his arm and drove his first straight into the guy's jaw, then did it again for good measure. When the guy stopped moving, he gave him a last kick to make sure he wouldn't get up anytime soon. The gunshots had stopped now, two of the men who had attacked them dead already, while the bastard who had shot Jawon tried to get away. The wolf went for his throat as he ran, and it was over in seconds.

On a rational level, Kean knew the sight of that gray wolf should terrify him, especially after what he had witnessed it was capable of, its muzzle still smeared with blood and other things Kean didn't want to think about too much. But he wasn't scared of the wolf. It was his brother, his master, his *Alpha*.

As the wolf, Lidon, howled in victory, Kean joined in.

Vieno woke up from his nap when his phone beeped. He frowned, irritated that Palani made him carry his phone with him at all times, even when napping. Who the hell was texting him now?

Then it hit him. His phone was on silent, meaning it hadn't been a text. The only alerts that got through the do-not-disturb mode were safety alerts. He shot up to a sitting position in bed, his adrenaline spiking as he scrambled for his phone on the nightstand.

Code orange. His heart raced. It was happening. Something was wrong or Palani never would've given permission to send that alert. Vieno was out of his bed in a second, grateful he had gone to bed with his clothes on. What was he supposed to do now? He shook his head, trying to clear the last remnants of sleep. Hakon and Jax were asleep in the crib. Should he wake them?

He closed his eyes and took a deep breath, willing himself to calm down and think. They had gone over this ad nauseam. His instructions were clear. He was to take the baby and make his way down to the basement, where he had hidden before during the previous attack. But that was with one baby. How was he supposed to carry two?

The door opened and Ruari came flying in. "Is he okay?" the omega asked, gasping for breath.

"Yes, they're still asleep. We need to go, now."

Ruari nodded, and they both hurried into the baby room. There was no time for slings or carriers, Vieno decided. Time was of the essence here. He wasn't sure what was going down, but a code orange was bad news. He held Hakon tightly against his chest and gestured for Ruari to follow him.

His phone beeped again. *Code red.*

Oh god.

This was the real thing. They were under attack. Even as he thought it, he felt his mates, felt the fear in all three of them. He pushed it down. Hakon was depending on him, and he would not fail his son. Or his mates.

Before he entered the hallway, he looked to the left and right, as Bray had taught him. When it appeared clear, he stepped out of the bedroom, Ruari on his heels. They had rounded the corner, on their way to the door that led to the basement, when gunshots rang out. The front door burst open with a kick, angry footsteps coming in. Sick with fear, Vieno turned and saw Grayson running in the direction of the door, growling with fury.

The back door was kicked in, the smashing sounds unmistakable. They wouldn't make it to the basement, Vieno realized, even as sounds of fighting ensued. Another gunshot, much, much closer. They had to find a place to hide.

Jax stirred in Ruari's arms, and before Ruari could do anything, the baby let out a little cry. It didn't last long, but it echoed in the empty hallway, and Vieno froze in his spot.

"Find that baby," a voice snapped, way too close to them.

Vieno opened the first door he saw, Grayson's room, and went inside, Ruari quickly following him. They heard it at the same time and looked at each other in shock. The shower was running, meaning someone was in the bathroom.

The bathroom, Vieno thought. It wasn't perfect, but at least they could lock it from the inside. It was better than nothing, and with the men already in the house, their chances of reaching the basement were zero. Ruari apparently had the same thought, and they hurried to the bathroom at the same time.

The water shut off as they closed the door behind them and turned the lock. "Is that you, Daddy?" Sven's voice called out.

"Hush," Vieno whispered urgently.

Sven pulled back the shower curtain with force, looking shocked when he saw Ruari and Vieno standing there. "What...?"

"Be quiet," Vieno whispered. "Please. There's a code red."

Sven paled, but to his credit, stayed calm. He gestured at Vieno to hand him a towel, and as they stood, listening with bated breath, he toweled himself off. He was still naked, though, Vieno thought. Not that it mattered, but if they had to get out of here, having clothes would help. But Sven solved that problem, tiptoeing to the laundry basket in the corner and grabbing some random clothes. The shirt obviously didn't belong to him as it was way too big, even with his baby bump, but the shorts did, and at least he was dressed.

He stood next to them, linked arms with them, the three of them hugging each other as they waited. Jax had fallen back asleep, and Hakon had never woken up, and all Vieno could do was pray that it would stay that way. If the baby started crying... He swallowed, pushing down his fear. His son needed him right now. There was no time to freak out.

Then he heard it. They all did. More gunshots, outside. Sven's grip on him tightened, and they huddled even closer together, joined in their fear. What was going on? Oh god, please, let Bray and his men be strong enough to fight off this attack. Please let his mates be safe.

There was shouting. Running footsteps in the hallway. Then they were hit with a wave of power so strong it made Vieno's teeth chatter. Lidon had shifted. There was no other explanation for that power surge. And it was comforting, knowing that his mate, his alpha, was out there defending him, defending them, but he was scared, so scared. Was one wolf strong enough to defend them all?

Another power surge, equally big. What was that? Howling that made goosebumps break out all over his skin. Sounds of a struggle coming from inside. Grayson's angry snarls, joined in by others. Vieno recognized Isam, Adar. Were they winning? He listened with all his might, trying to make out what was going on.

The door to the bedroom opened, the soft creak giving it away. Vieno's heart rate tripled in speed. He resisted the urge to press Hakon even closer to his chest, not wanting to disturb the baby. Footsteps sounded in the room, slow, as if someone was methodically checking it. Vieno knew what was coming. There was no way whoever was in that room would not check the bathroom. Still, he almost jumped out of his skin when someone tried the door and found it locked.

"Someone is in here," a voice said, followed by a crackle. They had a com system, Vieno realized. Not one of Bray's men, then, not that he'd had any hope it would be. It was only a matter of time before they would force their way into the bathroom, and the three of them were pretty much helpless. How could three omegas defend two babies?

Despair tried to force its way into his system, but he pushed it back. He couldn't give up now. There had to be a way.

He looked around for a way to escape, but there was nothing. Sure, the bathroom had a window, but it was too small for them to fit through. Anything to defend themselves with? Again, he looked around but came up short. There was nothing in that bathroom, except for them. And how could three tiny omegas fight off attackers?

He was almost ready to give up when it hit him. During the first attack, when Grayson had told him to do something, Vieno had refused. Not only that, he had been able to somehow tap into Lidon's powers and use alpha compulsion on Grayson. He had never done it since, but he hadn't tried either. There had been no need, but what if he could do it? He'd tapped into Lidon's powers during the delivery, hadn't he?

He forced down all thoughts it wasn't possible and nudged Sven. "I need you to take Hakon," he whispered almost soundlessly.

It was the hardest thing he had ever done, to hand over his son when he wanted to hold him and protect him the most, but he had to.

Sven nodded and held out his hands to take the baby, cradling Hakon as soon as he received him. "I'll defend him with my life," he whispered back, and for that, Vieno leaned in and pressed a soft kiss on Sven's lips.

He stepped away, taking a spot as far from them as possible. He closed his eyes and with his mind, tried to find

Lidon. He was in wolf form, Vieno could feel it, the power of his shift still running through his body. Vieno needed that power, so he sought it, embraced it, held it in until it rose in frequency, in force. It filled him until his body was shaking with it.

He was so close, but it wasn't enough. He needed more. Lidon had tried to explain how he shifted, but it had been hard because he still wasn't sure how he did it exactly. But Vieno thought of what the alpha had mentioned, how they could feel it when Lidon shifted because he took their powers for a few seconds, before returning them with force. That's what Vieno had to do, borrow all the alphas' powers.

He pinched his eyes shut, reached out even farther until he could feel them. Grayson was fighting inside. Bray was close to his father. He could sense some of Bray's alpha men around the house. He found Enar, then Palani. They were alive, angry and fighting.

Outside, voices closed in on the bathroom, and seconds later, someone rammed on the bathroom door again. "Open this door or we will break it in!" a voice shouted.

Fat chance, Vieno thought. He took another deep breath, then sucked in all the powers from everyone he could sense. It hit him like a lightning bolt, like he put his fingers in a socket and was about to get electrocuted. Then it rushed through him, and his adrenaline peaked so high he couldn't breathe. On instinct, he threw his head back and opened his mouth, not even shocked when he started howling. His body froze, then shook with a force that rattled his teeth, and in one glorious second, he transformed.

One second, he was a man, and the next, he was a wolf.

Sven and Ruari gasped in shock, but at the same time, the door shook with the force of someone kicking it in. Vieno braced himself, but he wasn't scared. If they wanted to get to his baby, to Ruari's baby, they would have to go through him. He would kill them before they ever put their hands on his son.

And how wonderful this wolf body felt, how familiar and powerful. He shook his limbs loose, readying himself for the fight.

The door splintered, then gave way completely, and it was dragged off its hinges by strong hands. Vieno didn't even wait for them to step into the bathroom, but attacked the first man he saw, his strong jaw clamping around the guys wrist, severing his artery in seconds.

It was amazing how he was man and wolf at the same time, how he had all these heightened senses and instincts, but his mind still worked the same. It was what Lidon had described, but it had been hard to believe.

Vieno didn't wait for a second man to appear but leaped through the broken-down door into the bedroom, where he encountered two more men. One went for his gun, so he jumped at his throat with all his weight. He wasn't sure how big he was as a wolf, not as big as Lidon, but he had no issues reaching the man's neck.

The force of the impact sent the man flying, and Vieno leaped on his chest as soon as the guy was down. He struggled, pushing Vieno away, even tried to land a blow, but with his wolf's senses, he was so much faster and stronger. His strong teeth clamped down on the man's arm first, then went in for the kill without queasiness or hesitation. He knew where to bite, ripping out his throat without blinking.

The third man scrambled away, was already halfway in the hallway. Vieno overtook him with a few leaps, his body graceful and fast, growling low and threatening. He crouched in front of him, content when the man paled underneath his sweaty face. God, he wanted to kill him, so badly, but he didn't. They needed survivors if they wanted to find out who had been behind this. That had been their issue last time, that no one had survived to tell.

So he threatened him until the man sank to his knees, his hands raised behind his back. He was an alpha, early fifties, with eyes that now shone with fear. Vieno stood, content to wait for someone else to show up, determined not to let this asshole out of his sight.

Seconds later, he smelled something. Something rancid and sour. He looked down at the guy and noticed with a deep satisfaction that the alpha had peed his pants.

26

W hen it was all over, it was a bloodbath. Bray checked, then double- and triple-checked before giving the all clear. But his instincts told him it was safe, and when both Lidon and Palani confirmed that, he felt confident to send out a code green.

"Vieno is okay," Lidon assured him. "I can feel him, and he's fine."

There was something in the alpha's tone that Bray couldn't identify, something that told him there was a lot more going on, but he let it go. In the same way, he didn't comment on the fact that Lidon was stark naked, having just shifted back. There were far more pressing things to worry about.

It had been a carnage. He'd watched Lidon shred some attackers to pieces, had killed two himself, and he'd seen his men fight valiantly. But had it been enough? Lidon said Vieno was safe, which meant Hakon was okay, and he would've mentioned it had he felt anything about Enar and Palani. But what about the others? What about Kean and Ruari and Jax? His chest was tight with worry.

When they turned the corner, Bray's heart stopped. Kean was leaning against the wall of the house, his shirt soaked with blood.

"Kean!" Bray called out, rushing over. Had Kean gotten shot? God, he looked like he'd been beaten, too, his eye swollen and turning blue and black, various scrapes on both arms. What had happened to him?

"It's Jawon," the beta said, his voice constricted.

Bray hadn't even seen the man slumped against Kean, the beta's arm holding him, too focused in his worry for Kean. Jawon wasn't moving and looked pale as a ghost, a sharp contrast with his shirt, which was crimson.

"Jawon!" Lidon said, kneeling next to Bray. "What happened, Kean? I thought he was okay when I left you guys."

"He was. I put pressure on the wound and held him, and I thought he was okay. Then he started bleeding like crazy." Kean's voice broke. "Alpha, I did everything I could."

Bray found himself choking up. Jawon was dead? Lidon reached out for Jawon, checking the pulse in his neck with trembling fingers. After half a minute, his hand dropped, the alpha pale and shaken. "He's gone."

Lidon gently took Jawon from Kean and laid him on the ground. With shaky hands, he closed his cousin's eyes for good.

"I'm sorry, alpha..." Kean said, ending on a sob.

Lidon grabbed the beta's head with both hands and kissed him on his forehead. "This is not on you, Kean. You didn't shoot him."

His voice sounded wobbly, as if the alpha had to push down his emotions. He had to, Bray thought, because he was feeling the same thing. He wanted to grieve for Jawon, but he couldn't. Not until they'd checked on everyone. Not until he was sure Ruari and Jax were okay.

"Bray," Kean sobbed and Bray gave in, pulling him close for a hug.

"I'm sorry," he whispered in his ear. "I'm so sorry."

He heard Lidon leave them, heading inside to check on the others, but he couldn't leave Kean yet. After about a minute, the beta finally let him go. When Bray released him, Kean yanked him back and kissed him, a desperate kiss that wasn't elegant or even practiced, but that somehow communicated everything Bray felt too.

He cupped Kean's cheek, his heart clenching at how lost and forlorn the beta looked. "I have to check inside," Bray said softly.

Kean nodded. "Isam dashed by earlier and said Ruari and Jax were okay."

"Oh god, thank god. I was so worried," Bray said, that tightness in his chest finally uncoiling.

Kean's eyes softened. "I know you were."

He shouldn't, but he kissed him again, then rose.

"I need to stay here for a little," Kean said. "Everything fucking hurts. I'll be there in a few."

Bray nodded and went inside. The main house was in pure chaos, his men dragging out bodies, while pack members sought comfort with each other. He found his dad in the kitchen, his lip split and his face already swollen. Both his hands were raw and bruised, and they held a trembling Lars, who was plastered against his alpha, his dad's hands putting pressure on Lars's arm.

"You okay, Dad?" Bray asked.

"Lars was shot. I need Enar or Maz."

"They're on their way," Palani called from the hallway.

"Where is Sven? Please, Bray, tell me he's okay," his

father asked, but before Bray could answer he hadn't seen him yet, running footsteps sounded from the hallway, and then the omega launched himself at Bray's father.

Bray's eyes watered as he watched the reunion, his dad cradling his two boys in such a sweet manner it made Bray almost look away because it was too private and intimate to watch. Kean had been so right. This wasn't about sex or kink. This was love.

He put a soft hand on Sven's shoulder. "I'm really glad to see you're okay," he said.

He was rewarded with a tentative smile that grew bigger as Sven realized Bray meant it. "Thank you. Ruari is fine," Sven said, and for that news, Bray could've kissed him.

Enar rushed in, his face tight with worry. "Lars, what happened?"

"He got shot," Bray's father said.

Enar was already reaching out for Lars's arm. "Grayson, I appreciate your protectiveness, but I need Lars to tell me himself, okay?"

"Yeah, of course, sorry, I'm..."

His father sounded out of it with worry, Bray thought.

"I'm okay, Daddy," Lars said, and for the first time, Bray could see the love behind that term. "Let Enar do his job."

Bray left Lars in the capable hands of Enar and walked into the hallway, where blood stains had splattered everywhere. Then his eyes widened as he tried to process what he was seeing.

A man lay flat on his stomach on the floor, his hands folded in his neck. His black shirt and fatigues indicated he was part of the group that had attacked them. That in itself wasn't so astonishing, though Bray was a little surprised to see one of them had survived unharmed by the looks of it.

What was mind blowing was the wolf standing right next to him, softly growling.

It wasn't Lidon, because the alpha was standing beside the wolf, holding his son against his bare chest, his big hand resting on the wolf's head with affection. He'd apparently found some shorts somewhere, though he was still barefoot. It wasn't Palani either. Bray had heard him call out, and he'd seen Enar as well. That left...

The wolf was light in fur color, almost white, and much, much smaller than Lidon was as a wolf. It had to be Vieno. How had the little omega managed to shift? And why was he still in wolf form?

"Ruari is in the bedroom with your son," Lidon told him. "They're fine, Bray. They're all fine."

The relief in the alpha's voice matched what Bray felt inside as he hurried into the bedroom Lidon had indicated. He almost stumbled over the bodies of two men, clearly taken down by a wolf. Blood was everywhere, and the gruesome sight made his stomach turn.

He found his son sleeping on the pristine white bed that had somehow escaped the carnage, looking pure and innocent, completely unaware of what had happened. Next to him sat Ruari, his small shoulders shaking as he sobbed.

"Ruari," Bray said, rushing over. "Are you okay, baby?"

Tear-filled eyes looked up at him, the horror of what he had witnessed clear on his face. "Oh, Bray," the omega cried. "It was horrible."

Bray wasn't sure who made the first move, but he opened his arms wide and held him, taking the omega on his lap as he sat down on the bed, careful not to disturb the baby, cradling Ruari against his chest. "I know, baby. Are you okay? Are you hurt anywhere?"

"I'm fine," Ruari said, his voice broken with tears. "Not

fine, but okay. I'm okay. Have you seen Kean? Please tell me he's not hurt."

Bray pulled him closer, allowing his own head to rest on Ruari's. "I saw him outside. He's okay, baby. The four of us, we're okay."

"Please, Bray, take me out of this room. The smell, the sight, I can't stand it anymore," Ruari begged.

"Hold on to Jax," Bray said, and once Ruari had lifted his son and pulled him close, Bray rose to his feet, cradling Ruari in his arms. The omega slumped against his chest in utter surrender, and Bray's insides went weak.

He carried him out and almost bumped into Kean. The beta had taken off his blood-soaked shirt, though a few red streaks were still visible on his chest, as well as the beginnings of what looked to be a broad arrangement of bruises. He'd fought hard, Bray realized. He'd fought for his own life and that of the others inside. They all had, alphas, betas, and even the omegas.

"Ruari, baby, are you okay?" Kean asked.

"Kean!"

Bray put Ruari down, and they kissed, then hugged, but Bray was part of it. Kean kissed him again, and he kissed him back, and he wasn't sure what it all meant. They stood in a tight hug, the four of them, careful not to squish Jax, and Bray's soul quieted with contentment and peace, the likes of which he had never experienced before, which was ridiculous considering everything they had been through.

And then he knew.

RUARI FELT safe and protected with both Bray's and Kean's arms around him as they walked into the hallway, where

Isam was securely fastening a zip tie around the wrists of one of the attackers, who had apparently survived. When Isam turned the man on his back, Ruari gasped.

"Dad!"

It flew from his lips before he could stop it, and he watched his father's eyes widen in shock. "James? What the hell are you doing here?"

Multiple faces looked from Ruari to his father and back at him again, all displaying a similar expression of confusion and shock. "This is your father?" Bray asked.

"Who's James?" Kean asked almost simultaneously.

Ruari closed his eyes and breathed in deeply. He had known this moment would come, though he had never expected it to be like this. And man, was he grateful for his honesty with Lidon and Palani. If he had not told them what he knew about his dad, he would've been truly fucked right now. As it was, things weren't looking too swell, but at least those two knew he'd been honest about his father's past and objectives.

Even then, he had never expected to run into him like this. The last time, his father had hired men do the job. This time, apparently, he'd deemed it safe enough to join in the attack himself.

It sank in, the fact that Vieno had pinned this man down. It had been his father, attacking them in that bathroom. If Vieno hadn't attacked, Ruari might have come face-to-face with his father as he broke through that bathroom door, and what would've happened then?

His only consolation, but it was a tiny one, was that his father's reaction made it clear he had no idea Ruari was staying here. That meant the attack hadn't been aimed at him or an attempt to extract him, and for that, he could only be grateful. It also meant the objective of the attack had been to kidnap Hakon, and that thought made Ruari's blood boil.

"Can you hold Jax for me?" he asked Kean.

He couldn't face his father while holding Jax. He needed no distractions now. Kean's eyes showed that he had already understood what was happening, who Ruari's father was. The beta took the baby with soft hands and nestled him against his shoulder. "Come here, buddy."

Ruari smiled despite it all, the sight of papa Kean too precious. Then he turned around, his face tightening, and gave his father an icy look. "I don't go by James anymore. I got rid of that name when I realized you would take my son away from me."

"He is an abomination," his father spat out. "He should've never been born. You have no idea what you are playing with, you stupid bitch. You're as stupid as your mother, going behind my back to get pregnant. Look at where that's brought us. A defective son who gave birth to a bastard child, not even a man, but an abomination."

Ruari had heard it all before, his father's hateful tirades against the wolf shifters, against his mother who had gone to that fertility specialist without his father knowing, against the CWP, against it all. And even though he knew the depths of his father's hatred, it still got to him. Would there ever be a time when it wouldn't hurt anymore? When he could hear his father's words and not feel rejected?

Bray shot forward, his foot suddenly on his father's neck, and the wince on the man's face told Ruari that Bray was putting pressure on it. The anger in the alpha's voice was dripping.

"You need to stop talking now," Bray said. "My son is not an abomination, and I will not tolerate you speaking like this about my mate."

At first, Ruari heard Bray defending their son, and it made his heart sing. Then the last part of that sentence hit. *Mate?* Bray was calling Ruari his mate? Had the alpha grasped the truth?

"Ruari, would you mind introducing us to this man?" Palani asked, putting a calming hand on Bray's arm.

Ruari straightened his shoulders, encouraged by Palani's friendly tone. "This is my father, Bennett Wyndham, the leader of the radical wing of the Anti-Wolf Coalition, the AWC. As you can hear, he's got some pretty nasty opinions on wolf shifters and the gene."

He met the shocked look from Bray head on. "I'm sorry I didn't tell you, but I was too scared you'd reject me."

"Of course they would reject you, who wants a—"

His father's words were cut off when Bray visibly put more pressure on his throat, and he made a choking sound, his tied hands flying up toward his throat to get rid of Bray's foot, which stayed unmoving.

"Bray, please make sure our guest gets enough oxygen to survive," Lidon said mildly. "We have questions to ask him, and he can't answer them if he's dead like the rest of his men."

With visible reluctance, Bray pulled his food back a little. "He'd better shut his mouth about Ruari, then," he growled.

"So," Lidon said slowly. "This is the man who was also responsible for the previous attack on our pack."

Gasps bounced through the hallway as those words sank in with everyone. It made it clear that Lidon and Palani had kept their promise to Ruari. They hadn't told anyone, except for Bray, but he hadn't known Bennett Wyndham was Ruari's father. That registered now, and Bray shot Ruari a look he couldn't decipher, before refocusing his attention on Lidon.

"Give us a status report, please, Bray, so Mr. Wyndham here can learn about the fate of his men." Lidon's voice was cool, but something simmered underneath.

"As far as we can tell, there were twenty attackers. Fourteen have been killed, and six have been taken prisoner, with one in critical condition and one seriously injured."

His father's face tightened at that news. Ruari figured the man had not been expecting those results. He had to have known they'd lost, and he had watched Vieno kill the other men in the room with him, but he might have harbored hope others had escaped or survived.

"And the death toll on our side?" Lidon asked.

"Two dead, one in critical condition, and multiple men with minor injuries."

Two dead? Pack members had died? Ruari couldn't hide his stress at that news. Who was it?

His father had paled visibly. "You killed fourteen of my men?" he asked Lidon.

"Oh, not just me. It was a pack effort. You went after my son, you bastard. You should've died a slow death as far as I'm concerned. You're lucky my mate has more constraint than I do." He gestured at Vieno, who was still standing there in wolf form, regal and beautiful.

Ruari couldn't even be upset at Lidon's words. His father *should* have died. In fact, it was a miracle he'd survived in the first place. More luck than anything else, Ruari figured. He had to have known that with an attack like this, going after the pack alpha's first son, they would show no mercy.

A chilling thought registered with him. His father was many things, but stupid wasn't one of them. He had to have known this would be the likely outcome, that even if he had counted on surviving himself, he'd suffer losses.

"He did it on purpose," Ruari said slowly. "He's counting on you to alert the authorities, and you'll have to explain how you killed these men. Everyone will know the shifters are back, but the first thing they will hear is that wolves are vicious, capable of killing fourteen men. They'll leak the pictures of what happened here, and the public opinion will turn against you instantly."

The words just fell from his mouth, and it wasn't till he was done that he realized this might've been better to discuss in private, but by then it was too late. Around him he heard murmurs and exclamations of shock, but Lidon and Palani didn't look surprised.

"I came to the same conclusion," Palani said. "But thank you for sharing your thoughts, Ruari. This can't be easy for you, knowing your own father did this."

Something changed inside Ruari, something that snapped and broke free. Even after everything his father had done to him, he had still considered him his father. Somehow, Palani's words changed that. This was not a man he wanted to call his father anymore. This was not a man he wanted to be associated with in any way, not ever again.

He exhaled, then spoke. "He's not my father anymore. I don't think he ever was. He's a stranger, a murderer, and you can do with him whatever the hell you want."

A wave of relief hit him. He felt light, as if he'd lost weight he'd been carrying around for a long time. Kean's arm came around him, and he leaned into his embrace, grateful for the beta's support.

And for the first time in a long, long time, Ruari felt free.

27

Kean was bone tired, his soul heavy, and he was grateful when Palani sent them away, stating that Ruari didn't need to be confronted with his father any longer. He was surprised when Bray joined them, and then he wasn't, because he belonged with them.

Ruari took Jax back, and when Kean stumbled over his own feet, Bray's strong arm came around him and he leaned in without a second's thought. He was tired, so tired, and everything hurt. His heart, most of all. His throat, with the grief that kept encroaching on him, but that he kept pushing back. But his body hurt as well, his eye that was almost swollen shut now. His belly, which had turned black and blue. His ribs, his hands, god, everything hurt.

They went to Omega One, where he wanted to collapse on the bed, but Bray's strong hand held him back. "You need a shower," he said quietly.

Kean looked at Ruari, though he didn't know why. "Go take a shower," Ruari said.

"But you..." Kean protested, not even sure what he was protesting.

"I need to feed Jax. Let Bray take care of you, love," Ruari said, and Kean surrendered.

The shower was brutally hot, just the way he loved it, and it wasn't till he registered that, that he also discovered Bray was right there with him. A naked Bray, standing quietly next to him in the shower, letting Kean hog all the hot water. And for some reason, that broke him.

He reached out blindly, his eyes filled with tears, sobbing with relief when Bray gathered him close and held him. He stopped fighting the sadness, the grief, the hurt, and it all came out. Bray was a rock he held on to; he didn't even know for how long.

It *hurt*. It hurt so fucking much.

Like a zombie, he let Bray handle him. The alpha shut off the shower and toweled him off, and somehow Kean registered how extraordinary it was to see the alpha on his knees in front of him. Bray gently lead him into the room where Ruari was waiting for them. He had clean clothes. Someone must've brought them, but he couldn't even find the energy to ask who he should thank.

"Here, Bray," the omega said. "Come sit with your son."

That did pierce through Kean's sadness, and he watched with warmth in his chest as Bray settled in a reading chair with his son in his arms, the look on his face pure awe and wonder. But it still hurt, his heart so raw and tender, his mind seeing the same images over and over and over again.

"Snuggle with me, love," Ruari said, and Kean didn't need to be told twice.

They settled on the bed, their bodies intertwining, Kean holding on to the omega as a lifeline. His heart beat strong, he thought, so alive. He shuddered, the image of Jawon forever etched in his memory.

"What happened?" Ruari whispered.

Should he tell him? Could he even talk about it? With Bray he had cried it out, but the alpha had seen it. He knew. Should he worry Ruari with this, knowing that his father was responsible?

"Don't shut me out because you think you need to protect me," Ruari said quietly. "I can handle it."

Yeah, he could. He would've had to, with a father like his.

"Jawon died," he said. Then again. "He died."

Ruari gasped, clinging closer to Kean.

He swallowed, not wanting to start crying again. "They shot him. One of the attackers shot him, point blank. He was okay and I held him, and then he started bleeding and he died in my arms. I watched him die, felt him take his last breath. They killed him, and for what? Because we refused to surrender. Because he spoke up and told them we'd fight to keep them out of the house. He spoke up, and he died."

"He died protecting the pack," Bray said. "With great honor."

And Kean couldn't say what he thought, what he felt, that he thought he was the greatest coward ever, because he should have spoken up. He'd let Jawon be the one to voice their resistance, and he'd died for it. It should've been him, and yet he was so grateful to be alive. Why was Jawon dead and he alive? It made no sense. Nothing about this made sense.

"I'm so sorry," Ruari said, his voice filled with sadness, and all Kean could think was how sorry he was, too. Sorry and yet so grateful, so happy to be alive. To be with his men. To have the chance to live and love.

He lay snuggling on the bed with Ruari, his head slowly

calming down as the omega simply held him, until Jax had fallen asleep and Bray tenderly put him away in his crib. The alpha stood in the middle of the room, hesitantly, but Ruari stretched out his arms to invite him.

When he still hesitated, Kean spoke up. "Bray, please. I need you. We need each other."

Kean could've wept all over again when Bray joined them, his big body comforting them both, completing their unit. They lay for a long time, silent, taking strength from each other as much as they gave it back. It was healing, Kean realized, restoring his sense of inner peace, of balance.

"So, mates, huh?" Ruari finally said, and Kean couldn't help but smile at his cheeky I-told-you-so tone.

"Yes," Bray said. "Mates." After a few beats, the alpha added, "And yes, you're allowed to say I told you so."

Kean grinned. "I told you so," he couldn't resist saying.

To his surprise, Bray pressed a tender kiss in his hair. "Yes, you did, my strong beta."

Kean's heart skipped a beat. "Yours?"

He turned his head to face Bray, catching the alpha staring at him with a look he'd never seen before.

"If you want to be," Bray said softly.

"I thought you didn't do relationships," Kean said.

Bray swallowed. "I came so close to losing you today..." His voice cracked, and Kean's eyes widened at the emotion that was painted all over the alpha's face. "When I saw you with that blood all over your shirt... I thought you'd been shot." He shook his head as if to clear a bad memory. "I know I've been an ass to you, and—"

"Stop. We'll talk about that some other time," Kean said.

The right corner of Bray's mouth pulled up. "You interrupted me."

"Someone told me that was not a big deal, and that I was overly sensitive," Kean fired back.

"What an ass," Bray said.

Kean studied him, the tightness in Bray's eyes betraying his insecurity. "Nah," he said. "Just mistaken."

He offered his mouth to Bray, who took it in the softest kiss he'd ever handed out, and Kean melted a little.

"So, mates then?" Ruari said, and they all chuckled.

Bray let go of Kean and they both turned toward Ruari, who looked at them with dancing eyes.

"If you'll have me," Bray said, and Kean's heart squeezed at his tone, his carefulness.

"I do," Ruari said, and those loaded words made a smile break through on Bray's face.

Ruari leaned in and he, too, got a tender kiss from the alpha. When Bray leaned back, Kean was amazed to see tears in the alpha's eyes. He held him close, his heart finding peace again.

They stayed like that for a long time, three bodies as close together as they could be on the too-small queen size bed, but their hearts were even closer. Finally, Ruari turned off the light, and it didn't take long before Bray and Ruari fell asleep. Their breaths danced over Kean's skin, warming more than his body.

Kean lay there, wondering how he could be so intensely happy and grateful and yet so profoundly sad at the same time. He thought of Jawon, that wonderful, quiet man who'd never said much, but had spoken up when the time came, who had defied alphas against all odds, protecting his alpha's heir. He'd have to live for him now, Kean thought. He'd have to make that sacrifice worth it, to prove that he'd been worthy to be spared.

And as he drifted off to sleep between his two men, with

a baby's quick breaths in the corner of the room, Kean vowed that he would love them for all eternity. Because he did.

(To Be Continued...)

MEET NORA PHOENIX

Would you like the long or the short version of my bio?

The short? You got it.

I write steamy gay romance books and I love it. I also love reading books. Books are everything.

How was that?

A little more detail? Gotcha.

I started writing my first stories when I was a teen...on a freaking typewriter. I still have these, and they're adorably romantic. And bad, haha. Fear of failing kept me from following my dream to become a romance author, so you can imagine how proud and ecstatic I am that I finally overcame my fears and self-doubt and did it. I adore my genre because I love writing and reading about flawed, strong men who are just a tad broken...but find their happy ever after anyway.

My favorite books to read are pretty much all MM/gay romances as long as it has a happy end. Kink is a plus... Aside from that, I also read a lot of nonfiction and not just books on writing. Popular psychology is a favorite topic of mine and so are self-help and sociology.

Hobbies? Ain't nobody got time for that. Just kidding. I love traveling, spending time near the ocean, and hiking. But I love books more.

Come hang out with me in my Facebook Group Nora's Nook where I share previews, sneak peeks, freebies, fun stuff, and much more:

https://www.facebook.com/groups/norasnook/

Wanna get first dibs on freebies, updates, sales, and more? Sign up for my newsletter (no spamming your inbox full...promise!) here:

http://www.noraphoenix.com/newsletter/

You can also stalk me on Twitter:

https://twitter.com/NoraFromBHR

On Instagram:

https://www.instagram.com/nora.phoenix/

On Bookbub:

https://www.bookbub.com/profile/nora-phoenix

ACKNOWLEDGMENTS

This book was written in a relatively short period, even shorter than I had panned because of some personal shit that made it impossible for me to write. I owe a massive thank you to Zolie and Vicki who helped me breathe during those weeks. Literally.

Vicki: you made another gorgeous cover, and I didn't even make you do fifty revisions on this one. I'd say that's a win, haha. You make my life better and my work easier. Thank you for being awesome. #SnarkyBitchesForever

Jamie: you were once again super flexible and delivered top-notch editing. Thank you so much. And you're welcome for the hilarious dictation-typos, haha. All those eyebrows shutting up, LOL.

My fab beta readers: Kyleen, Karina, TA, and Vicki, thanks for your awesome job on the beta read. You all caught different errors, including some potentially embarrassing ones (hello, blue eyes, haha...and fuzzy babies, LOL). Plus, your comments alone while reading make it worth it for me (cue Lion King music!).

My fellow authors from Reading Past the Realm: how much fun we had this month with all our releases! I'm so grateful for your support. Let's do this again.

Nookies: my sweet Nookies (the readers in my Facebook group), you are all so unbelievably awesome. Those tough weeks when all that shit went down, you guys lifted me up. I am so grateful for this group. It's my happy place.

Thank you, dear readers, for reading my books and supporting an independent author like me. If you loved this book, please leave a review, as it's one of the most helpful things you can do for an indie author!

ALSO BY NORA PHOENIX

No Shame Series:

No Filter

No Limits

No Fear

No Shame

No Angel

Irresistible Omegas Series (mpreg):

Alpha's Sacrifice

Alpha's Submission

Beta's Surrender

Alpha's Pride

Ballsy Boys Series (with K.M. Neuhold):

Ballsy (free prequel)

Rebel

Tank

Heart

Campy

Stand Alones:

The Time of My Life

Layover (novella)

Kissing the Teacher